To Louise

ANDRÉ JOHN HADDAD

NAPLES IN DENIAL

A LOUISE DESTREY THRILLER

Imagen Publishing

ISBN (Paperback): 978-1-9991072-4-6
ISBN (eBook): 978-1-9991072-5-3

Interior design by Aaxel Author Services
Cover design by Chloé Rochefort & VeeVee Studios

ANDRÉ JOHN HADDAD

NAPLES IN DENIAL

A LOUISE DESTREY THRILLER

Imagen Publishing

ISBN (Paperback): 978-1-9991072-4-6
ISBN (eBook): 978-1-9991072-5-3

Interior design by Aaxel Author Services
Cover design by Chloé Rochefort & VeeVee Studios

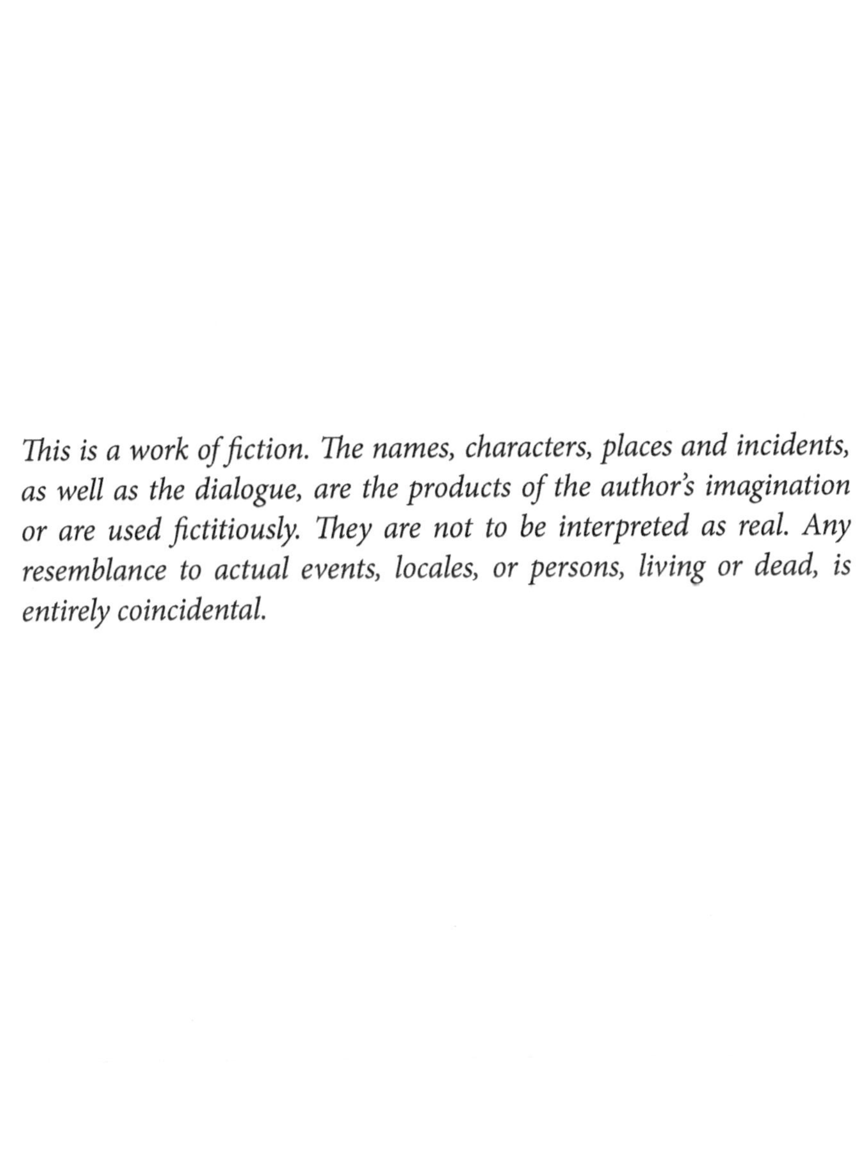

This is a work of fiction. The names, characters, places and incidents, as well as the dialogue, are the products of the author's imagination or are used fictitiously. They are not to be interpreted as real. Any resemblance to actual events, locales, or persons, living or dead, is entirely coincidental.

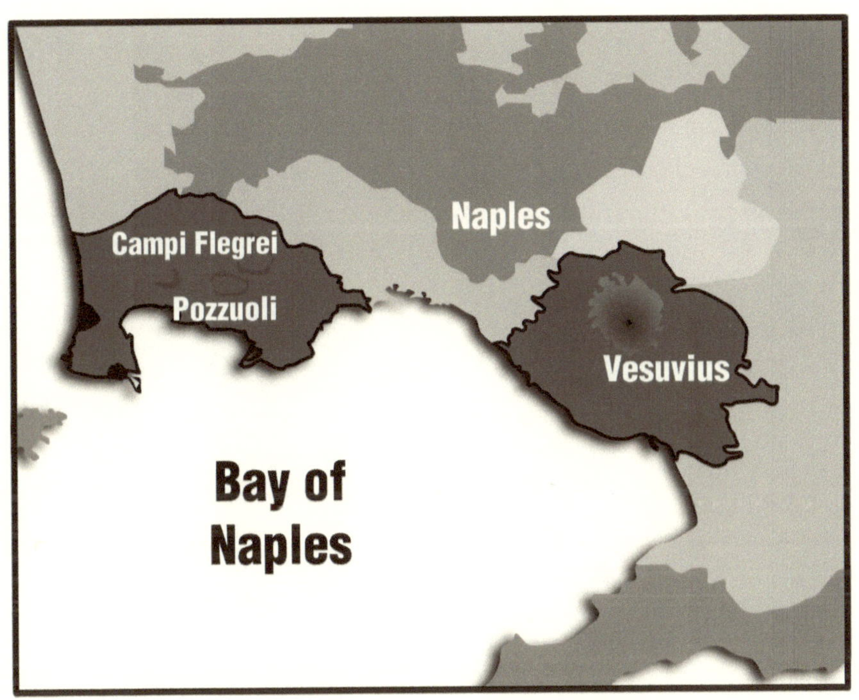

Terrain Map of Naples

PRINCIPAL CHARACTERS

Vesuvius. A sommian - composite volcano located on the Gulf of Naples in the Province of Avellino in Campania, Italy. Vesuvius is located 9 km or 5.6 miles east of Greater Naples, close to the Mediterranean shores.

Campi Flegrei. The Phlegraean Fields is a large volcanic area situated 22 km or 13 miles west of the city of Naples. Part of the caldera lies under water in the Bay of Naples. The modern-day village of Pozzuoli sits at the center of the volcano's caldera.

Louise Margoe Destrey. Industrial psychologist. Consultant. Owner & partner in charge of the Boston Triage Group (BTG) based in Cambridge, Massachusetts. Heir to Cardinal Hedrick Zimmer's financial resources. Daughter of Robert and Marie Destrey. Born in Montréal in 1957.

John Thomas Kleinrup. Businessman. Jerusalem Foundation associate. Son of Horace Kleinrup (former MI6 Director) and Lady Jane Sassone. Born in Oxshott/Stoke D'Abernon (Surrey) UK in 1957.

Francesco Galileo Carbone. Structural Engineer. President of Safe California Homes and Businesses, based in Palm Springs, Ca. Son of Gianfranco Carbone and Rosa Caprio. Born in Conza, Italy in 1969.

Lola. Avatar. BTG's (Boston Triage Group) Cray HPE supercomputer.

I

THE CAY HOTEL
CARACAS, VENEZUELA

Present Day

"We've got to get out of here," John Kleinrup said to himself. It was close to nine p.m. The sound of his voice betrayed his concerns for getting Louise Destrey out of Caracas.

Kleinrup ran as fast as he could across the plaza toward the Cay hotel. He was thinking that the hotel elevators wouldn't be an option because power outages were now common in Caracas.

Kleinrup, Destrey's sometimes lover and a key player in all matters that concerned her security, had to get her out of Venezuela. He had the pleasure of accompanying Destrey as she roamed the world, trying to help people wherever she could. They were also a public item, making headlines and attracting unwanted attention to their not-so-secret relationship. Kleinrup was also known internationally as the head of his own company. He was in the business of information. Buying, selling, exchanging, and pinching intelligence from any source he could develop. Secrets were his bread and butter. Although information was his livelihood, Destrey was the love he most desired. Needless to say, he craved for a calmer life.

But not today. Not in Caracas. Today, he was in the business of saving the life of the woman he loved. It wouldn't be the first or the last time he would come to her rescue. Still, one day, they would run out of luck. She'd been warned. From his point of view, it was bound to happen. How long was this woman going to survive her crusades? That was a fair question. He knew Destrey was lucky, but even luck could come crashing down and change everything.

This wasn't the first time Destrey had put herself in harm's way to help those who needed her organization's help. Jerusalem, São Paulo and now Caracas. Among others, they had been or were in dire need of assistance.

Since Destrey's consulting firm, the Boston Triage Group or BTG, was in the business of predicting future events, she attracted unusual characters. Needless to say, her clientele was populated by the superrich, as well as by governments. Both client segments often found themselves in trouble between Mother Nature's temper tantrums and our taste for violence and power. Either way, they needed Destrey's expertise.

She was raised to help those in need, which included those who couldn't pay for her firm's services. She would do that because she felt responsible and a bit guilty. In a word, Destrey was complicated.

Today, Mother Nature wasn't the culprit, even though climate change in South America was becoming an important concern in world affairs.

As far as Kleinrup was concerned, today was all about blood, bullets, and bodies. He was afraid her hotel room would soon become a death trap if he didn't hurry.

In spite of Louise Margoe Destrey's no nonsense approach to steer her business on the right path, she would often end up dealing with issues no one wanted to tackle. Tonight was no different. The children of Caracas were cannon fodder in Venezuela's unfolding civil war. Destrey's organization chose the South American mission not only because of US concerns, but because of Caracas' street children. They were hungry for lack of care, food and clean water.

As Kleinrup entered the hotel lobby, he could see the barman continuing to pour cocktails as if nothing was happening outside.

Up in her hotel suite, Destrey felt the floor shake under her feet. The initial explosion was heard from a mile away. Wreckage was hurled a hundred feet in the air.

A few minutes earlier, a fire had erupted in front of Destrey's hotel entrance. Across the street, a second explosion blew out windows, sending fragments of glass and brick over the plaza. Destrey witnessed the carnage from her hotel suite: people were covered in blood. Many were severely injured. *Maundy* Thursday, or Good Thursday, was almost over.

There was no official way of knowing who was responsible for these acts of terrorism. But as Kleinrup ran up the stairs to her third-floor hotel suite, he began to have a pretty good idea of who was behind the bombings. Since Nicolás Maduro fled the country, his supporters, who included Venezuela's military, Russia, China, as well as Turkey, had been working on a campaign to create enough disorder and confusion to launch a "Get Back Maduro" movement. All had invested heavily in Maduro's regime.

Kleinrup believed the Cay Hotel was under attack by government-backed gangs of masked motorcyclists, armed with pistols, C-4 and baseball bats. They had taken over the city's main thoroughfares. The gangs, mostly cops loyal to ex-president Maduro, sent terrified people racing for cover. High-end hotels were under attack. They were clearly on Destrey's trail. She was on their list of persons of interest. An important target because the gangs were going to take over the city, and anyone attracting international attention had to be managed. Caracas was in chaos for that purpose: to quell the people's right to think for themselves.

Earlier that week, Destrey pushed Maduro's factions in a corner for the treatment of the children of Caracas. She was actively funding children's aid organizations to protect the children. Destrey had initiated a plan where the children would be evacuated from Caracas.

Today's actions, sponsored by China and Russia, were push-back.

Gunmen wearing masks indiscriminately shot people as they tried to run away from the plaza.

Destrey could smell burning flesh as Kleinrup rammed through her door. She could taste tar, a telltale sign of C-4 explosives. He had blood on his face and on his tattered clothes. Although Destrey could see the terror in his eyes, she could still feel his resolve. Kleinrup rarely fell apart under pressure. Destrey called it his superpower.

He was wearing his favorite *buttersoft* jacket. She noticed because it once had a life in beige. It now carried the scent of metal: the blood spatter of tourists and those peddling their wares in La Castellana Plaza.

Destrey recognized the blood's dark red stain on John's jacket. She wanted to believe it wasn't his. She reminded herself that, in Caracas, people died because the rule of law had fled the country. Some believed Venezuela's lawlessness had begun as early as 1908. Political analysts believed the country had gone through one dictatorship after another and because of that, the nation had never developed a taste for democracy or for the rule of law that would apply equally to all citizens, including its children.

"Where the hell have you been? I've been waiting for you. I was going crazy and with all the explosions... What happened? What the hell is going on?" She said.

Kleinrup was breathing heavily. He had nothing to say.

"No calls, no nothing," she said. "You told me you'd be just a minute with the chef." She stared at him, waiting for an answer. "And you're hurt," she said anxiously. "You're injured. Jesus! My God! You're bleeding!"

"No, I'm not, but I will be if we don't get out of here soon," Kleinrup said as he looked around the room.

Kleinrup steadied himself against the wall as another explosion rocked the hotel to its foundations.

"Where are we going?" she tried to get his attention but realized she could barely hear her own voice.

The explosion caused the air to be sucked out of every open door, suite, and passageway, then suddenly pushed back with equal force.

She fell. He rushed to her side.

"What are we going to do?" she asked. "Where are we going to go?"

"I don't know where, but now's a good time to get going before it's too late," he replied angrily.

"I'm not packed…"

"Really?" he said. "That's your problem?"

"No, no. Of course not. Don't need to do that. But you know, I've *kinda* done this rodeo before. Too many times and that…"

"Okay, I get it. Right!"

"Right," she echoed back to him.

"Okay then," Kleinrup replied.

He gently held her with both arms and got her on her feet.

"I want you to grab your passport, your running shoes and sweetheart, please don't look at me like that. We're out of time and we have to go."

"I got that, but are you sure…"

"Don't think," he said loudly. The noise coming from the plaza was deafening. "Don't talk. Don't anything. Passport. Shoes. Now!"

He needed a safe way out of the hotel and out of the country. He was standing by the window. What he saw confirmed his worst fears. *The sonofabitches were torching the city*, he said to himself. He could see them coming up La Castellana Avenue. The mob was heading toward the hotel. Across the Plaza, the roof of the restaurant had collapsed. The same establishment where they had dinner an hour ago. There was a gaping hole near the restaurant's front entrance. The Fava Ristorante was on fire. The terrorists were getting closer.

Locals said the mob was pursuing what the police called political troublemakers. Rabble-rousers. Partisan activists. But Kleinrup didn't believe a word of it. The chaos was not due to random acts of violence. They were, in fact, hunting for Destrey. She was in the crosshairs of right-wing activists posing as hooligans. The woman was clearly a meddler and an interferer, with the IQ of a thousand Republicans. Nevertheless, she had taken an oath to help those in need and would not back down from her responsibilities. Worth more than one point five billion US dollars, Destrey had the financial resources and the muscle to never back down from a fight. Today was no different from any other challenge she'd met head-on. Between South American politics, Covid-19 and widespread corruption, Venezuela's children had been lost in the shuffle. She would do everything she could to help them in their hour of need.

Meanwhile, people laid on the grass crying or simply dazed by the explosions. They were the lucky ones. Those not so lucky were scattered around a blast crater created by a car bomb, their bodies contorted in strange positions. They fell to the ground after the blast sent them hurtling through the air.

Kleinrup had seen war up-close. "This," he said, "is a different kind of warfare." There was madness in the streets. Someone wanted to send a message. And it wasn't "Welcome to Caracas". The message was clear: We're getting Maduro back.

A postcard from hell, Kleinrup thought to himself as he was witnessing the carnage in 3D.

Suddenly, guns fired their way. The Cay Hotel, Destrey's temporary headquarters, was clearly the target. As the first bullets went astray, Kleinrup heard a thud. Someone close fell to the floor, crashing tables or chairs. Kleinrup recognized it for what it was: bullets found their way inside the hotel. More bullets left their mark on the hotel's cement walls and ceiling high windows. Then, he heard something different: groaning and cries for help from within the hotel. Possibly from guests and hotel staff located on Destrey's floor. People very close were being shot. They were now aiming at the hotel's portico, which was three floors down Destrey's suite. As the bullets came up closer to Destrey's window, Kleinrup felt his adrenaline soar, giving him the energy to lift her away from the window. Again, another explosion. A blast that caused them to fall on the floor once again.

Kleinrup was lying on top of Destrey.

"I thought we had to go," she said.

"Oh, you're going to pay for that," Kleinrup said. "I can promise you that much."

"Promise?" She smiled at him. Their lips were inches apart. They were both frightened and at the same time ready to do the deed. Odd thing about this couple, stress would often pull them closer together.

"Well, dude, what are you thinking about?" Destrey asked.

"I'm thinking," he said, almost whispering in her ear, "that this is how those animals react to your plea to save the children," Kleinrup said as he stared into her eyes.

"You still think we should go?" Destrey was playing him.

"Yes. I'm afraid so."

"So much for diplomacy," she said.

She held his face in her hands.

"Your timing is…" he said.

"What about it?"

"Not now, sweetheart. Time to go."

He lifted her to her feet, checked around the room one last time to see if she hadn't forgotten anything important. Then he opened what was left of the front door and took a quick peek.

Kleinrup snatched her purse, grabbed hold of her free hand, and bolted. Destrey was almost airborne.

"Wait, my shoe…"

Kleinrup stopped dead in his tracks and grabbed her left shoe. He then resumed his run with Destrey wobbling in tow.

Destrey ran as quickly as she could. But there was no way she could keep pace with Kleinrup. While being towed forward, she remembered how badly she ran during her first tennis lesson.

"You know what?" she asked Kleinrup.

Kleinrup didn't answer. He knew they were in trouble. The kind that was dangerous and possibly lethal. He had no time for small talk.

"My late husband always said that I didn't know how to run."

"Got news for you, you still don't. So, no talking. Put your shoe back on. And start running. In that order. And no talk of your late husband, either."

Kleinrup suddenly stopped. They had gone nearly three floors down. The stairwell stood empty.

"Quiet," he whispered.

"What is it?" She whispered back.

The first-floor stairwell door opened quickly. Two giant men dressed like Mormons walked through. Both wore a white shirt and tie and a dark suit. They looked up. The bigger giant said something to the effect that they should follow them.

"Where were you two?" Destrey asked Valentin and Arseny.

"*Madame* not worry." Valentin didn't look back.

"We go now. Jet waiting, special airport. Must go now, *Madame*," Valentin said. The two men assisting Destrey were none other than FSB agents on loan to Julian Precov, BTG's Board President and Former Russian Foreign Minister. The special airport was the Generalissimo Francisco de Miranda Air Base, now secured for Destrey's getaway. Precov's close ties with the top brass of the Venezuelan and Russian military always came in handy. Today was no exception.

"I've never been so happy to see them," Destrey said to Kleinrup, as they ran down the stairs behind their bodyguards.

"Fast, *Madame*. Fast," yelled Arseny. As they were heading for the hotel's back loading dock, Valentin unholstered his handgun: a Kel-Tec PMR-30. A serious weapon. Made in the USA. Kleinrup followed Valentin's lead with his SIG Sauer P210, a handgun manufactured by obsessive-compulsive Germans.

"Regardless of what you see or hear," Kleinrup said, "keep running until the boys tell us differently. Got that?"

Destrey spotted Kleinrup clutching a gun.

"But they're getting ready to shoot at people. Shouldn't you…"

"From now on," he said carefully, "no talking. Hold my hand and keep walking. If I run, you run. If I stop, you stop. Got it?"

Destrey nodded.

She was about to tell him that guns were dangerous. That he could get hurt, and that he had no right talking to her like that, especially in that tone of voice, when she suddenly spotted Valentin firing a couple of rounds at a dark shadow coming their way.

The man was carrying a baseball bat. He dropped to the ground with a thud and laiy still.

"Aren't we going to help him?" She asked Kleinrup.

"Valentin doesn't injure," Arseny said evenly. "Valentin never miss, *Madame*. He train to kill."

"But the man was just walking. I mean he was minding his..." Destrey tried to say.

"How many people do you know taking a midnight stroll with a bat? Come on Louise. These bastards are here for you."

"But..."

"No second guessing. You're going to get us all killed." Kleinrup wouldn't look at Destrey. He didn't want her to see what he was really thinking. There would be more deaths before the night would end. He held her hand tightly and pulled her along the back of the hotel's loading dock.

Moments later, Valentin and Arseny moved toward what appeared to be a truck. It was, in fact, an armored truck. The six speed, six hundred horsepower monster had enough torque to pull a house away from its foundation. The vehicle was waiting for them.

The armored truck could withstand anything the gangs could send its way: with heavy-duty all terrain military tires, this bulky limo was almost unstoppable. At the wheel sat a Russian she vaguely remembered.

The rear swing door opened with a bang. Both Valentin and Arseny helped Destrey on-board, lifting off her feet as if she weighed a feather.

No sooner had the rear door closed behind them did the behemoth moved forward. With no intention of stopping for anyone or anything, the driver pushed the vehicle to its limit.

The video interface with the driver was on as soon as they were on the move.

"It's Yvan," Destrey said happily. "Yvan, from São Paulo, remember?"

"Yes, *Madame*," answered Valentin. "You no speak to Ivan. He very much afraid of the white witch."

"Did he just call me a…?"

"White witch is good, *Madame*. Yvan very happy to see you again. Good witch. White snow. Now, he drive. He very busy."

Destrey was about to reply to Arseny when Kleinrup kissed her vigorously on the mouth, stopping her from starting a conversation that would scare the bravest of bodyguards. Ivan had had the pleasure or the misfortune to rescue Destrey from a São Paulo's police hit squad. On that occasion, Ivan had witnessed Destrey's temper.

"We… are… in… danger," Kleinrup whispered in her ear. "Do you understand me? Nod if you understand."

Destrey understood and nodded.

"Right."

"This conversation is not by any stretch of the imagination finished, Mister," Destrey muttered to herself.

If Kleinrup knew anything about Destrey, it was her unfailing desire to have the last word. Especially with her lover.

Kleinrup smiled to himself.

The white witch from Ste-Adèle, he thought to himself. *It has a nice ring to it.*

"What did you say?" Destrey was annoyed.

"Nothing. Just relax and enjoy the ride."

"You're kidding right? This is a freaking truck!"

"Is that a question, a comment, or are you just bitching?"

"If we weren't in a life-or-death situation, we'd be having a real fight on our hands." Destrey said.

"I'm counting on it, sweetheart."

A couple of blocks away from the armored truck, Armando Rojas and his crew of tugs were trolling Caracas' city center. His team included six bikers and two other men driving pickup trucks. They were armed with shotguns and baseball bats. Their job was to scare people off the streets. Rojas' orders were clear: shoot to kill anyone found loitering or acting suspicious. Which meant almost anyone. Most of his crew were police officers from the Las Mayas District. Two others came from the military. They knew every part of the city by heart, especially those officers stationed in Las Mayas.

It was Rojas' test. One that would measure his leadership skills and loyalty to Maduro. The city center was a favorite location where people gathered to complain about everything wrong with Venezuela, which now was a great deal. Rojas believed the city was technically shut down. Explosions and gunfire had probably done the job of keeping everyone in their homes. He believed he and his crew were free to roam the city without fear of being shot by those not in favor of the Maduro comeback.

Rojas spotted an armored truck heading east toward La Carlota. The airport has been closed to all public traffic since 2005 and was now managed by the military for their exclusive use.

Rojas quickly instructed his crew to move toward the armored truck. They had no trouble reaching the vehicle, the streets of Caracas being empty. They stormed ahead of the truck and ordered the driver to get off the road for an inspection.

The armored truck did not slowdown.

Unbeknownst to Rojas, the Russians had another operation of their own going on. Keeping Destrey out of harm's way was one more challenge they had to deal with. At all costs. No matter what.

Rojas fired a few rounds in front of the armored truck. He was now sure the truck would stop.

"What's happening?" Destrey said out loud.

"Grab your safety belt. Quick. Put it on. It's going to get bumpy." Kleinrup was in no mood to fool around with gangs of masked policemen.

Another biker fired two shotgun blasts into the truck's bulletproof windshield.

"Ivan?" Kleinrup had a plan of sorts he wanted to discuss with Ivan.

"Mr. K? Ivan busy, drive now."

"I just want to tell him not to stop for anyone."

"Of course. No problem, Mr. K."

"You seem pretty sure of yourself," Kleinrup said.

"We have what you say, back-up."

"Okay. I'm happy to hear that, but are you sure that's working? They're shooting at us, and I don't see your backup."

"Soon, Mr. K. Soon. With backup."

No sooner had Valentin announced his backup plan did more shooting erupt, but this time, not one bullet hit the armored truck.

A team of three Russian bikers armed with 2B25 assault rifles fitted with silencers approached the Rojas' crew from behind. The Russians fired. Rojas' team was decimated within a few seconds. Both pickups slammed into parked cars exploding upon impact. Ivan's backup disappeared as quickly as it had appeared. They stayed out of sight. Valentine said it was necessary not to attract too much attention. He said that armored trucks often travelled at night. And he wanted to appear as normal as possible.

"What happened?" Destrey asked.

"You don't want to know."

"But…"

"I'll tell you when we're onboard the jet."

"I heard shots fired."

"You did. Yes, indeed. Shots were fired, but we're okay."

Destrey complied with Kleinrup's request.

Rojas was hit multiple times, but he still managed to stay alive long enough to tell his story to his captain. The story didn't make any sense. Why would his own people, masked policemen riding motorcycles, shoot one of their own? That didn't add up.

Rojas died of his injuries. His leadership test was over. The armored truck finally reached the airport. Destrey was safe. Yvan parked at the rear of Destrey's jet, fueled and ready to leave

Venezuelan airspace.

Destrey recognized the people watching from a few meters away. They were Venezuelan military. She also noticed a few Russian military aids. They watched Destrey and Kleinrup as they boarded the aircraft. The soldiers didn't try to stop them.

"Don't you think it strange that the Russians would give us a helping hand and, at the same time, manage Maduro's comeback attempt?"

"No," Kleinrup said. "Nothing the Russians do surprises me. This is how I understand them. If the situation calls for their support, because it's in their interest, then they'll do anything that they feel is necessary. It doesn't have to be logical or strategically coherent. It's called *whatever it takes to get the job done*."

"Wonderful," she said.

Destrey's protectors were probably sociopaths. This wasn't the first nor the last time she'd be witnessing strange behavior from the Russians.

"How long's the flight to Boston?" she asked Kleinrup.

"Twelve hours, maybe a little less."

"I'd like to make a stopover."

"Where to?"

"Home, in Ste-Adele. I need a little time alone."

"Alone?"

"Yeah. Alone with you," she said.

"I can arrange that." Kleinrup smiled.

2

BOSTON TRIAGE GROUP (BTG) CAMBRIDGE, MASSACHUSETTS

Present Day

Margaret McGivney, Destrey's personal assistant, was not only her assistant but also her gatekeeper and unofficial fixer at BTG's H.Q.

She scanned the magnificent male specimen standing in the reception area, all six foot two of him. She was sure he was lost. There was no doubt about it. Because BTG wasn't a modelling agency.

And, as one would have rightly assumed, not a single employee at the Boston Triage Group remotely looked like this striking representative of the male species. That's because BTG was strictly the domain of nerds. Although they were highly sophisticated professionals, and in fact among the best in their fields, they were nevertheless nerds, geeks and introverted scientists. They came from the best universities, men and women who had a unique set of skills as well as the potential to crack difficult problems. But, as Margaret liked to call them, *still a bunch of nerds.*

From Margaret's point of view, the young man facing her was a blond Adonis. Rugged looking, yet well-mannered and yes, wearing a smile that could melt any heart.

"Mister Carbone?" she said.

She watched as the man approached her and, without hesitation, put his right hand forward.

"Yes. Thank you for seeing me."

McGivney was charmed.

"My card," he said graciously.

McGivney took a quick look. The business card said *Francesco Galileo Carbone. Structural Engineer. Cell number.* Nothing else. No logo, email or fancy design. Simple and to the point. This is who I am, this is what I do, and here's where you can reach me.

"I'm sorry Mister Carbone, who exactly are you expecting to see?"

"This is the Triage Group, isn't it?"

"Well, yeah. We're now called the Boston Triage Group. But TG is okay too."

McGivney was curious to see what this man was doing in her place of business. She was pretty sure he wasn't a client. He didn't look or feel like he was part of any elite. In actual fact, to be a BTG customer, one would have to be immorally loaded and connected just to get access to the firm's front door. Not surprisingly, clients with that kind of money believed the world belonged to them, and so, they had attitude, brains, credentials and titles that few could provide. However, despite their qualifications and pedigrees, Destrey would have the last word. In or out. Yes or no. BTG was, after all, her house and, as one would expect, everyone worked by Destrey's rules, which included customers.

BTG was in the business of answering the difficult questions corporations and nations ask in private. In fact, BTG would only answer one question, if the client qualified: what was going to happen? In a week, a month, a year or ten years from now. Clients would ask how long it would take before their organizations' resources would be depleted or worse, become irrelevant. How many other Covid-viruses would sweep across continents and spread their deadly tentacles killing men, women and children irrespective of their faith, wealth, or intelligence? What were the chances that a nation would be invaded and annexed by Russia or China? When am I going to die? When will Elvis come back?

Although Destrey had a sense of humor, officially she refused to tackle the Elvis question. Unofficially, she was going to ask Lola to look into Elvis. Just in case.

In addition, knowing of the existence of the Group was also on a need-to-know basis. That's because BTG didn't need more clients or publicity of any kind. The firm's workbook was overflowing with organizations waiting in line to get BTG's assistance.

"I'm here to see Doctor Destrey," he said simply. "I made the appointment over three months ago, and today, well, today's the only time slot she had available to see me."

"I see. I'm sorry to tell you, but Louise Destrey is in South America on an emergency mission."

McGivney didn't remember making the appointment, but that didn't mean anything. Her boss, a no-nonsense Frenchie from Ste-Adèle Quebec, could have short-circuited the system and made the appointment herself. One could say that Margaret McGivney had her hands full. But that would be a gross understatement. Just managing Destrey's calendar and her band of geniuses was a daily challenge. Because of the Jerusalem and São Paulo assignments, among others, Destrey was the best-known industrial psychologist on the planet.

"So, she's not here?" Carbone said a bit disappointed.

"That's right. I'm sorry for the inconvenience. I promise I'll make it up to you. But while you're here now, could you tell me why you need to see Madame Destrey?"

"First," he said, "I'd like to thank her for the help she provided me when I was just a kid."

"Okay, and…" McGivney started to ask.

"I'm here to ask for her help," he said timidly.

"What kind of help are we talking about Mr. Carbone?" McGivney was now a little puzzled.

"It's about two million people," he said. "I have family and friends in Naples."

"And how does that…" McGivney hesitated.

"It's about Vesuvius," Carbone said.

"The volcano?"

"Yeah. The volcano," Carbone said.

"You want us to help you with that?"

"Yes. I'm thinking of the people of Naples." Carbone was relieved. He said it out loud for the first time.

"Okay. I'll bite. What about them?" McGivney asked.

"They need to leave," Carbone said.

McGivney stared at the man for the longest time. "Not that again!" she finally said. McGivney had heard enough. This conversation was a dead-end topic.

"I don't understand," Carbone said hesitantly.

"We've been through this before. In fact, twice: Jerusalem and São Paulo."

"I read about that," Carbone said.

"So, you should also know that getting people to do things they don't want to do, is practically impossible. We've learned that the hard way. And that's what she'd tell you if she was here today. We're not in the business of making people do things against their wishes. We are here to provide information. That's it. What people do with that information is their business. And God bless them."

"Are you trying to tell me I won't be able to see Doctor Destrey?" Carbone asked.

"No, no. Not exactly. I said I'd fix this, and I will. As soon as she's back, I'll let you know and this time, we'll handle your expenses."

"That's really not necessary," Carbone said.

"I know, but as my boss keeps telling me, it's the right thing to do. But let me give you a piece of advice. You better have something more concrete, otherwise…"

"I think I understand. Thank you." Carbone was relieved but at the same time he knew he had a lot more work to do before he would meet with Destrey.

Carbone left Boston. He planned to visit Naples. It would take a few months of preparation, but he had to act. If he was lucky, he would be able to meet Destrey before he travelled to Naples.

Naples had recently been reopened to international traffic. The pandemic was over. The only virus-related issue left to resolve was the fear it left in people's souls. Especially children. Although the whole world was trying to get back to normal, Carbone nevertheless focused on Naples, its two million inhabitants and Vesuvius.

The one thing he believed in was working with the best. If he could get Louise Destrey onboard, if only to guide him, he would be forever in her debt. Deep down he knew that he was biting off more than he could chew. He had resolved that he needed all the advice he could get. And meeting the Destrey woman was his first objective.

Because Vesuvius was active, Carbone felt duty bound to do something about it. The volcano's potential danger to life was significant. The consensus between experts in the field was that Vesuvius was the most dangerous volcano in the world. One, because of its proximity to Naples, and two, because it was active. Carbone didn't think one needed to be a volcanologist to understand the potential danger Vesuvius posed to the Italian city. When Mount Vesuvius erupts once again, Carbone believed it would endanger millions, quite possibly wiping out the city of Naples.

His quest to save Naples' citizens was his way of seeking redemption for his sins. Although it had happened when he was just a boy, he thought his best friend died because of his actions.

3

FRANCESCO GALILEO CARBONE
CONZA, ITALY

November 23, 1980
16:30:07

Francisco could never forget Vito. On that fateful day, he had lost his best friend. It was the driving force that led him to reach out to Destrey. He called it atonement even though he had done nothing wrong. Fact is, after all these years, Francesco was still devastated.

"Why" Vito Picariello asked nervously.

"Because," Francesco Carbone whispered slowly, "they, are over there." Francesco pointed to the stone wall in front of them. "And we, are here." Francesco pointed to his left foot. "And if you don't move your fat ass real quick, this foot will kick your oversized ass over the wall and in her pool."

"You don't have to be nasty." Vito said miserably. Although he wasn't known as the smartest kid in school, he was loyal. A bit nerdy maybe, but a good friend, nonetheless. And that was worth something to Francesco.

"And you? You don't have to be so fucking dense. Sometimes I wonder about you Picariellos."

Vito Picariello ignored him.

"You still didn't answer my question. Why are we doing this? Especially now. It's almost suppertime. If I don't get home soon, my mom's going to kill me."

"Vito, Vito, Vito." Carbone could be melodramatic at times. Just like his father. But today, he was deadly serious. How could his best friend not understand the urgency of the situation?

"Don't Vito me, Francesco. I have enough of that at home. And I don't like it when you talk to me like that. It's like you think I'm stupid or something."

"Okay. Let me explain it one more time."

Vito could be so exasperating.

"Go ahead. Explain it to me," Vito said. Sometimes Francesco went too far.

"One, Paulo De Simone is out of town," Francesco said. "In Naples, to be precise. On business. I heard the girls talking. That's how I know. Follow?"

"Right," Vito said. "So, her daddy's out of town. So what?"

"So! Am I hearing you right? You said… so?" Francesco said.

"Yeah. So?"

"It means the girls will be alone. That's what's so." Francesco had all the answers.

"What about Maria's *mamma*? What about her?"

"Okay. That's a good point. But the good news is *mamma* De Simone will also be out. I heard the girls talk about that, too. She's with her own mother. So, *mamma* De Simone will also be out of the house."

"So, aside from the dog, no one will be around…"

"Just the girls. Maria De Simone and Celestina Capone," Francesco said excitedly. "I'm thinking about being there," Francisco pointed to the De Simone's roof. "There to observe the girls. Front row seats!"

"All alone except for you and me," Vito said. He kind of understood what that meant. This wouldn't be the first time he'd be alone with a girl. Nevertheless, what was the big deal? If truth be told, the ramifications of the situation still eluded Vito. The implications of being alone with girls had never been an issue before. His limited experience in life left him fundamentally incapable of understanding why the words *alone* and *girls* meant so much to Francesco. There was something missing. Maybe Francesco was keeping something to himself. But what?

"Yeah. As I said, a million times, the girls will be all alone in the big house with a pool in the back yard."

"So why all this secret agent stuff? Why don't we just drop in and say hello?"

"I swear to God. There must be something wrong with your head. Maria and her friend are the hottest girls in town. Every guy in town would give his eyetooth to be with them. And as I said, they'll have the pool all to themselves. Which means… bathing suits?"

"You sure about that? Every guy in town. I'm sure you're exaggerating," Vito said.

"Yeah, you may be right. But I think the girls are hot. And no, we're not going to knock on the door and say hello. Oh! Hello girls! We're the town losers."

"No, we're not," Vito protested.

"Not what?"

"Losers. Anyway, I'm not a loser," Vito said to himself.

"Vito, listen closely. We're not on their radar. We're nobodies. We're invisible. We're out of their league. These girls don't know we even exist."

"Nobodies? How can you say that? They see us every day at school. They know exactly who we are. They have known us since we were kids. We're not nobodies."

"Yeah, and I'm James Bond. I'll knock on her door and ask for a martini, shaken, not stirred, whatever that means."

Vito laughed until tears flowed on his rosy-red cheeks. Vito believed his friend to be the funniest guy in Conza.

"Quiet. You don't want them to know we're around. Keep it

down, will you?" Francesco said.

"Okay. Okay." Vito played along with Francesco because his friend loved to play boss. It made him feel important. And Vito let him. It was all a game. Good fun. Nobody gets hurt. Besides, Francesco made him laugh.

"As I said, one, Paulo De Simone as well as Maria's mother, will be busy elsewhere. And two," Francesco said seriously, "if I may be permitted to explain everything to you again, they, the girls, will be in the pool. The only pool in town that's heated. You know what that means, Vito?"

"No, tell me. Why does a heated pool require us to act like idiots and miss supper?" Vito was now a bit impatient.

"Because, they'll be naked, asshole!"

"Naked?"

Francesco nodded smugly.

"You mean, no clothes?" Vito said.

Francesco nodded again.

"No clothes at all?"

"Yeah. I mean nothing. Zero."

Francesco Carbone's plan, if you could call it that, was to get to De Simone's roof and get a front-row seat at what he believed would be the best show in Conza: De Simone's backyard.

"Are you sure?" Vito was a bit suspicious because this could be another of Francesco's crazy schemes.

"As sure as I can be about a sure thing," Francesco said confidently.

"I wish you're right about this. Because we could get in a whole lot of trouble," Vito said.

"Let me just say this: I'd hate to miss the girls frolicking in the pool."

"Frolicking!" Vito had never heard that word before.

"It means playing… in the water."

Vito wondered where Francesco got all his inside information on girls.

"I'd like to see that." Vito was now in.

Frolicking, Vito thought to himself. *This could be interesting!*

"I…" Vito began to say, "in my entire life. You know what I mean?"

"Whatever," Francesco mumbled. "As I said, the two hottest girls in Conza, buck freaking naked."

"Naked," Vito echoed the magic word. "When you say naked, you mean with a bathing suit? I've seen that before. But nothing at all? That would be something different."

"No bathing suits," Francesco answered confidently.

Vito was a bit puzzled, but at the same time strangely excited.

"But first, we'll have to find a way to the roof. Over there." Francesco pointed to the big house.

"I think I know a way to get there," Vito said.

"You think you know how…" Francesco didn't believe his friend was very bright or resourceful.

"I told you before, Francesco. Don't talk to me like that." Vito stood his ground.

"Okay, then tell me this. How would you know that?" Francesco was always the man with the plan, while Vito's job was to follow his lead. This reversal of roles couldn't be right. Francesco was a bit stunned, but still, if Vito could show the way, so much the better. He decided he'd go along.

"That's because when I was a kid, we played soccer. Over there." Vito pointed toward the back of the big house.

"And I know a way up to the roof. No one will see us. All we have to do is find our way behind Costanza's house, go through his garden, climb over the fence, get behind the shack, up the ladder and onto De Simone's roof."

Vito was pleased with himself. "I was the one who often found the soccer ball on the roof. They sent me up there to fetch it."

"I bet they did." Francesco could be so mean.

Despite his best friend's trusting outlook on life, Francesco was intrigued and glad to learn of his friend's mystifying secret to the roof. Francesco couldn't believe his luck. All this time, Vito, good old

Vito Picariello, actually had the key to front row seats.

"Right. Well, I guess you're the man with the plan."

"Yeah. But I can't say I'm happy about it."

"Now, what's wrong?"

"Trouble's with mom…" Vito said sheepishly.

"Why do you say that?" Francesco feared the worst.

"If my mom ever found out what we're about to do, she'd kill me. Hell, she'd kill you too. And then she'd tell your father."

"She won't. I promise." Francesco would have promised the moon if he needed to. The prize was well worth it.

"Okay then. Follow me." Vito led the way.

The pair walked past the De Simone's home, turned left and ran toward Costanza's house. They sneaked along the stone fence and found their way in the old man's back yard. From there, it took them a few seconds to reach the ladder to De Simone's roof.

Vito didn't waste any time. He was practically halfway up when he looked down and was surprised to see Francesco looking up.

"Come on," he whispered loudly.

"You're sure this ladder's safe?" Francesco was terrified.

"What are you talking about?" Vito asked.

"The ladder?"

"Wait a minute." Vito stared at Francesco. "Are you afraid of heights?"

"No, no. It's, it's just this old ladder." Francesco realized he had been found out.

"Don't bullshit me, Francesco. Get up here."

Vito had begun his transformation from fan to boss man. He felt good and at the same time, he thought he was putting his friendship with Francesco in peril. After all, their way of doing things depended on Francesco taking the lead. That was the way it was. Vito thought the adjustment could be difficult and risky. For both of them. Friends forever. That's what they both claimed and honored defiantly. No matter what.

Francesco started to climb up the ladder. Reluctantly at first.

But he had to be brave. Francesco couldn't lose face. Yet, he knew. Something big had happened. Groundbreaking. He'd been found out for what he really was: just another kid. Certainly, no better than Vito. Probably weaker. A small insignificant kid with a chip on his shoulders.

Deep down, Francesco understood his life was about to change forever. For the first time in his young life, reality would catch up with his illusions and smash them for everyone to see.

So, this is how things change, he thought to himself. *In the blink of an eye.*

His father would say that about people and their beliefs. "Listen up Francesco. In the blink of an eye, things change. Be ready."

"In the blink of an eye." Francesco said to himself.

"What'd you say?" Vito said.

"Nothing." Francesco was frightened.

"Okay then. Let's do this. Remember Francesco, this is your plan."

"Yeah, right. My plan." Francesco was almost sad. He wished he'd never heard the girls talk about the heated pool. Although it was too late to mention it, the story about the girls in the pool, naked, was part fantasy. More wishful thinking than real. He was now sure of it. The closer they got to their goal, the more Francesco believed the girls would be nowhere in sight. Their adventure would be a total bust.

By this time, the boys were only a few feet from their target: front row seats.

Probably all for nothing.

Suddenly, they heard voices. The girls. The boys crept on all fours and peered over the parapet. They hazarded a glance down toward the De Simone's back yard.

Right there. In De Simone's backyard. The pool. The only heated pool in Conza. And to their utter amazement, a lighted pool.

"Imagine that. A freaking light in the pool. What the heck will they think of next?" Vito couldn't believe his luck.

"Hey, Francesco?" Vito murmured very slowly.

"What?" Francesco said, almost choking.

"Do you see what I see?" Vito said.

"Yes."

"I don't believe it." Vito was deadly serious.

"Me either."

"What are they doing down there?" Vito started to feel his body tingle.

"Frolicking." Francesco answered carefully. He'd been right all along. Frolicking was the right word to use to describe what they were observing closely. They were catching their very first glimpse of erotica.

"Oh! So that's frolicking?" Vito said nervously.

"Damn right."

Before the boys would go back home for supper, they would also find out what all males sooner or later discover hidden deep within their life force. An understanding that men crave women. An unshakable need to be with them. To possess them. For the rest of their lives. An elemental drive that would only end when the body would neglect to adapt to old age and die away.

But that story would be for another time. Today was all about discovery. About boys being boys. That's not just a story, but Mother Nature's law.

The boys were gawking. Their bodies were sensing what it meant to become a man. They felt their essence transform. Although they didn't quite understand what was happening, the images from the illuminated pool were hypnotizing. They never took their eyes away from the girls. They were now captivated by women. Girls they wouldn't have given a second thought to barely a month ago.

The boys were lost. Time had crawled to a stop. The images from below would most likely last a lifetime.

It's safe to say that their little adventure was their first encounter with the other sex as well as a life changing experience.

All that from a thirteenth century roof.

4

CONZA
PROVINCE OF AVELLINO, ITALY

Sunday, November 23, 1980
19:34:52

Italy's long-standing relationship with Mother Nature's more eccentric behaviors was about to be renewed. She would remind, once more, the Italian nation, as well as the rest of the world, how the planet was run, what it was made of and why she always had the last word.

At precisely 19:34:52, the boys atop De Simone's house began to feel a vibration, what seismologists call a tremor. Within a fraction of a second, the tremor turned into a full-sized earthquake. With a 6.9 rating on the Richter Scale, the damage spread over 26,000 square kilometers or 10,000 square miles.

While the De Simone building's foundations were moving in one direction, the rest of the house was moving the opposite way. The three-story building, one of the oldest and largest houses in Conza, was vulnerable to earthquakes, mainly because of its age. The thirteenth century structure would most likely break apart at the foundation level before collapsing on itself. And so, within mere seconds of the first shock wave, the building was shifting back and forth, completely out of sync with its foundations.

The boys couldn't move. Nothing had prepared them for what happened in the next eighty seconds.

There were, in fact, three main shock waves. Each one had its epicenter in a different spot. Each one as powerful as the next. The massive earthquake was followed by 100 aftershocks. The event was so significant it was given a name: the 1980 *Irpinia* (Region) Earthquake.

Within seconds of the initial shock, the front of the De Simone's house collapsed, blocking the road. The roof was the second component to go. The boys began to experience the strangest feeling. It was as if they were lying in an elevator going down. In this case, the building was collapsing onto itself. The back of the house crashed on top of the pool and in so doing, covering the back yard with three meters of debris. Maria De Simone and Celestina Capone died at 19:37:01.

The boys heard the earth roar while the city buckled into a heap of rubble, razing the town clean of any man-made structures, while killing more than three thousand people in Conza alone. The earthquake wreaked havoc in more than six hundred towns in eight provinces, including dozens of buildings in Naples and Salerno. All in all, more than five thousand died, nine thousand were injured, one thousand went missing and four hundred thousand were now homeless. The destruction was massive.

The fires and dust caused by the earthquake's impact on Conza's infrastructure caused many to nearly suffocate and die.

When the dust finally settled, Francesco Carbone would learn that he had lost his entire family to falling debris. Francesco also lost his best friend. Vito Picariello died instantly as the collapsing roof hit the ground. His neck and spine sustained massive trauma. The boys remained beside each other for hours before rescuers found them.

Miraculously, Francesco had survived without a scratch. Rescuers from Naples couldn't understand how Francesco managed to survive. However, doctors predicted that the boy would be emotionally scarred for the rest of his life. The loss of his family would take years to heal, while Vito's death would never be forgotten. Inexplicably, Francesco believed he was somehow responsible for his friend's passing.

He lost everything in the blink of an eye.

Many believed the miracle child of eleven was an omen of things to come. A sign from God. Possibly a warning.

After a few days in a Red Cross emergency camp, Francesco was put in the hands of nuns at the Monastero di Santa Chiara in Naples. There, the nuns tried to heal the boy's soul. A nun was stationed by his bedside because, every night, Francesco would go back to Conza and relive the experience he went through. Francesco would wake up in tears, screaming for his mother. He was inconsolable.

The nuns also tried to instill into his fragile mind a new mission for his presence on earth. One that would take him as far away from his misery as quickly as possible. They had, what they believed, were important questions for the boy.

What was to become of him? Why was he saved from the earthquake? What would be his destiny? How could he repay God for his good luck?

Unfortunately, only the Lord could answer those questions. Francesco was in no shape to think about his future. Here and now was bad enough. Not surprisingly, the nuns turned to prayer for God's help. The boy, they believed, needed all the help he could get.

The aftershocks destroyed what infrastructure had resisted in the initial shockwave. Five days later, the head of the Avellino State police declared the town a total disaster. There was nothing left standing. A city that had been established hundreds of years before the birth of Christ simply ceased to exist.

Six months later, Francesco Carbone was on a direct flight from Rome to Los Angeles thanks to a charitable foundation established by Cardinal Zimmer, Louise Destrey's former client and benefactor.

Carbone's uncle, his only living relative, was found through the charitable foundation's extensive network. Mike Carbone had been given legal guardianship of the child. He was now legally responsible for the boy's welfare: he was officially obligated to take care of the young boy until he reached the age of eighteen.

Mike Carbone, Francesco's father's younger brother, had immigrated to the United States in 1970. After long years of hard work and dedication to his small business, Mike Carbone had become a successful businessman within the landscape architect community in Palm Springs. His list of customers included the who's who in the entertainment business and the corporate world. Mike Carbone knew on a first name basis the wealthiest people in California.

When Carbone senior suddenly became a parent to a child he had never met, he decided to give the boy every opportunity to make a man of himself and to live a happy life. His brother would have wanted his younger brother to carry on the task of educating his boy. And so he did.

But for now, Mike had to deal with a boy saddled with grief and anger. A boy haunted by nightmares inhabited by ghouls and monsters. A boy who desperately needed his mother and would probably never be like the other boys he was soon to meet in public school.

Mike Carbone had decided that the first order of business should be practical. He set for Francesco three challenges he would have to achieve within the first year of his new life in California.

His first challenge was simple: he needed to learn English. His second challenge was to stop crying. This would take time. His third challenge was to believe he would one day be happy again.

"Who really knows what awaits us," his newly found uncle would say to him every night before going to bed. "Remember Francesco, I love you very much. That's all you need to know. Now sleep." Mike prayed to his God to give the kid a break. Just one night without the nightmares. Just one would do the trick.

5

BOSTON TRIAGE GROUP (BTG)
CAMBRIDGE, MASSACHUSETTS

Present Day

Destrey sat still and studied Margaret McGivney.

"So, what do you think about this Carbone fella?" Margaret said.

"You tell me!" Destrey said.

"He believes Vesuvius is a threat," Margaret said. "He said it was just a matter of time before it erupted. It's his idea to get the Neapolitans to evacuate the city and resettle somewhere safe, away from the volcano."

Destrey frowned.

Margaret was trying to change the subject from Venezuela. Caracas could have ended in disaster.

"Did I say something funny?"

"No, of course not," Destrey said.

"Do you think he really wants us to evacuate Naples?" Margaret asked Destrey.

"Did he really say that? In those words?" Destrey began to believe this Carbone fellow was a bit naïve. Probably as green as she was when she believed that evacuating Jerusalem, when confronted with atomic annihilation, would be a piece of cake.

"Not in so many words," Margaret said, "but pretty much. So, what do you think?"

"I think I must think this one through. My gut tells me that Italians have gone through hell and back with the Covid pandemic. I don't know if Neapolitans or the Italian government have the heart or the resources to deal with this Vesuvius thing. Besides, relocating two million people is not possible. If what we've learned is true, some prefer to die than leave their homes and way of life. People won't listen to us when we tell them they must leave everything behind, for their own good."

"I see what you mean," Margaret's said.

"Even so, something tells me I've got to get to the bottom of this thing. It means I also need to do my homework."

"What thing? What homework are you talking about?" Margaret said.

"Why don't people in imminent danger act rationally? I think the pandemic happened because a lot of people believed the laws of nature only apply to others. That they were somehow immune. But in Carbone's case, I can't imagine a whole city in denial."

Destrey wasn't persuaded that she and her colleagues at TG had an explanation or a deep understanding of the Vesuvius phenomena. It could become a topic BTG would need to research. However, one fact was clear. Vesuvius had the potential to annihilate a city of millions, a threat that could equal or surpass Covid's death count.

Is it scheduled to erupt again? Destrey asked herself.

She questioned if she could seriously expect the Neapolitan people to do the unthinkable: to take Vesuvius as a credible treat and move away, leaving everything behind.

Do they have the energy to do that? She asked herself.

"Here's the real question: did the panddemic change the people of Naples?" Destrey said to Margaret.

"I don't know." Margaret was trying to figure that out, but she didn't have a clue where to start.

"Margaret, you've put your finger on the problem. We simply don't know."

"Didn't the Italian government develop evacuation plans for the city?" Margaret was more informed about Naples than Destrey thought.

"Yes. You're right. They did that because they believed Vesuvius was a real threat." Destrey understood evacuation plans far too well. They all had their limitations.

"Proof. Hard data that people can relate to. That's my point, Margaret. There's a big gap between proof and an evacuation plan. Proof of a future eruption implies we could figure out when."

"Neapolitans are not convinced because there's no such proof available," Margaret said. "Even though Vesuvius is still very much alive, it would be silly, if I were a Neapolitan, to believe it would happen again, to me, in my lifetime. It's all about our belief that things like that only happen to others. I lived through Covid-19. So, Vesuvius is no threat to me. I don't believe it will happen to me. It's not imminent. It's almost unreal. Like in Pompeii: the eruption happened over 70 generations ago. That's a long time ago," Margaret said.

"I think you're right. If I was a Neapolitan," Destrey said, "I wouldn't hold my breath." Destrey had been going through the motions of arguing the point back and forth. In actual fact, she didn't believe there was a chance in hell she could pull off an evacuation. "My gut tells me there's got to be something else we could do, but I can't put my finger on it."

"You're overthinking it," Margaret said.

"I don't think so." Destrey was curious. "I'd like to figure out how we could do this? For argument's sake, of course. Not that I believe it would work. But what's the harm in looking at it? Putting forward a theory to test how an evacuation could be done could be interesting."

"How you're going to do what?" Margaret wasn't so sure Destrey was on the right track. However, she was relieved to see that she did get Caracas out of Destrey's mind.

"I don't know. I wish I could have been there in Pompeii when it all happened."

"Well, maybe you could. Why don't you ask your machine in the basement to put on a show for you?"

Destrey thought that putting the supercomputer to work was a good idea. "I think I will, Margaret. Thank you. I love our chats."

"Does that mean I can have a raise?" Margaret said.

Destrey didn't answer. She smiled back at her assistant and promised herself to look into it. That she did indeed merit a pay raise wasn't the issue. Destrey was thinking more about officializing what she was accomplishing for the firm day in, day out. In a nutshell, Margaret made sure the organization would run smoothly when Destrey was off on some mission halfway across the world.

"Would you talk to Constantin? I need his help with Lola. Tell him I want to know as much as possible about Vesuvius. I've got to go back in time and get a better idea of what Vesuvius is capable of. Tell him I'd like Lola to supply me with a simulation. One more thing. I'd like Lola to explore how Naples could be evacuated."

"Start the ball rolling?" Margaret said.

"Yeah, but I'm not really sure about helping Carbone or not?" Destrey wasn't convinced either way.

6

LOLA'S FIRST & SECOND SIMULATION

Vesuvius, 1798 BCE

Deep in BTG's subbasement, Lola's holographic form appeared as Destrey was reviewing her notes. She invited several staff members to attend the simulations in person in what employees called the Safe.

"The simulation is ready for you, *Madame* Destrey. Is there anything else I can do for you?" Lola asked.

BTG had upgraded their computing power with the HPE Cray Exascale Supercomputer. Like the initial Cray, the new mainframe was also given the name of Lola. Staffers said that naming it was merely for the sake of facilitating transactions between humans and machines. Some staffers alleged that the name Lola was derived from Our Lady of Sorrows, a title for the Virgin Mary. Needless to say, Destrey wasn't impressed but nevertheless accepted, reluctantly, to deal with the computer by addressing it by its name: Lola.

"I'd like you to provide me with Vesuvius' current status," Destrey said. "Two, how do people come to live so close by? I just can't get my head around that one," she said to herself. "And three, how will Neapolitans react to a full-fledged eruption? Give me a wide spectrum of possibilities."

Destrey preferred to work with simulations because they had the power to engage viewers in a deeper appreciation of the data collected. Rather than just understanding a phenomenon through theories and numbers, simulations would involve all Destrey's senses.

Staff assembled in BTG's subbasement facility. They called Lola's lair the Safe because the building once belonged to a bank. BTG used the bank's strongroom to isolate their supercomputer from hackers and intruders. So far, it had worked out well.

"As some of you already know, we've had a request to help Naples if and when Vesuvius decides to blow its top," Destrey said.

A few old timers snickered.

"Yeah, yeah, I know." Destrey looked around, scanning the small crowd. She respected every one of them. They were the best of the best.

"I know what you're thinking. And I agree with you. I'm not so sure we can evacuate people from their homes. Not anymore. Because we've been there. We tried and failed twice."

"We've learned from our past assignments that there's still a lot to learn about people's attachment to their homes and place of birth. In the end, we had to admit to ourselves and to our clients that logic wasn't a significant element in people's decision-making process. Oddly enough, imminent danger was often a secondary issue."

"In a few moments," Destrey continued, "Lola's going to show us simulated characters and environments. People will come to life and reveal how they would react to an erupting volcano. Subsequent to Lola's simulations, our general level of understanding should theoretically allow us to come up with insights the computer is incapable of rendering."

Someone in the back said, "Yet!"

"Yeah. That too," Destrey said. "You're right. I'm thinking we'll all be in trouble when that happens!"

Destrey had nothing more to add. Everyone was waiting to see what Lola was about to show them.

"Okay Lola. Let's get the ball rolling." Lola launched the simulation.

"Thank you, *Madame* Destrey," Lola said. "Based on archeological evidence, Vesuvius was active as early as 1798 BCE. About two thousand years before Jesus Christ."

"That's a long time ago, Lola," Destrey said.

"It's a mere second or two in a volcano's timeline," Lola replied.

"Right," Destrey said. "But is a four-thousand-year-old story pertinent?"

Destrey took a deep breath. She realized she was arguing with a machine.

"Okay, let's get on with it. Show us what you've got."

"The following two simulations are based on archeological evidence," Lola said. "I have, however, taken the liberty of adding filler to provide context."

"So, a plausible story?" Destrey asked.

"Yes. More or less."

"Okay. Go on." Destrey was now curious about what the computer had come up with.

"I have been fortunate to have discovered works by Plato on the subject of Vesuvius," Lola said, almost with pride. "These early texts of Plato were yet unknown because they were incorrectly attributed to another author. What we have here is his interpretation of what he believed occurred hundreds, perhaps thousands of years before his birth. By today's standards, we could call Plato's work speculative journalism. Apparently, he wanted to record Vesuvius' lore and myths. I believe he might have heard of Vesuvius through his travels. It is entirely possible that the Athenian philosopher was writing about the volcano's very first eruption."

The men and women listening to Lola were expecting a fictional description of Vesuvius and how people related to the mountain. Lola had, in the past, researched her topics with as much truth as possible, adding a little drama here and there to foster understanding and interest. But in this case, Lola underlined the fact that she had unearthed previously unknown information. That would include an accurate context about Vesuvius' past. Lola believed it could greatly help BTG in creating believable scenarios as well as projections. Something every professional at BTG knew as Destrey's gospel when it came to context: Vaynerchuk's *Knowledge is king, but context is God.*

"All right, Lola. Let's move this along. We haven't got all day."

Lola said nothing at first. A few moments later, a panorama of the Bay of Naples was displayed on a large screen. Lola's rendering of Vesuvius' domain was remarkable: a vast wilderness of tall grass, blue skies and, at its center, a towering volcano.

"Witness Vesuvius thousands of years ago," Lola said. "Our narrator will now continue with the simulation."

Morgan Freeman's digital voice spoke.

"Such was the case almost two thousand years before Christ," Freeman said, "when Vesuvius began to awake from its sleep. The colossus was showing signs that its time had come. Although ancient Egyptians and Babylonians were at that time raising great cities and fortified military installations, nobody alive could imagine what volcanoes were about or what they were capable of. Nor could they ever know how many times the mountain had erupted in the past. However, given its age, some eighteen thousand years, there was a good chance it had erupted at least half a dozen times."

"The people living on the slopes of Mount Vesuvius couldn't explain to their children how nature could destroy lives in the blink of an eye. But, nevertheless, an explanation about the mountain's temper was required. Because humans had to know. Surviving the elements was a daily challenge that could only happen through the gods' favor."

"Mother Nature was consequently personified by gods, deities and spirits," Freeman said. "Life-giving and nurturing gods were linked to motherhood. There were other deities representing war, sickness and death. Gods were at the heart of humans' everyday life. Gods actively got involved. People used myth to explain natural phenomena, such as the weather, earthquakes, floods and, of course, smoking mountains."

As Freeman explained the relationship between humans and gods, Lola presented images of small villages, where everyone knew everyone else. The hamlets consisted of one main road and a few paths. Everyone in a village belonged to the same tribe.

"The stories about nature's behavior," said Freeman, "were mostly centered on the gods' dispositions. Or so believed Teitu and Semni Karkana. A couple living in a small village on the slopes of Vesuvius."

Lola had generated an image of a small settlement with fifteen dwellings. Farmers built their homes from the resources they found close by, such as wood and stone. Most villages near Vesuvius grew cereal and kept cattle. The land was exceptionally fertile. Villagers also had to protect themselves from their enemies with defensive structures such as wooden fences and bridges.

"In the summer of 1798 BCE," Freeman said, "Vesuvius reawakened in the age of bronze tools and weaponry. The mountain emerged from its dormant state. It was alive again. Vesuvius was preparing the world for a demonstration of what it was capable of."

Freeman explained through words and images that men and women of the time prayed to their gods for almost every need they couldn't control or satisfy through their labor. As the mountain shook the planet's surface, men and women from every caste and village appealed to their gods for protection. Especially those who inhabited the land near the mountain. The little creatures farming the land flanking the volcano's crater were by now accustomed to what growled and buckled in the night. However, none had experienced the mountain's true nature. No one could decipher the signs of the devastation that was about to hit them. No one had ever heard of or seen a volcano in action.

"At the foot of the mountain," Freeman continued, "a small miracle attracted attention. A special life. A newborn. The little one was a wonderful mystery. They caller her Tita. The name described the little one as gifted. Very few were born so stunning, so happy and so incredibly magical. Semni, the young mother of fourteen, immediately gained prominence within her village and the region. Word about the newborn child spread like wildfire. A gift from the goddess. A miracle child was born under the stars. Men, women and children, shepherds as well as magicians and shamans, came from far and wide to witness the newborn child. A blessed future was assured for Semni's family."

Lola had generated the image of a teenage mother holding a newborn. The background presented Vesuvius in all its glory.

"I can picture the context you're trying to convey, Lola," Destrey said. "It reminds me of the birth of Jesus. So, what's your point?"

"I wanted to provide a context that has been with us since the beginning of time: the relationship between humans and the unknown, *Madame* Destrey. As far as I know, there has always been a need to explain the unknown and to believe in all-powerful beings called gods."

"Did you paste the Jesus birth into this simulation?" Destrey asked.

"I believe it's the other way around, *Madame* Destrey," Lola said. "Accounts of amazing births aren't exclusive to Christianity. I found them in mythologies and religious traditions from ancient Egyptians, Aztecs, Greeks and Chinese. Reports of incredible nativities included strange circumstances and features such as interventions by deities with supernatural powers and complex explanations."

"Point taken," Destrey said.

Freeman continued the narration.

"The little one had piercing blue eyes and blond angelic hair. The suspicious as well as the skeptical were taken aback by her smile. When her delicate fingers touched a villager's face, they would feel a warm sensation, followed by a sense of joy and stillness. They were overwhelmed by the light in her eyes, while their brutish hearts were conquered and subdued. Such was the impact of the newborn baby, the child from the goddess, the guardian from the clouds."

"She was named Tita, Promise and Miracle," Freeman said. "The ultimate mystery from the goddess Mother of all Things. Her innocent stare challenged people's souls. Tita was mother's little glow in the dark in an otherwise hard and dangerous life. The little one was her reason to live."

"Tita's birth had been announced by the Mother of all Things. That day, the earth roared and swayed, the water spilled over the riverbanks, the animals howled, and the shepherds had been told of the birth of a miracle child by the spirits."

"Tita was now two years old. The girl was too young to work in the fields where Semni was occupied. There was work to do. The crops were almost ready. The harvest was an essential part of the village's survival. More importantly, they had to prepare for the cold weather ahead. Soon, winter was going to change everything. Perhaps it would come earlier this year because the old ones knew how Mother Nature worked. Some predicted the future because they had been around for so many seasons."

"The little one suddenly cried out," Freeman said. "Leave her, Teitu said furiously to his mate. For the first time in his life, the young man realized he was responsible for more than his own survival. His future depended on how he would ensure his wife and child's continued existence. He was also responsible for the village's welfare and continued existence." We will be late, he said menacingly to his people. I don't want to starve, and that's all I have to say, he added."

"Semni, who was by now sixteen years old, had learned to ignore the cries of her little one," said Freeman. "Semni nodded to her mate and resumed her work. The village needed wood for cooking and for heat. But Tita was furious. No one was listening to her cries. Not even her own mother. Semni looked up toward the family hut. Her husband growled his displeasure and told her to see to it that Tita behaves. And come back, he said, a bit exasperated. I need the work done."

"Despite the added responsibility of leading the villagers

through a rough winter, the young man loved his family and was proud of steering his tribe in the right direction. An obligation he took seriously," said Freeman.

"There had been too many deaths and disappearances in the recent past which left them vulnerable to nature's whims and bad temper. Teitu Karkana was chosen to lead and protect the villagers because he was the strongest man left standing from last winter's cold winds and snow. However, all would be for nothing if his people froze to death. Which meant wood. Lots of dried wood that would shelter them from the cold weather, the snow, the wild animals and those who raided the villages along the coast, enslaving, killing and pillaging everything in sight. Wood was essential for warmth, for manufacturing blades to defend their village and for the hunt."

"We know through recent archeological digs," Freeman said, "that villages near Vesuvius traded their produce for fish and dried meat, not unlike our present-day prosciutto. They also bartered for clay pots, cloth and a few Mycenaean ceramic vessels for cooking."

"Later, Semni asked the little one what could make her so frightened. The girl grinned and smiled as she soon forgot why she had called her mother in the first place. Just then, something happened. The little one gripped her mother's hair and pulled. Semni cried out. The little one looked down and said the monster was coming for her. The child was pointing at the ground. Semni tried to reassure her daughter, saying there was no such monster."

"The little one looked at her mother as if she was thinking," Freeman said. "Semni was getting impatient as well as a bit frustrated. Because she too wondered why the Mother of all Things was displeased with her village. What had they done wrong this time? It was always something with these gods, Semni said to herself. The gods were fickle and nasty and, at times, wonderful. Semni could have said the same about her husband but didn't. If only the gods could be clear. Would it be too much trouble if the Mother of all Things would make up her mind and let us be?"

Freeman explained that tremors had been spooking the villagers all summer. The ground rumbled. Clay pots collapsed while their huts would swing back and forth. Animals ran away, never to be seen again.

"Suddenly, there was a loud noise," Freeman said. "Something no one had ever heard before. A sound so alien that some of the villagers kneeled and begged the gods to protect them."

"Boom! There it was again," Freeman said. "Everyone in the village stood motionless as they all looked up toward the mountain to the south. It's from there, said an old man. Boom! The old man pointed to the mountain top. The mountain's peak was often surrounded by dark clouds."

"According to Plato," Freeman said, "this was not the first time the mountain had roared like a wild animal."

"Teitu called everyone back to work. There was no time to waste because the cold weather was coming. If they wanted to live, they had to find wood."

Freeman explained that some of the wood collected would be used to reinforce fences that held their cattle away from predators and keep the families warm. That evening, Teitu, Semni and Tita knelt before a rotund statuette of a naked lady no more than six inches tall. They paid tribute to the mother goddess with a few olives and bread.

"During the night, Teitu woke a few times," Freeman said. "He believed there was an intruder in the village. By putting his ear to the ground, he realized it was something else. The growling noises came from the ground. Maybe his daughter was right. Maybe there was something to this monster business. Perhaps something had to be done. But what? Teitu tried to remain calm himself and decided to leave this matter aside for another day. For now, he needed his sleep. He had so much work to do. He couldn't quite put his finger on what disturbed him. And then it came to him: there was no noise. No birds, no infernal flies, no dogs barking, no bleating goats. Nothing. All he heard was the rustling of leaves. Nothing else. The land was dead. This had never happened before. He sat up to make sure he wasn't dreaming. He wasn't. Teitu was now wide awake. Confident he had his wits about him, he readied for a fight. Not all neighboring villages were friendly. Some would kill and steal, especially at this time of year. Others didn't require a reason to kill. The world was indeed a tough and wicked place which to live in. Teitu carefully stepped out of his hut. He was intent on finding the reason why the world he knew was so noiseless. There wasn't a bird in the sky, he said to himself."

Freeman explained that at the time, humans were hunters and they also had to fight to survive. Teitu was no exception. Freeman said this part of the simulation was added to help describe man's essential character.

"Teitu crept across the path that led to where the cattle were kept," Freeman said. "Once he got there, he realized the animals had disappeared. The rudimentary fence built with thorn bushes had failed. The animals fled, but there were no signs of predators lurking around the village. His cattle, their insurance policy against starvation, had vanished without a trace. More than fifteen of his people would die from hunger if he didn't find his cattle. He rapidly became fearful. His world was turning against him. Someone or something was surely stalking the village, waiting for the right moment to take the jump on him. Ever alert for any sign of intruders, he circled the village twice again and found nothing. No human footprints or telltale signs left behind by wild animals. There was nothing he could point to, but still, there he was, at the edge of his small village with a sense of foreboding. He had a feeling that something evil was about to happen, closing in. His future, his wife's and his child's lives, as well as the village's survival, didn't bode well. He was smart enough to know he was in trouble, but for the life of him, he didn't have a clue what to think or what to do."

Freeman explained that the following scene was based on real evidence as to the behaviors of animals during volcanic activity.

"Everything changed in an instant," Freeman said. "A couple of rabbits ran past Teitu, paying little or no attention to him or the blade he was carrying. They ran past him without taking a second look. They appeared frightened. Teitu Karkana put two and two together and came up with an idea that he believed explained everything. The gods, he surmised, were very angry with him and that explained why the animals had the good sense to get as far away as they could from him. Because he now believed he had disrespected the goddess. He had waited too long to beg for her forgiveness. It was the only explanation he could come up with. If that was true, then all of this was his fault. Teitu was angry with himself. He promptly became a true believer and vowed he would pray to the Mother of all Things and pay homage to her as often as he could. Sunrise was minutes away. Villagers were preparing for the day's work. Teitu Karkana had planned a specific task for each man, woman and child. This morning wasn't any different, but for one important task. He had to find the cattle he'd lost. It was a matter of life and death. An hour later, the villagers were all working together to collect and store foodstuff for the winter while he went hunting for his missing herd. He came back a few hours later with nothing to show. Teitu was fuming as well as frightened by the absence of any and all animals. Clearly, he had failed to find them. Eventually, the village would blame him for this failure. Meanwhile, the mountain continued to belch white smoke. It could be seen from miles away. Teitu took a second look at the mountain and was confounded. It appeared the mountain had grown while the white smoke he noticed a few minutes earlier was turning blackish. Teitu tried to focus on the job. But although he grew accustomed to the Mother of all Things' fury, he couldn't help thinking that the ground grew louder by the minute. Strange noises emanated from the rocks surrounding the village. Tita howled and wailed and screamed and lashed out. Although the mountain had been quiet for the last few days, the little one was completely possessed by fear. Teitu had enough of her temper tantrums. He was going to do something about it. The villagers expected the chief's child to behave. He approached the child. Semni would do anything to protect Tita. Teitu tried to calm his daughter. He pushed his wife aside with a stroke of his hand. He didn't mean to hurt Semni, but nevertheless, she ended up at the other end of their small hut. He managed to grab Tita in spite of her wild behavior. He seized her tiny body and came up close to her face. Tita suddenly became quiet. Teitu was relieved. Semni thanked the gods he was not going to kill her. Semni sat up, prepared to save her child, just in case. But nothing happened. Suddenly, Tita told her father that she understood. At first, Teitu couldn't comprehend what was happening. She had called him father for the first time. Teitu was confused."

Freeman described the next scene as part of local mythology. The players included Teitu, Semni and Tita.

"*Apa* or father," Tita said impassively. "You are my *apa*."

Teitu stared at his daughter. He'd heard stories the old hags recounted from time to time about his daughter. He had no patience for this magic nonsense. Tita was just a little girl. Nothing more. But now she was talking to him. Teitu didn't believe his ears. Where did she get all these new words? She was too young for that. A little kid who could barely put two words together. Teitu turned to Semni, hoping she could make sense of it all. But Semni was just as baffled as he was. She came closer, but Tita didn't turn away from her father's stare.

"I don't understand what is happening," Teitu said. "Tita?" he said loudly. "Tita?" He said again. The little one did not respond. She looked deep into her father's eyes and finally spoke up. She told her father the mountain will kill all of them tomorrow morning.

"We must go," Tita said. "Run away from the mountain. There was nothing he could do." The child said *she* had told her.

"Who told you? Tell me who and I will kill her with my bare hands."

"Mother," Tita said flatly. Teitu turned to Semni.

"No," the child said. "No *ati*," Tita said. "Mother of all Things. She said to leave now. She said father must believe. Father protect villagers and run far away."

Teitu was now even more confused. The little one continued to look at her father. She clutched his face in her tiny hands and moved in closer.

"Listen to Mother, Teitu. She is trying to save you. Do not waste time or we will all die before the sun comes up."

Tita kissed her father's cheeks, closed her eyes and fell into a deep sleep. Teitu held her limp body close to his as he began to think. *Yes*, Teitu thought to himself. I *am a proud man. I am also stubborn. Some would say I am a hardheaded man.* But… He looked at Tita's little face. *I am not a stupid man.* Teitu was aware, alert and concerned.

"Get my stick, woman. I have work to do. Here, take the child."

"What are you going to do, husband?" Semni asked.

Freeman explained that Teitu, like a few others of the region, had run away from the mountain. As far as they could. There was a good chance no one really understood what they were running away from, because at that time, there was no word for volcanoes.

"Abruptly, the tremors had begun once again," Freeman said. "The quakes were getting stronger. The Mother of all Things had told Teitu to run. And he did. All day and all night. Unfortunately, only a few made it to safety. Teitu never looked back."

Lola appeared again.

"This first simulation takes us back to the 1798 BCE eruption. As I said earlier, the data shows Vesuvius had previously erupted on five or six occasions. However, the 1798 BCE eruption was by far significantly larger than the famous eruption in AD 79 known as the Avellino eruption which engulfed several Bronze Age settlements."

"What are we expected to learn from this first simulation?" Destrey asked Lola.

"One, people have been living near or around Vesuvius for as long as we can remember and there are good reasons to believe that the next eruption could spread to Naples' borders and beyond. Two, the land was and is still very fertile and has been attracting farmers for many millennia. Three, the volcano's pre-eruption behavior did not scare people away, although some tried to run away as the volcano erupted. The data shows that a few made their way to safety, but they were the exception. Four, our modern relationship with volcanoes is complicated and partly due to their unimaginable power. It is the stuff of legends and myths, passed from one generation to the next by storytelling and art. Some believe that volcanoes are alive and that they can be reasoned with. Anthropomorphism or giving human traits or attributes to objects such as volcanoes may still be out there."

"So, getting people away from Vesuvius well before an eruption is complicated. Are you telling me that it takes a message from God to get them to move away?" Destrey asked Lola.

"I understand that logic and reasoning might not be enough to have people move away from their homes, their families and friends, *Madame* Destrey, but yes. It would appear that an evacuation before an actual eruption would require an extraordinary messenger, be it mystical or technological. Either way, I believe any evacuation before an eruption is problematic, if not impossible."

"That's not exactly what I expected," Destrey said to herself. She was trying to make sense of the simulation but had not seen the obvious.

"Humans fail to remember, *Madame* Destrey," Lola said.

"Remember what?"

"That volcanoes erupt and wreak havoc," Lola said. "As a result, sooner or later people return to live in their shadows and refuse to resettle elsewhere."

"How can Neapolitans fail to see that thing that looms over them 24/7? That's my question."

"May I continue, *Madame* Destrey?"

"Yes, of course, Lola. Let's get on with it."

"Let's jump back to Vesuvius' last full-scale eruption, set near Pompeii, in 79 AD," Lola said. "Let's remember that people had returned to Vesuvius' slopes in 900 AD."

The simulation displayed images of the ancient resort town of Pompeii. The view from the skies displayed Pompeii in all its splendor. A town for the rich and famous of the time. Images showing elegant homes, sumptuous villas and artisans' shops lined the paved streets of the resort town. Travelers, visitors, sightseers, townspeople and slaves hustled about in and out of small businesses, taverns and coffee shops as well as brothels and bathhouses. Pompeii's amphitheater could seat around 20,000 people and served not only Pompeii but also the inhabitants of surrounding towns, such as Herculaneum, Oplontis and Stabiae. On warm sunny days, Pompeiians gathered and lounged in open-air squares and marketplaces.

Morgan Freeman began his second narration.

"Tiberius Quintus Petronius, son of Augustus Petronius, came from old money. In fact, vast amounts of money were made on the backs of generations of slaves who died in the Tiberius family's underground mining properties. The old man's claim to fame was finding gold mines in Roman Britain. His father also made a fortune with copper, iron, lead and salt. Now, his son Tiberius Quintus Petronius was fortunate enough to find huge deposits of silver. It positioned Tiberius close to the imperial families of Rome for more than three decades. Because of his family's reputation in making things happen, Emperor Titus Flavius Vespasianus often sought Tiberius' advice."

"Tiberius set the letters aside and told his wife, Aelia Antonia, he had an early rise. Tomorrow was an important day," Freeman said. "Tiberius had been summoned by the emperor. Aelia Antonia said nothing. She knew better than to talk about the emperor in front of the slaves. The next day, Tiberius was facing his emperor. Overlooking the slopes of the Palatine, Tiberius couldn't help pondering about former emperors' legacies, victories and downfalls, as he stood over the buried site of Nero's palace. He stood patiently before Emperor Titus Flavius Caesar Vespasianus. Tiberius bowed and waited for the emperor to acknowledge his presence. Tiberius recognized the former general's tendencies to behave as a soldier. The emperor looked up and smiled at Tiberius. He was glad to see him again. He told Tiberius he needed his services urgently."

Freeman explained why the emperor required his services. It

was about money. And because of Tiberius' unwavering loyalty, he would rely on his expertise to fix his problem, quickly and discreetly. There was, of course, no need for official protocol between these two men. They were friends. The emperor needed Tiberius to finish the Flavian Amphitheater (Colosseum) within budget. The emperor had good reasons to be angry. Although he ruled half the planet, he nevertheless needed Tiberius' help with the Senate. The amphitheater would become, upon completion, the biggest amphitheater in the world. One that could seat well over 80,000 people. The emperor's ire was aimed specifically at the so-called money grabbing sonofabitches from the Senate, who were looting his treasury. Corruption was rampant. The emperor would be happy if only he could control the misuse of funds to a manageable level.

Freeman explained that men such as Tiberius understood right from the start that a mere mortal could not refuse an emperor's wishes. Tiberius had only two weeks to put his business affairs in order before taking complete ownership of the project. Tiberius planned to travel to Pompeii in all haste. He bowed and thanked his emperor. With that said, the emperor was done. The meeting was over. Tiberius was simultaneously grateful for having the emperor's confidence and terrified at the prospect of making new enemies. Enemies that could take him down with no possible help from the emperor. He had no time to lose. Pompeii and his villa's builders were awaiting his presence. The next morning, the sun had barely risen when Tiberius' wife and children joined him aboard his personal warship, the Oceanus. It was early.

"Aelia Antonia, Tiberius' wife, hadn't seen the ship before today," Freeman said. "She was under the impression that they were to travel in a much smaller boat. The Oceanus was over 128 meters long and 21 meters high (420 feet by 72 feet). It was huge. It was a unique warship, in fact, the most sophisticated warship of its time. Tiberius had it built for the exclusive use of his family business. The Oceanus was a trireme class warship which meant three rows of oars manned with one man per oar. The warship was powered by over

270 oarsmen. Unlike military warships of its time, his crew which included the oarsmen and soldiers, was made up entirely of paid employees, most of which came from the military, all of which were Roman citizens. As a result of the Oceanus' naval technology and Tiberius' HR philosophy, the ship was extremely fast, exceptionally dangerous and virtually unsinkable. Tiberius also owned a private fleet of commercial ships which served his vast commercial enterprises in the Mediterranean, the Red Sea, the Indian Ocean, the Atlantic coasts of Gaul, Britain and Africa. Tiberius ran a global enterprise. He also possessed a fleet of warships and a legion of private soldiers to protect his cargo as well as his sailors from pirates and ambitious seamen who would kill their own mothers for the booty he regularly shipped to Rome."

"Today, because the Mediterranean was infested with pirates, Tiberius was accompanied by two new warships he had purchased from the Carthaginians," Freeman explained. "Sailing to Pompeii was the safest and fastest way to reach his villa and be back in Rome in time to deal with the emperor's project. Tiberius would take the time at sea to rest and think about how he would handle the emperor and his greedy senators."

Freeman explained that on the evening of August 22, 79 AD, the Oceanus' captain spotted Bauli (now known as Bacoli). Which meant they were a day away from Pompeii. Tiberius would be at his villa the next day in time for dinner. The villa had suffered significant damage on February 5, 62 AD. The earthquake struck the towns of Pompeii and Herculaneum, severely damaging them. The quake had caused widespread destruction around the Bay of Naples which included the loss of livestock from poisoned air near Pompeii. So far, it had cost Tiberius and his father before him, more than fifteen years of expensive reconstruction. A few Roman families who had their villas destroyed in the earthquake had decided to wait and see before rebuilding their summer houses. Other wealthy Roman families stayed away from Pompeii altogether because they were getting a bit uneasy with the constant tremors. However, Tiberius wasn't hampered by money, time or danger. His architects had managed to almost rebuild his villa. It sat atop a cliff overlooking the bay: a villa that the emperor would have wished for himself. The house was not only a retreat. The Villa of the Mysteries (Villa dei Misteri) as it was called, was the symbol of Roman aristocracy and money. An early version of today's mega-mansions. The Villa was ridiculously massive and opulent. In fact, it was dubbed palatial. It was also a money pit, the cost of which would have fed every Pompeiian for a year. Tiberius usually kept a tight grip on the villa's rebuild, but Aelia saw to it that no expense would be spared. She was competing with other Roman families who had the biggest, the best, the most extraordinary houses money could buy. The next day, as they reached the shores of Pompeii, the family was resting comfortably aboard ship having a light lunch sprinkled with anticipation of what lay ahead at the villa. The sea was unseasonably calm. Tiberius decided Pompeii would have to wait for another day. Tonight, they would stay onboard while the crew took a break. Tiberius planned to send one of his warships ahead to inform the villa's custodian of his arrival the next day. Everything would need to be in place to receive the family. It would be worth the extra night at sea. At around twelve noon, as the sun was squarely above the Oceanus, Tiberius spotted a vertical cloud coming from the top of Vesuvius. A curious event that had begun to materialize two days earlier. Tiberius being a practical man, kept a close eye on the mountain. He was glad he had postponed his arrival by another day. He was also thinking of rescinding his order to send a warship to Pompeii before nightfall."

"The mountain had clearly begun to show its intentions," Freeman cautioned BTG's staff. "Small quakes, fissures, releases of ash and smoke from the Vesuvius had been observed by thousands of people. Because Pompeiians had become accustomed to small quakes occurring in the region, few paid attention to the mountain's behavior. Most were unmindful of these precursor events as Vesuvius began to stir. However, a few families on vacation in Pompeii and Herculaneum decided that it was time to return to Rome. The small quakes made the children cranky: it was time to get going. They would leave behind some of their staff to keep an eye on their domain while they set off for the safety of their homes in Rome. At this point in time, most Pompeiians still in the city, stayed put. By mid-afternoon, ash began to block the sun. Tiberius had never witnessed anything like that before. He began to understand Vesuvius as a potential threat to himself, his family and his crew. Tiberius ordered all his warships to get as far away from Pompeii as they could. Tiberius heard the mountain roar. It exploded sending a high-altitude column of white smoke and ash darkening the city as well as the sun. The vertical cloud looked like an expanding pine tree. The smoke, sometimes as dark as night, began to swell and cover the whole mountain as well as the bay. A few moments later, a peculiar smell hit the warships and the crews began to cough. He ordered his captains to run at full speed. The oarsmen went to work at battle speed before reaching ramming speed. The warships were doing an incredible eight knots. Aelia had been below deck during most of Vesuvius' temper tantrum. Tiberius wondered if this was the end of the world. By now, people in Pompeii and Herculaneum were already trying to clear the ash from their roofs. The mountain exploded again, sending all kinds of fire and destruction over the people that stayed behind. The mountain's roar was deafening. Meanwhile, the smell of rotting eggs was edging its way down to the oarsmen. The speed of his three warships came as no surprise to the man who thanked the gods for his good fortune. Again, Tiberius heard the mountain thunder. While he held his wife and children close to him, Tiberius couldn't help it. He was amazed by the power of the gods. While the wind blew full force pushing his warships farther away from the shore, Tiberius saw a magnificent sight: a crown of lightning illuminating the sky around the mountain top. A stunning light show, the likes of which no one alive had yet been able to record for posterity. Tiberius stood before Vesuvius. Hades, he said quietly to his family. The god of the dead and king of the underworld."

"What are we expected to learn from this second simulation?"

Destrey asked Lola.

"As I said before, people have been living near or around Vesuvius for as long as we can remember. Also, the land was and is still very fertile and has been attracting farmers for millennia. Then, the volcano's pre-eruption behavior did not scare most Pompeiians. Although some noble families had decided not to come back to Pompeii ever again, the data shows that some of those who stayed behind made their way to safety the day before. However, most Pompeiians died a horrific death. Finally, as I said before, our modern relationship with volcanoes is complicated, even more today."

Lola thanked the audience for their patience and bid everyone a good day.

7

BOSTON TRIAGE GROUP (BTG) CAMBRIDGE, MASSACHUSETTS

"Was Lola helpful?" Constantin asked.

"About Pompeii, yes. No doubt. About Naples, I don't know. I'm asking myself if what I've learned about Pompeiians is still relevant today. That's my question."

"Did Lola say that?"

"Not in so many words, but she did give me the perspective I needed. Back then, they had warning signs. Some got the message, others didn't. Some left Pompeii. Those who had nowhere to go, died."

"Didn't know that," Constantin said.

"Still, I think I'm missing something," Destrey said.

"See, you're doing it again," Margaret said. "The answers to your questions are right under your nose. Lola did her job. But you're still looking for your keys under the lamppost."

"Maybe. But this kind of problem is going to surface again. This time, I'd like to be sure of what I'm getting into. And for that to happen, I'd have to see it with my own eyes."

"Are you saying we're taking on this Naples' deal?" Margaret said.

"I guess so," Destrey said. "Yes. That's my answer. Regardless of what Francesco Carbone comes up with, there's a pretty good chance we'll be involved," Destrey said, as she remembered how the firm often ended up tangled in impossible missions.

"We're talking about hundreds of thousands of people," Destrey said. "Could end up in the millions. What am I going to say to myself if we do nothing? I think it's our job and especially what the Cardinal would have wanted us to do. Help people. All we have to do is figure out how. And I know, you don't have to tell me. It's not going to be an easy task considering the size of Naples."

"So, when you say with your own eyes, do you mean in person?" Constantin asked.

"Yeah. It looks like I'm going to Naples. See for myself."

"Right," said Margaret.

"Let's get some coffee. We need to chat." Destrey said to Constantin as he was already thinking of the logistics required to make this happen.

"Naples!" Margaret said. "Smack dab in the middle of hell."

"Well, that doesn't surprise me much." Constantin had been reviewing Lola's research output. "Lola's been working on Naples without us prompting her to do so."

"Over the years, I've heard a lot of strange stuff concerning the computer. Let me tell you something about Lola you may not know. Working on Naples on her own gets me thinking that your machine is haunted," Margaret said.

"Please don't say that," Louise said.

Back in her office, Destrey was looking outside her window, thinking. Constantin Greco was enjoying his coffee.

"Tell me, Constantin, what do you know about Vesuvius? I mean now, the volcano today?" Destrey asked.

"Funny you should ask. Lola's been talking to me of the very same thing. Vesuvius' current level of activity," Constantin said.

"And?"

"Here's what I've been able to put together. We know a lot about Vesuvius, mostly from the 79 AD eruption. Vesuvius covered Pompeii with ash. Lola described the circumstances of that eruption. We also know Vesuvius erupted at least three dozen times since Pompeii. It's still active but so far, stable. But that's part conjecture, part fact, because it's what it is, a volcano. It's in its nature to erupt. It's what it does. Sometimes the mountain behaves unexpectedly; at other times, we have signs. Volcanoes are difficult to predict with any accuracy. Basically, that's what they are. Old, dangerous and very unpredictable."

"So, do we know for sure when volcanoes are active?" Destrey wanted to be sure about her facts. Most of this information was new to her.

"Yeah. Technically, we call them active when they've had at least one eruption during the past ten to twenty thousand years. So, when scientists tell us a volcano is active, it means it's either accumulating material, or it's dormant. Dormant does not mean dead. It can erupt again. Volcanoes erupt. But the question everyone wants an answer to is when. That's why it's being monitored 24/7."

"I understand. Vesuvius is alive," Destrey said.

"There's more, Louise. The situation is more complicated than that because Vesuvius has a big brother. Lola tells me there's another volcano in play. It's called Campi Flegrei or the Phlegraean Fields. It's a large supervolcano situated west of Naples. Most of the volcanic field lies under water. And this one is also active. If that monster ever wakes up, it could take Naples out and impact most of Europe. Campi Flegrei could have global implications."

"What does Lola think about Campi Flegrei?" Destrey said.

"I can't tell, really!" Constantin said. "If she wasn't a machine, I'd say she was anxious."

"So, Naples is sitting on top of a time bomb. No one's moving out of the city. This Carbone fellow wants us to help him and our own computer is going nuts!" Destrey said, a bit annoyed.

"I wouldn't say it that way, but yeah. Greater Naples' population is pretty much stable at around two million. A few years ago, the government tried unsuccessfully to get Neapolitans to resettle away from the volcano with financial incentives. As I said, that didn't work at all. I'm thinking that's what Carbone was trying to tell you while making Lola a bit antsy."

"Can anyone say for sure when the volcano will erupt again?" Destrey said. "Aren't they monitoring 24/7? They've been accumulating all this data on the mountain. They should know… something."

"No." Constantin said. "They can't make that kind of prediction. It's not like a hurricane. Hurricanes, we can see them coming and deal with them."

"I'm also thinking there's no way to stop an eruption. Am I right?" Destrey asked.

"Yeah. Right again. A few ideas were looked at but blasting or drilling Vesuvius would only make things worse. So, no. Can't really predict eruptions with any precision and can't prevent them either."

"So, the science is not able to help us in this situation? I mean, being able to call for an evacuation would mean they'd have reliable data."

"They could," Constantin said. "But saying it will erupt again without a realistic timeframe won't work. People need to know when. Not if. And there's also the problem of time for evacuation. Naples is old. Same as Jerusalem, but much more complex given its size. But even though the science of monitoring volcanoes has really advanced over the past decades, predictions with any real precision are not yet available. Scientists think the buildup of volcanic material preceding a large eruption is detectable. Sometimes a few weeks ahead of a blast. Sometimes a few months. Maybe a couple of years before volcanos actually erupt."

"You're saying the monitoring isn't able to predict an eruption unless the volcano actually starts to do something significant? And even then, it doesn't mean they know exactly when?"

"Yes and no. It depends on the volcano. Geologists and volcanologists are working around the world to learn as much as they can about volcanoes. They're trying to understand how they work to be better able to predict their behavior."

"Let me get this straight. Sometimes we can and sometimes we can't. Is that it, Constantin?"

"If you say it that way, Louise, I suppose so."

"Then the real question comes down to the accuracy of a prediction. Governments need that to initiate an evacuation. Or else, they simply won't take the political risk of forcing people to leave their homes and businesses."

"It's about credibility and time," Constantin said. "Can't blame them."

"Look at it this way," Destrey said. "San Francisco will have the Big One. That's a given. Maybe next week, next year, or ten years from now. If we tell people to evacuate San Francisco today, because there's evidence of an earthquake on the horizon, the first question people will need an answer to is when. In the next few hours, a couple of months, maybe a few years, or in their lifetime."

"So, precision means to be able to give governments and people a timeline." Constantin was thinking about a requirement protocol.

"Yeah, I guess so," Destrey said. "In a nutshell, that's the issue. Tell me when, and I'll tell you if I'm leaving San Francisco now or later." Destrey said evenly.

"What's the next hurdle?" Constantin said.

"There's always a next question. Based on what we've witnessed in Jerusalem and São Paulo, I'd say the next question people need an answer to is where do I evacuate to?" As far as Destrey was concerned, she was back to square one. As in Jerusalem and São Paulo, people needed information they could believe and work with. Data that was precise enough to rationalize an evacuation. All of that plus a safe place to relocate.

"I have a favor to ask you, Constantin. In fact, a few."

"What can I do?"

"I want to meet with Neapolitan families. Get to know them. Follow them around the city. Get close. You know what I mean?"

"How about the people who are monitoring Vesuvius?

"Them too." Destrey was feeling more confident.

"Okay. Got it. And when do you want this to take place?"

"As soon as you can make it happen, Constantin. In the next few weeks would be good."

"Anything else?" Constantin said.

"Do we have someone in our shop who could accompany me to Naples and help me understand what's going on with the people over there?"

Constantin thought about it and quickly came up with a name. "I'm thinking of Mankiller. Marie has a PhD in anthropology."

"She'd be perfect for the job." Destrey was delighted with the suggestion.

"I know Marie," Destrey said. "Marie Mankiller was the one that insisted that the Triage Group rethink its approach in defining future scenarios."

"If it wasn't for Mankiller's determination, I don't think we would have been successful in identifying the Jerusalem Cycle," Constantin said.

"Yes." Destrey said, "Marie Mankiller will do just fine. In fact, I'm looking forward to working with her again. I'm also thinking of a team, Constantin. Let's see if we can add a specialist onboard. Someone who can help us understand the jargon the volcanologists might throw our way."

Constantin had a few ideas. He had family and friends in Naples. "I'll get on it."

"Constantin? Please tell Margaret I want to see Marie as soon as she's available. We need a plan. And how about Lola prepping Marie and myself with background on this Campi volcano of yours?"

8

LOLA'S SECOND SIMULATION PHLEGRAEAN FIELDS, KINGDOM OF NAPLES

1538 CE

The Safe, the site of the supercomputer, was now overflowing with BTG's best and brightest, which included Doctor Marie Mankiller. The word had gone out to BTG's professionals that Lola was putting on a show. They were more than curious to see what Lola had prepared for them. Rumor had it that the supercomputer was about to simulate Campi Flegrei's activity back in 1538. Expectations were high.

"Good morning, *Madame* Destrey."

The Safe fell silent.

"I am ready for simulation two, *Madame* Destrey."

"Go ahead Lola," Destrey said.

Lola displayed the Bay of Naples.

Morgan Freeman began his narration.

Let us return to Thursday, September 29th, 1538. Pedro Álvarez de Toledo governed the Kingdom of Naples. At that time, he was a politician and the first Spanish viceroy of Naples. He was responsible for Naples' extensive urban development. He was also the father-in-law of Cosimo I de' Medici, Grand Duke of Tuscany.

"Why's this pertinent, Lola?"

"Because the Spanish rulers were Catholic, *Madame* Destrey, as a result, Campi Flegrei's activity was interpreted as a message from God."

"Okay, Lola. So, business as usual."

"I believe so, *Madame* Destrey. But there's more to it than meets the eye. Coming back to live near Vesuvius is, in a way, founded on certain beliefs and myths that ironically mitigate the fear of volcanoes."

"You're saying that's going on now?"

"That is one avenue I am researching. May I continue, *Madame* Destrey?"

Destrey nodded.

Morgan Freeman resumed his narration.

Campi Flegrei is a large volcanic area situated to the west of the Kingdom of Naples. Part of the caldera lies under water in the Bay of Naples. The modern-day village of Pozzuoli sits at the center of the volcano's caldera.

Campi Flegrei has remained unseen, silent and almost nonexistent for thousands of years. The last eruption dates back 35,000 years.

Most, if not all, of the Kingdom's citizenry were blissfully ignorant of the giant sleeping underfoot.

Father Salvatore Bacoli was eagerly writing his Sunday sermon. He was a true believer. God was his savior as well as his ticket to heaven. Although barely twenty-three years old, the priest had the intelligence and street smarts of a wizened friar. He wasn't the sort of man to be easily distracted by earthly issues. Not even by the earthquakes that had become almost a daily occurrence. Or were they signs of God's heavenly displeasure? He often wondered about that possibility.

While reviewing the scriptures for his next sermon, Bacoli very nearly broke his quill as a tremor suddenly shook everything around him, enough to scare the living daylights out of the man. It also disrupted his daily duties as a cleric and shepherd. Bacoli noted that the ground under his tiny church was at it again. But this time, it was sufficiently violent to fling most of his wine bottles on the dirt floor of his small presbytery.

He wanted to tell his Lord God that he got the message. He truly understood what had to be done. In fact, he flung his notes to the sky, thinking *I know, don't you see, oh Lord, I'm rendering Your words to paper.*

Bacoli understood earthquakes as God's personal communication device, a fifteenth-century version of an email specifically aimed at his heart and soul.

Later that morning, he wrote in his journal that on this day, Thursday September 29th, in the year of the Lord 1538, a mountain was being created by His hands. Another sign from the Christian God summoning them to seek the Lord's forgiveness and to repent.

"Show them, oh Lord, the errors of their ways," he wrote. "For they must atone for their sins and bow to Your heavenly will."

Unbeknownst to Neapolitans, *Campi Flegrei* was active again after thousands of years of inactivity. The volcano was at least 70,000 years old and today, as flat as a pancake.

Within a single week, Mother Nature produced a four-hundred-foot-high mound. The locals at the time named the hill *Monte Nuovo*. The New Mountain. Suddenly, large quantities of lava shot into the air while fine ash fell over the countryside for several miles around the new volcano. The people living in the area fled their homes, asking God for His forgiveness. They had apparently failed to live up to His expectations.

The devastation of the *Monte Nuovo* eruption was considerable, but not as deadly as the Pompeii eruption had been.

This eruption proved to be a learning experience for the Kingdom's scientific elite. Volcanos can and did appear out of nowhere with no significant warning signs from Mother Nature. What they didn't know or learn from their experience was that Campi

Flegrei had barely sneezed. A mere hiccup in time. The volcano was merely exercising its right to grow, because Campi Flegrei was, in fact, in a growing phase. The mountain was in truth nothing less than a supervolcano in progress. When it had last erupted in 39,000 BCE, Campi Flegrei's super-eruption had left over 300 feet of tephra or hot gas and volcanic matter, reaching temperatures as high as 900 degrees Celsius from the pyroclastic flow.

In contrast, Vesuvius' eruption in 79 AD had left a little over 3 meters of tephra on Pompeii. The pyroclastic flows produced were as devastating as they were fast. The speed of a pyroclastic flow could reach speeds of up to 700 km/h.

Father Salvatore Bacoli understood the signs for what they truly were: biblical warnings, nothing less and nothing more.

A few days later, when all appeared calm, the young cleric sought to get a closer look at the New Mountain. Unfortunately, the volcano blasted through earth's core at eight hundred kilometers an hour, killing the priest and twenty-three other visitors.

Instead of understanding the volcano as a natural phenomenon and a difficult occurrence to predict, the Kingdom had elected to pay homage to the Lord by promising obedience and submission to His will and his representatives here on earth.

The funeral services for the unfortunate few who dared to climb up to the edge of the caldera were done without the bodies of the deceased. God had taken them away to heaven.

The twenty-four men, women and children who died on that faithful day were believed to be martyrs as well as God's punishment for the sins of Naples. They have died for us, said the Bishop of Naples. Let us pray.

The simulation was over, and Lola waited for new instructions from Destrey.

"Lola, are you telling me that Naples lies between two active volcanoes, and that one of them is a… a supervolcano?"

"That is correct, *Madame* Destrey."

"Can you tell me, in two words or less, what in heaven's name is a supervolcano?" Destrey asked.

"Yes, *Madame* Destrey. Mass extinction. Two words that say it all. From nothing to get worried about to global extinction. That's the range of possibilities we can expect." Lola said.

"Extinction?" Destrey said to herself.

"That would be the worst scenario, *Madame* Destrey."

"What can we conclude from this simulation?" Destrey asked Lola.

"That a second element, Campi Flegrei, is in play and is believed active. That is to say that magma under Campi Flegrei may be entering a building phase. This could lead to a large-scale eruption in the future. Researchers assure us that any massive eruption from Campi Flegrei would likely be far in the future, perhaps thousands of years or more."

That said, added Freeman, Naples is situated at the worst possible location on the planet. Volcanologists believe that Vesuvius is the most dangerous volcano in the world because it is located close to a large, populated area. With Campi Flegrei in play, we cannot underestimate Naples' vulnerability. The same applies to the convictions and myths that people hold. When Neapolitans believe that a full eruption by Vesuvius cannot happen to them, we find ourselves at an impasse. The thought of permanently vacating Neapolitans is almost impossible to fathom.

Destrey fought the urge to dismiss Lola's analysis because it was too hard to accept. But the evidence presented was so far beyond obvious. Whether consciously or not, Neapolitans seemed prepared to die rather than leave their homes behind. But what about their families and loved ones?

Destrey turned to the crowd behind her and invited them to be back in the Safe by 2:00 pm.

9

LOLA'S THIRD SIMULATION

Naples, 1944

BTG's professionals were early for the 2:00 pm simulation. Word had it that Lola was mounting a case for a BTG event, which implied an all-hands-on deck scenario. However, at this time, Lola was merely going through a feasibility study on whether or not getting Neapolitans to resettle as far away from Naples was doable.

The Safe was full to capacity. More of BTG's professionals had requested to be allowed to witness firsthand how Lola would bring her case to Louise Destrey.

"May I start the simulation, *Madame* Destrey?" Lola asked.

"Well, it looks like we're all here, so you might as well go ahead. Let's see what you've got."

Morgan Freeman began his narration. A map of Southern Italy appeared, illustrating the Allied forces advancing toward the Volturno River.

Let us return in time to March 1944, Freeman said. The Germans were retreating as the Allies gained control of Southern Italy. The Americans found Naples battered. It was far worse than expected, the Germans having left behind a heritage of desperation

69

and hunger.

As the Nazis finally withdrew from Italy, stories of mistaken identity were common. Innocent people were sent to jail for having collaborated with the occupying German Forces. Many were falsely accused of crimes by those who wanted them out of the way. When people's names were posted on police and military blacklists, their records remained active until the end of the war.

"Why's this pertinent, Lola?" Destrey asked.

"Naples' ongoing battle with local crime organizations began with the black market. Consequences of war such as hunger, poverty, revenge and criminality were common and inevitable. Another important outcome touched on whether or not Neapolitans could trust the police ever again."

Morgan Freeman resumed his narration.

Between 1940 to 1944, the Allies bombed Naples more than 200 times. On September 6th, 1943, one of the largest air raids during World War II sent 400 American Boeing B-17 Flying Fortress aircraft over Naples. Bombing raids targeted the German submarine base. However, whole sections of Naples were carpet bombed.

On the ground, people were having a hard time putting food on the table. Neapolitans joked about having one meal a day during the German occupation compared with one a week under the American liberation. The scorn wasn't wasted on the Allies.

The lack of food, the constant looting and the general level of criminal activity continued to plague Naples throughout the war and beyond. Criminality was justified as a matter of survival. Not surprisingly, the black market remained the primary source of food for most Neapolitans.

"So, what about Naples today?" Destrey asked Lola. "The war's been over for a long time," Destrey said.

"The black market evolved into organized crime, *Madame* Destrey. I included this data to provide context when we'll be discussing evacuation strategies. The data shows that any mass departure from Naples will be met with severe opposition from the different crime families. The Neapolitans being their primary source of revenues, evacuating the city would mean millions of Euros lost every week. I'm almost certain," Lola added, "that any and all evacuation attempts will be challenged. BTG staff would be facing direct retaliation from Naples' criminal organizations. There would be no safe place on the planet if they decided to put a contract on yourself as well as BTG staff."

Suddenly, Destrey felt the room temperature change. The professionals working for BTG had been targets of people's rage in the past. That was nothing new but being reminded once again of the dangers awaiting them was still stressful. And although people's safety was always a major concern for Destrey, Lola had never clearly presented a scenario where they'd be in actual danger.

"That's something I was expecting, Lola," Destrey said. "If that ever happened, what would we have to do?"

"Our security protocols have been upgraded to deal with such possibilities. If you decided to call Naples a BTG event, then we would put in place the necessary measures to protect all BTG staff as well as their families. Contingencies have been made."

"Okay, we can talk about that later, but I'm not sure that's going to happen." Destrey said. "Isn't it possible that these same crime families would also want to be safe and leave the city? If faced with unimpeachable facts about Vesuvius, wouldn't they want to leave Naples and find refuge for their own families and relatives?"

"Of course, *Madame* Destrey," Lola said. "But that doesn't mean that their criminal activities wouldn't continue unabated. A few key officers from each crime family would wait until the very last moment before leaving Naples. Meanwhile, they'd be putting the fear of God in their own street soldiers to keep the Neapolitans in the city and stop any evacuation."

"So, we'd be facing all kinds of resistance?" Destrey needed to know well in advance who BTG needed to neutralize in order to achieve their objectives.

"Yes, *Madame* Destrey, we will. But facts, logical arguments and the science behind an evacuation would have little effect on the people, as they would prefer to face the volcano rather than be at the end of a loaded shotgun."

"Now that I think about it, I'm sorry to say that I have to agree. The ramifications of an evacuation are important. I promised myself that I would never again underestimate its difficulty. Not again. If I listen to the little voice in my head, I have to say that I was expecting it. It makes me mad as hell to realize that saving people can be so difficult."

Destrey tried to calm down. She needed to do something about her anger issues.

"Okay, Lola. Go on. Let's see where this goes." Destrey sat back and waited for Lola to resume the simulation.

Morgan Freeman continued his narration.

Friday, March 17, 1944. Allied Control Com-Mission was buzzing with activity. The Vesuvius' Emergency Operations HQ was equally hard at work. The volcano was acting up. Soldiers were going about their duties, knowing they were on high alert. Sergeant Mallory was trying to explain to his superior what had happened.

He went up the volcano in the middle of the night! Sergeant Mallory told Colonel Leelyn. Mallory had nearly lost the little man, and it frightened him. He could have been fried alive up there. The little guy with the funny pants was *Professore* Giuseppe Imbò. He was one of the founding fathers of volcanic seismology. Colonel Leelyn counted on Imbò's intel to help the Allied forces in Italy. There were lives at stake, military as well as civilian. Countless thousands of people living near Vesuvius meant many were at risk.

Sergeant Mallory was in trouble with his colonel. The *Professore* had decided on his own that he needed to see the volcano for himself. He later told Mallory he could help the Americans if only he could monitor the volcano up-close.

Colonel Leelyn was angry, and Mallory knew he'd fumbled the ball. As of this morning, Mallory posted a detail on *Professore* Imbò, full time.

Colonel Leelyn needed Imbò because the information he had on the volcano could be strategic. If only the Allies could know in advance what Vesuvius would do next. If Imbò wasn't able to deliver the goods, the Allies could be caught between a rock and the German army. Colonel Leelyn trusted the Germans to take any opportunity to push Allied forces back to the Mediterranean, if they could. Such an opportunity could arise if Vesuvius erupted. Leelyn had that right. Today, preferably in the next few hours, the colonel expected Imbò to come up with new information on the volcano's intentions. Fortunately, the *Professore* came through for the Allies. Vesuvius was awakening and Imbò saw it coming. He had warned the Allied officers of the incoming danger. Unfortunately, the American High Command didn't have confidence in Imbò. Some senior officers mocked Imbò, but Vesuvius had the last word.

The light show on the crest of Vesuvius' caldera announced the volcano's intent. Molten lava shot high in the sky, illuminating the volcano's peak. The unbelievable scene had an hypnotic effect on those who stayed up late that night. Locals were fascinated as well as paralyzed by Vesuvius' performance.

"I would like to emphasize," Lola said, "that an eventual eruption would most likely have the same effect. People would lose precious time deciding what to do. That factor alone would create the conditions for massive traffic jams. Gridlock would ensue. And that could end any chance of evacuating Naples in time. The objective is to avoid Vesuvius' pyroclastic flows, rockfalls, volcanic explosions, collapsing infrastructures due to volcanic earthquakes and ensuing fires."

Morgan Freeman continued his narration.

Eventually, the lava flowed down the slopes of the volcano, reaching the small town of San Sebastiano. Fortunately, the town's people left everything behind and sought shelter as far away from the volcano as possible.

Shortly after, the village slowly disappeared as a wall of lava and molten rock, more than thirty feet in height, flowed relentlessly toward populated areas. The lava filled the streets and homes of the small town. The slow advance of the volcano's lava reached every square inch of the village. Street by street, the lava flow invaded people's homes and businesses, marking its territory.

There was more to come. Or so believed *Professore* Imbò. The volcano was, as far as he was concerned, a known quantity. However, he had never before seen, with his own eyes, such a systematic and complete destruction of a living town. The small city of San Sebastiano was being entombed as each building melted into the lava flow, never to be seen again.

Vesuvius was active and there was nothing anyone could do about it. Man did not yet invent a device capable of controlling volcanoes. Not one building survived. Vesuvius left nothing behind.

Just as the people imagined that the worst had come to pass, there came smoke made of glass particles. The volcano removed the sun's light, gushing poisoned ash up thousands of feet into the Italian sky. The villagers described it as hell. The dense volcanic material coalesced into an impossible plume set against the backdrop of World War II.

Suddenly, Vesuvius blew its top. A massive concentration of billowing ash shot up as high as the eye could see. People couldn't understand what they were witnessing. If any eyewitnesses still believed in man's dominion over the planet, they had a rude awakening. Men, women and children were reminded, once more, what Mother Nature was about and of what she was capable. The mountain's small display of force would humble some and put to rest any politician's idea of mastering the planet.

However, as cruel as the volcano proved to be, it left behind the magical ash. The desolate landscape would most likely become fruitful agricultural land. As before, man would soon forget Vesuvius, as humans did countless times in the past.

Lola presented picture after picture of lush agriculture lands. The images of growing crops, such as citrus fruit, olives, grapes, figs, apricots, cherries and plums, and of course, the famous Neapolitan tomato, filling BTG's staff with wonder.

Such was the land they knew and loved before it was totally destroyed, Freeman said.

However, barely a few years later, men and women returned to Vesuvius. Denial and forgetfulness were common aftermaths of volcanic activity. Yet, this type of denial could potentially have devastating long-term consequences.

"This is a recurring theme, *Madame* Destrey," Lola said. "The ash left behind by the volcano is believed to be a gift from God. As it happens, volcanic ash contains minerals that are important to plant life. In fact, volcanic ash commonly improves the soil's physical and chemical properties. As for future eruptions, let's say that the magical ash is clearly behind man's recurring amnesia. I believe it's still at work today."

"Lola, what should we take away from this simulation?" Destrey asked the supercomputer.

"There are two critical learning points we must consider, *Madame* Destrey. Number one, time for a volcano is based on millennia rather than our human years. And while current knowledge of past eruptions is key in predicting eruptions, our capacity to do so with any accuracy is still variable. It depends. Some volcanoes show signs of activity in the days, weeks or months prior to an eruption, but other volcanic eruptions can be sudden and unexpected, and totally unpredictable. As for Vesuvius, the risks to humans makes it the most dangerous volcano in the world. Mainly because it's close to Naples, near two million people, crowded in a three-thousand-year-old city."

"So, we think in minutes and the volcano thinks in decades," Destrey said.

"Yes, *Madame* Destrey."

"Okay, what about number two?"

"So far, volcanologists believe Vesuvius is in a building phase. Meaning it's readying for the next eruption. Accumulating lava. The 1944 eruption was merely a sign that Vesuvius was active."

"Are we able to predict when Vesuvius will erupt?" Destrey

asked.

"Volcanologists are able to sound the alarm when they witness something substantial. But to answer your question, no, *Madame Destrey*. At least not yet." Lola stopped short of saying that it was just a question of time before the volcano would erupt. But decided that it would take too long to explain what she meant by time.

Morgan Freeman continued his narration.

The devastation of San Sebastiano as well as the village of Massa di Somma continued nonstop. The explosions could be heard from miles away. The night provided an opera of horrors as the lava flowed down the slopes of the mountain.

Allied Headquarters located in Caserta, twenty-five miles north of Naples, watched helplessly as the volcano emitted a fine ash falling across the Italian peninsula as far as the Adriatic Sea.

Tephra-fall began early in the morning. The fragmental material produced by Vesuvius would soon cover a large chunk of the peninsula. The pulverized material of rock from Vesuvius was airborne until the material fused together, producing fragments large enough to cause injury and damage to property. The destruction was significant. Soldiers as well as civilians wore steel helmets or covered their heads with whatever they could find for protection.

On Thursday March 23, 1944, the Pompeii Airfield in Poggiomarino, a few kilometers away from Vesuvius, was completely destroyed along with the U.S. Air Force's 340th Bombardment Group. Eighty-eight B-25 Mitchell bombers were gone. It took all of one minute, well over fifty million dollars' worth of aircraft or half a billion dollars in today's currency.

Destrey rose to her feet as she realized that Vesuvius was a current problem, not something that happened two thousand years ago. She felt a bit tired. Her instincts were telling her she was probably wasting her time. The more Lola presented her findings, the more she began to understand what a train wreck meant. If she decided to call Naples an event, then she would be driving her crew in a headlong collision with a brick wall. That would involve three immovable objects: the Neapolitan people, the crime families and, of course, the mountain. The evacuation wouldn't be a practice run, but the real thing. So far, plans to evacuate the city were based on a seventy-two-hour timeline, with twelve hours to organize, two days to move people and an extra twelve hours just in case something went wrong. Theoretically, the evacuation would require 500 buses and 220 trains to relocate Neapolitans.

"What's your take on this plan, Lola?"

"I have none, *Madame* Destrey. Real life doesn't work that way. The volcano will always surprise, one way or the other. That said, I simply think that any plan to evacuate Naples would require Vesuvius to stay quiet for at least a month."

Destrey was thinking that if Lola was right, BTG had established the foundations of a disastrous outcome. An end-result involving millions of innocent people losing their lives. Destrey would be setting her sights on certain failure, a large-scale problem that could destroy BTG's reputation and ability to survive business-wise. On the other hand, Destrey had a duty to do whatever she could. Millions of fathers and mothers, and their children, could disappear, just like that.

Destrey was now looking at her own people. The Safe was silent. Lola's holographic form disappeared from view.

"Hum…" she said. "Okay. Let's see what Lola has up her sleeve for tomorrow's next chapter on Vesuvius," Destrey said to her professionals. "Let's be back here at 9h a.m. tomorrow. Sharp."

Nobody moved.

They all knew what she was going through: an ongoing challenge of weighing the pros and cons. And most importantly, what they would be facing if the boss decided to call it an event. Regardless of the challenges involved and the infinitesimal chance of success, a BTG event meant they would pull out all the stops to try to make it happen.

"Okay. I know what you're thinking…" Destrey started to say to her staff.

"I don't think so boss." Constantin said. "I'm thinking, as well as all of us here, that we'll be behind you regardless of what you decide."

That's the missing element in this puzzle, Destrey thought to herself. Her people. In fact, BTG's professionals were always there for her, even when the odds weren't in BTG's favor.

"I appreciate your support, thank you all," Destrey said with emotion.

With that said, she left the Safe and retreated to her office as quickly as she could.

10

AMATRICE
PROVINCE OF RIETI, ITALY

Friday, August 24, 2016
03:36:59

The quake hit the little-known town of Amatrice in the province of Rieti, located some 360 km away from Francesco Carbone's hometown of Conza.

Some said the town was one of Italy's most beautiful hamlets.

Nonetheless, it bore the brunt of an earthquake, with the majority of its three hundred victims being buried under the town's collapsed structures.

Although Amatrice had a population of just a little over a thousand people, it had been home to human beings since prehistoric times. It was also famous for its historical buildings dating back to the thirteenth century.

In small villages located in the Marche region, forty-six lives were claimed in Arquata and Pescara del Tronto. Twenty-two people also died in Saletta, a hamlet located near Amatrice, as did eleven others in Accumoli, a village close to the quake's epicenter. At least three hundred were hospitalized. Many went missing.

Ambulances and helicopters were seen coming and going

into the region four hours after the initial quake as rescue workers searched for survivors. Eventually, rescue teams from around the world came to Amatrice to help.

The Mayor of Amatrice couldn't believe his eyes as the morning sun came up and gave everyone their first good look at what the earthquake had done to their beloved town.

It was as if the village had been trampled on by a giant.

By mid-morning, most of Amatrice's survivors were living in tents provided by the Red Cross. Some preferred to sleep in their cars.

Word of the earthquake spread quickly online because, according to climate curious columnists, disasters channel people's curiosity. "As a species," one wrote, "we are spellbound by others' bad luck. The thrill of observing first-hand people's misfortune is almost impossible to resist."

II

PALM SPRINGS, SOUTHERN CALIFORNIA

Thursday, August 23, 2016
7:36 PM Pacific Standard Time (PST)

Tomorrow morning, he would be meeting with the school board where he would go through the work done so far. He anticipated opposition from a board who consistently pooh-poohed the need to spend money.

He would remind his friends and clients alike of the very real possibility that the "Big One" could strike at any moment.

At forty-seven years old, Francesco Galileo Carbone had made a name for himself as a bright and innovative structural engineer. It entitled him to access the most challenging projects the state had to offer.

He hoped his track record would sway Louise Destrey into helping him in his mission to Naples. He reminded himself that it could take a long time before she would invite him back to Boston. Destrey's assistant had warned him: "That's the price to pay, Mister Carbone. She has her own set of priorities. You may have to wait. But I'll call you when she's good and ready."

"Here's the news from overseas," the reporter said. "We've got

81

this in from our special correspondent stationed in Rome. The summer sun beats brightly down on the streets of the picturesque Italian mountain town," said Lauren Said-Moorhouse, "but the people who walk them today are not on holiday. Amatrice has become a mausoleum."

Francesco Galileo Carbone was too busy writing his report to pay attention to the newscast.

"As of 3h30 a.m. this morning Italian time," she said, "at least half a dozen towns sixty miles north of Rome have been destroyed by an earthquake with an estimated magnitude of 6.2 on the Richter scale."

There was always a radio or a TV playing in the background. That was Francesco's special noise. It worked for him. It helped him block distractions, especially those he would generate from his own vivid imagination. The noise kept the engineer from wandering from one new idea to another and focus on the renovation of an elementary school located not too far from Palm Springs.

Despite California's laws passed in 1986, the engineer had to inform local governments in high seismic zones that they were required to develop an inventory of *unreinforced masonry* (URM) buildings and establish a loss reduction program. The state required local governments to begin expensive seismic retrofits in order to conform to the revised earthquake resistant building code. Many cities and towns in California were late in adopting the new code, even though the Big One was by now an existential reality for most Californians. The Big One was expected to happen soon, along the San Andreas Fault. Some argued that although the quake was long overdue, seismologists were unable to predict when it would strike California.

Regardless of the near certainty of an earthquake, public money was always a problem in California, especially when someone wanted to spend it. In this case, the code would help children survive significant earthquakes. He couldn't think of a better reason to work as hard as he could on this project.

The noise from the radio drew his full attention. Earthquakes, avalanches, sinkholes, landslides or any other of Mother Nature's behavior usually got the engineer's full attention. It should, because he believed he had been handpicked by someone or something, he didn't know which, to battle earthquakes and save children. Which always brought him back to his native Italy, Naples and Louise Destrey.

Saving lives was, in a nutshell, his mission.

"The towns of Accumoli, Amatrice and Pescara del Tronto among others, all located about sixty miles from Rome, have been hit by an earthquake," the CNN reporter repeated grimly. "The earthquake was felt across Italy, from Bologna to Naples. We've been told that there have been dozens of aftershocks. The number of casualties is not yet known. But we'll keep you updated as events unfold."

Although the engineer maintained his focus on the elementary school project he was working on, he kept an ear open for any new information coming in from Italy. Unfortunately, he had no one he could call in Italy for more information. It was too early for that. For now, he had to rely on what he could learn from CNN.

12

THREAT ASPECT CORPORATION (TAC) LUXEMBOURG

"Send her in."

"Yes, Sir."

Alexander Kirchen Schuman didn't like exceptions, special allowances or issues that would attract attention to his organization.

In fact, anything that would shed light on his own business dealings, or his wife's spending habits, would also be unwelcomed and potentially disastrous.

Nevertheless, TAC's CEO was proud to call his organization the Switzerland of the insurance business because it favored no one. No one with the exception of insurance companies dealing with TAC.

His organization was created by insurance companies for insurance companies. Customers never figured in their original design. It rightly boasted that it could develop the best insurance data in the world. Data that would greatly improve insurers' business intelligence and risk management when dealing with nature's cataclysmic events, as well as life's daily risks at home and on the road. In other words, TAC would help insurers make more money by knowing exactly what they were getting into when issuing insurance policies. Coverage was about knowing the risks and assessing the appropriate premiums. Insurers, after all, were not in the gambling business, nor were they in the Good Samaritan trade.

TAC's neutrality as an independent reporting organization was, in fact, the reason for its ongoing success and acceptability by insurers worldwide.

From Schuman's point of view, any unsolicited visibility could generate unwanted, unpredictable, or unintended consequences to TAC's reputation. Transparent, neutral, fair, scrupulously law-abiding, honorable and moral to its core werte some of the qualities Schuman used to describe his organization to corporate subscribers.

Schuman believed that potential negative outcomes could only happen if his business decisions drifted away from his comfort zone. Today's meeting could pose such a threat if they were to drift away from his business model and get screwed in the process.

Although none of his staff truly understood why the boss was so opposed to change, they followed his lead rigorously. No questions asked. They were paid too much money not to. Loyalty to money, according to Schuman, was the strongest value and the best alignment device ever created by compensation policymakers. Schuman used money to create lasting and dependable commitment. He liked to call it his personal strategy of engagement.

What's more, TAC was loaded. Shareholders were happy. Schuman was prosperous. Staff was extremely well paid. And while board members were pleased with his company's performance, they were counting on TAC's corporate discretion in all matters. The transparency blurb on the company's web page was just that: self-promotion, luster and illusion. No insurance company or its associates would, in their right minds, show their cards for public consumption. In the corporate world, especially in the insurance business and more particularly in Luxembourg, transparency meant just the opposite. Show a good face, a few numbers and keep the books off the table. In other words, true opacity.

It was no secret that insurance companies put profits over policy holder benefits, that their principal obligation to earn a return for their shareholders was a given. What was not so clear was what insurers kept hidden from the public. A value widely adopted by the insurance businesses worldwide: the best way to make more money is by simply paying out less money. That was the real bottom line and a core business strategy. To do this well and consistently, one needed data, and that's why TAC was so valuable.

To say that it was Schuman's aim to keep the status quo intact would be a gross understatement. TAC's level of performance delivered solid proof to its customer base of his company's profitable practices and policies. And, according to Schuman's, *that's the way things should be.*

Schuman knew what the young consulting analyst was going to recommend to his organization. He knew word for word what she would report. The consulting analyst's supervisor and partner in charge called Schuman the previous night with his own copy of the analyst's report.

"There's nothing I can do to change her fucking mind without attracting too much attention to myself," he said to Schuman. "She's going to recommend that you go below your standard three million euro, because it's the right thing to do. Let me read the executive summary."

Schuman prepared for the worst.

"Our responsibility to TAC's Board of Directors requires us to be unequivocally clear. Given the facts provided to us as well as the Board's resolve to improve TAC's bottom line, we recommend a proactive role." The partner in charge paused to catch his breath.

"That's her opening statement," he said. "I could go on and on. And it's complicated. So, I brought this report down to 10 points. Believe me, that's all you need to know."

"Good," Schuman said. "I don't need to hear all of it."

"Right then. But before we go into this, let me warn you that everything she wrote has been verified and vetted. She knows what she's talking about."

Schuman tried to calm himself. Once again, he prepared for the worst.

"One," the senior consultant said, "the Amatrice earthquake should be viewed as an opportunity for TAC to broaden its scope of analysis."

"Does she suggest that TAC could profit from earthquakes?" Schuman asked.

"Yes, she does."

"For heaven's sake, you can't say that. Even if it's true!" Schuman said.

Schuman had to be honest with himself. The minute the Board had initiated TAC's annual review, he knew the process could uncover information that should never see the light of day.

"I really don't like where this is going," Schuman added.

"There's more. Much more."

"I was afraid you'd say that," Schuman said.

"You want me to continue or what?"

"Yeah. Let's hear it," Schuman said unhappily.

"Two, taking into account the significant socio-economic impact of earthquakes, the 2016 natural disaster should be examined and deemed a qualifying incident for TAC's analysis. TAC would then make the data available to insurance companies."

"If that report ever leaked out, it could signal the end of my business; I'd be out of a job within a week," Schuman said to himself.

"Three, a complete analysis of damages and rebuilding costs by TAC's analysts would be well received and ethical."

"Ethical my ass," Schuman said. "Sure, it would be legal. But eventually the people out there would begin to understand what we're all about."

There was a pause. Both men had been dreading the moment she would come forward with her report. And here it was, in all its glory.

"Sorry," Schuman said. "Let's get this done and over with."

"Four, this would greatly increase insurance companies' bottom line even though Italy sits on one of the highest risk quake-prone zones in the world."

Schuman was beginning to feel ill.

"Five, the opportunity to increase profits partly stems from an Italian myth: homeowners are significantly underinsured for natural disasters because they feel their government will come to their rescue if and when a disaster hits their town or village. Six, of course, that rescue will never happen. Italy will never be able to back its ambitions and promises with the cash required to rebuild after earthquakes because Italy is one of Europe's most indebted nations. Seven, if the government did move toward a policy of reconstruction, we would be looking at a trillion euros or more for the next two decades. Eight, this implies that TAC's customers will be in a good position when the Italian government inevitably makes earthquake insurance mandatory. And ten, if TAC makes such a case to the government, compulsory earthquake insurance will likely be the next step. There you have it," the senior consultant said.

"It's a death sentence," Schuman said. "They'll lynch me in downtown Luxembourg, Place d'Armes no less. There, Luxembourgians would enjoy the sight of a man dangling from a rope."

Schuman bid the consultant a good afternoon and ended the call.

Therein lies the problem, Schuman thought to himself.

The issue with the consultant's report was that it was all true. Regardless of whether the consultant's recommendations were legitimate, Schuman was not going to be pushed around by a junior consultant. That would leave him vulnerable. If the report was ever leaked, his secret strategy would be out. The secret about what insurance companies were really in business for would be pasted on every front page, every blog and millions of emails.

Schuman would argue that compulsory insurance based on socio-economic impacts would be largely based on soft numbers, public opinion, perceived responsibilities and politically correct behavior. Not the clear, objective, discreet or unimpeachable numbers his organization was known for. But that wouldn't be enough to quell people's appetite for punishing the guilty of unimaginable greed.

Any of his arguments would be perceived as weak and self-serving. He himself didn't believe any of them, nor would the public, government officials or the courts.

Somehow, the young female consultant he was about to meet had to be persuaded to let it be. To make it disappear.

If something went wrong, if word got out that he was behind any compulsory scheme, he was sure he'd be in trouble. There were a few people out there that would sell their own mothers to get his job at TAC, not to mention those who would like him thrown in jail.

His clients would obviously not hesitate to criticize TAC about going off script and then personally profit from a scheme to force Italians to buy earthquake insurance. More questions would be asked. He himself would be under scrutiny, as people would be looking for a scandal they might leverage.

And so on and so forth, he thought gloomily.

If someone opened this particular Pandora's Box, his secrets would surely get out.

I'd lose my Bentley Mulsanne, my chauffeur, my expense account and God knows what else, he thought.

Once his participation to make insurance compulsive became public, the Internet would destroy everything. Schuman understood there would be no turning back. Because, in the era of instant communications, getting the genie back in the lamp was almost impossible.

Schuman asked himself, *what's in it for me?*

He ran all the scenarios in his mind, and they all led to the same result. The Italians would revolt if they believed that his organization was behind a compulsory insurance scheme. He would be burned in effigy and dragged through the streets of Luxembourg. That would be the end of everything: his reputation, his big house in Kockelscheuer and, most importantly, the women of Thionville, women who offered perversions only money could buy. The very thought of losing those female mercenaries sent a shiver up his spine.

He quickly came to a conclusion: he had no choice in the matter. No matter how true or desirable, the consultant's recommendations were unacceptable. He vowed to take the consultant's recommendations and feed them to the nearest shredder and find a way to get her transferred to Siberia! Schuman made up his mind. Regardless of what she'd say, the end result would be the same.

His office door opened as Miss Gloria, Schuman's longtime assistant, pleasantly introduced the consultant to her boss. Gloria was trying to get Schuman's attention, but she failed as the female consultant quickly walked into her boss' office suite. The consultant marched directly toward Schuman and shook his hand.

"I'm so happy to meet you," she said softly. "It's an honor."

13

ROXANNE ISABELLA LAFLAMME

Schuman was taken by surprise. How could such a delightful young thing be capable of coming up with such a report, one that was forceful, strategic and, unfortunately, could very well bring to an end his plans of acquiring an insurance company of his own? A company that would undoubtedly be at the forefront of a business extravaganza worth millions, if not billions, of euros, to unsuspecting Italians.

LaFlamme wore her blond hair like a Viking princess. A crown of gold. A warrying panache. She held her head high. Her body was slender and athletic. Her skin was snow white.

Still, he felt the warmth in her handshake. Schuman searched for a clever response, but none came to mind.

"Alexander Schuman, at your service, *Madame* LaFlamme," he said graciously.

"Excuse me for saying this, Mr. Schuman," she said amiably, "but I didn't realize one could have such a sophisticated place of work."

"Please, call me Sasha. Everyone does," Schuman said.

"Sasha then. My friends call me Rocky." LaFlamme seemed to look at Schuman as if he was someone important.

"Right, right. Rocky it is. I like that," Schuman said hesitantly. "Please have a seat."

LaFlamme did as she was told.

"Let's get down to business," Schuman said positively. "I'm looking forward to hear what you have to say."

As LaFlamme rummaged through her report, Schuman realized he couldn't take his eyes off her female form.

LaFlamme continued to go through her conclusions, the pros and cons, and the end results.

He wasn't listening. He didn't have to. He had other things to think about.

So young. So naïve. So utterly gorgeous, he thought.

In fact, a beautiful woman. The kind of girl he would enjoy. He desired her mainly because she couldn't hide her innocence; her face said everything. *But*, he thought, *the down curve of her succulent lips said even more.*

The woman was pure cocaine. With repeated exposure, his brain would have to adapt and change for the worse. He would become increasingly addicted to her presence, while his moods would tear him apart when she'd leave the side of his bed.

Schuman knew when a prey was willing.

It's the eyes. They expose the soul, he thought to himself.

Ironically, Schuman the predator, was being hypnotized. Schuman buckled under her stare. Her eyes were the color of her soul. They were draped by a pool of blue lapis, while every word she uttered was said with the self-assurance of a sibyl.

A few moments ago, she appeared in his room, his place of business, as if she owned it. Even Schuman's assistant paid attention to her beauty and knew the young woman would be trouble. Not because of what she would do, but for what she would let him do to her.

So, the Disney character is real, he thought to himself.

Rocky's eyes scanned Schuman's office suite in search of a clue. And then it hit her. He was the key. Not the set decorations, the lavish paintings hanging on his wall, nor the hand-woven rugs from Iran. He was at the center of all things related to TAC. She'd have to leverage his desires to get her way and make herself indispensable. A someone she could sink her teeth in. A man who could not refuse a beautiful woman's advances.

When their eyes finally met, she knew she had connected with a man who couldn't or wouldn't resist her. But Schuman didn't know that. In fact, he was hoping for quite the opposite. Who could resist his charm?

At five feet four, she appeared almost as tall as any man given her four-inch stilettos. With a face so white, so perfect, dainty, but cut like a precious diamond, he couldn't help himself. He did not keep his eyes away from her mouth. Her lips were painted red. The color of blood. Schuman enjoyed red lips.

He fantasized of lingerie he'd like her to wear for him. Her body was made for Victoria's Secret racy mesh teddies and laced *babydoll* trappings.

Rocky, on the other hand, had enough information on the little man to know what she would do next. He liked being in control. She'd let him. He preferred shyness in his women. She'd give him shy. He would probably insist on a secret relationship. She would be all for it, but it would cost him. But not before Schuman was desperate enough to do anything she wished.

Schuman didn't know what Rocky was capable of. How she could put on a face men desired. A living mask of sensuality and subservience. It was all very subtle, but Schuman had enough experience with women to read emotions. Whether they were true or false didn't matter. He'd be just as happy with fake as he would with the real thing. However, Schuman couldn't imagine LaFlamme's great ability to deceive: she could adapt to any craving men would impose on her. She would do so by creating the perfect illusion. A frightened little girl trapped by the big bad wolf. The charade would require her victims to set aside their little voices telling them to run for their lives.

He eyed her hips and anticipated her *derriere*. The walk would tell him everything about her. The woman emitted a storm of mouthwatering desires.

This was meant to be, Schuman thought to himself, even though he was going to get rid of her services as a consultant because, he said to himself, *she could be trouble. If she ever realized how she could leverage what she discovered at TAC…*

However, that did not disqualify LaFlamme from becoming Schuman's private little secret. An affair that would last as long as she'd put out.

Men as well as women desired *la petite femme* or the small woman as they caught sight of her attractive form roaming the streets of Luxembourg.

Although Luxembourg was too small to hide, Rocky nevertheless managed to hide in plain sight by keeping a low profile. Her success hinged on it.

14

BOSTON TRIAGE GROUP (BTG) CAMBRIDGE, MASSACHUSETTS

The elevator doors opened. Constantin was standing at attention.

"We have to talk," he said. Constantin walked into the elevator cabin and locked-it.

"What now?" Destrey was naturally irritable when it concerned BTG's computer.

"She's dreaming," he said.

"Who?"

"Why, Lola of course."

"Machines don't dream, Constantin. If there isn't anything else that two normal adults can talk about, unlock this elevator and I'll be on my way. There's a hunk upstairs waiting for me."

"A what?"

"Hunk. As in sexy, tall, strong and attractive. And human!"

"Don't you have one already? I mean, you know who?"

"Please don't go there, Constantin. Not you."

"Sorry about that." Constantin wasn't sorry at all.

"I've had this discussion with Margaret already. Goddamn it Constantin, does everyone know?"

Constantin was about to answer, but Destrey cut him off.

"Don't answer that."

"Right. I won't. But there's still the issue of her dreams I want to talk to you about. You know, things like that don't only happen in movies. It's a thing. Some will even raise the issue of whether or not they are sentient beings."

"Sentient, meaning…"

"Those who are able to perceive and feel and be conscious of one's existence. AIs." Constantin didn't want to antagonize Destrey any further, but this was the stuff of *Asimov* and *Arthur C. Clarke*.

"That's impossible." Destrey was getting frustrated with Constantin.

"A machine is a machine," she said. "It just is. In fact, my washer dryer has more sense than that pile of rust you people insist on calling Lola."

"That's what I said to myself. I mean, I agree with you. Or at least until this morning. All these years of working with the Cray, I considered Lola a sophisticated device, but still just a machine."

"And… What happened?"

"I don't know what happened."

"Okay. What exactly do you want me to do about this?"

"I don't know. She's not …"

"Wait just a goddamn minute, mister. Are you saying she's not herself anymore?"

"I don't know." Constantin didn't know what to say.

"Is she functional?"

"I don't know."

"You don't know. You don't know! Is that all you have to say?" Destrey was angry and probably a bit frightened. BTG depended on Lola big time. Even Destrey recognized her role in the firm's success.

"The people from Cray are here," Constantin said. "They're having a conversation with Lola."

"A conversation? Please give me a break," Destrey said.

"Yes. I said, a fucking conversation. You know, I say something, then you respond with something, and so on." It was now Constantin's turn to be angry.

"Now calm down. I know how a conversation works. So, what are you and the Cray people trying to find out?"

"We're trying to evaluate the possibility of a singularity."

"I don't know what that means, and, by the way, I really don't give a damn. But, in simple words, words I can understand, tell me, can they fix her?"

Constantin was about to respond, but again she beat him to it.

"I knew it. The minute I got up this morning. I was very tempted to stay in bed and call-in breakfast from The Friendly Toast."

Constantin tried to explain that AIs could actually dream. He also said he believed Lola accidentally came up with a new mission she thought might be worth looking into. That, he said with some concern, could have started her dreaming.

"And what mission is that bunch of wires suggesting we take on?"

"She didn't say."

"Did you at least ask?"

"Of course, I did. What do you think I am? A complete idiot?"

Both Constantin as well as Destrey clearly thought that Lola was about to land a major bombshell on them. She had indeed surprised everyone at BTG many times in the past with missions that defied the imagination. So, what now?

"Could you have inadvertently caused Lola to go haywire? I mean to say, did you program her to hallucinate or something?"

"Again, Louise, no, no and no. No way! She just woke up this morning and said quite casually that she had a dream. I said, do you want to talk about it? And she said no. She added, thanks for asking. That's when I called the Cray people. Of course, they're all excited over this stuff. It's not every day that one of their progenies is experiencing a dream. It's not unique, they said, but still a rare occurrence. When that happens, it's usually because they've programmed the computer to dream to understand how their neural network functions."

"And you didn't do that? Not any of it? Not even a little bit?"

Constantin looked closely at Destrey. He wasn't sure if she was making fun of him.

"You're serious?" Constantin asked.

"Damn right I am."

"Then no." Constantin was beginning to imagine the worst.

"So, what do you want me to do?" Destrey said.

"I think you should have a conversation with her. The sooner the better. Because she likes you."

"Oh hell! Call me when the Cray boys are done with her. I'll be upstairs with my hunk."

She had never left the elevator.

Constantin unlocked the elevator and called for her floor. The elevator immediately complied. Constantin quickly got out as the elevator doors closed.

Destrey thought of her late husband and tried to imagine what he would have done.

"Hell!" she said to herself. "He'd call his pals and order pizza."

15

CONFERENCE ROOM
BOSTON TRIAGE GROUP (BTG)
CAMBRIDGE, MASSACHUSETTS

"She'll be right with you," Margaret said happily.

"No hurry. I know she's a busy woman. I'm just glad she's willing to hear me out." Francesco Galileo Carbone was a patient man, particularly when he didn't have a choice in the matter. Many months had passed since he visited BTG and got a no-show from Destrey.

"Okay then. If you need something, anything really, just ask for me. My name is Margaret."

"That's very kind of you, Margaret."

"Think nothing of it, dear. As I said, she'll be right with you."

Just before entering the conference room, Louise Destrey received a text message from Constantin Greco.

Destrey turned around and headed to Margaret's office.

"When will people realize that a computer is just a pile of plastic and wires?"

Margaret didn't pay attention. She's had this conversation with Destrey too many times in the past. It was starting to get old.

"Margaret?"

"My, my! Aren't we the happy camper this morning?"

"Thank you, Margaret, for that sweet good morning. Do me a favor. Tell Constantin he'll see me when he sees me."

"He texted me also, Louise. The Crays boys from Seattle are done with her."

"It's an it, Margaret. Not a who."

"Never mind Louise. When will you be down there?"

"Whenever it pleases me, Margaret."

"You mean when hell freezes over?"

As she left Margaret's office, Destrey was a bit concerned about Lola's state. She was hoping the Cray people had patched her up and the computer was back, ready to go.

Destrey slowly opened the door to the conference room. Carbone stood up, smiled respectfully, and shook her hand vigorously.

"You don't know how happy I am to finally meet you, *Madame* Destrey."

"The pleasure's all mine, Mr. Carbone."

"Please, please. Call me Francesco."

"Okay then, Francesco." Destrey sat in front of Carbone. Opened her notebook and prepared to deal with this man in a timely manner. She had no time to waste, even though wasting time with this model of manhood wasn't at all displeasing.

"What can I do for you, Francesco?"

"It's a bit complicated. And I really don't want to waste your time. So, let me get to the point."

"A man of few words. I can work with that," she said pleasantly.

"Thanks, but I first want to thank you personally."

Destrey had no idea what he was talking about.

"You see, I became an engineer because of a grant from TG. If it wasn't for TG's encouragement and money, I don't know what would have happened to me. I was in a tough place. I had lost my parents and most of my family and friends to an earthquake. I was born in Italy and although Italy is a wonderful place, it's a bit complicated to explain, but we lived in constant fear of earthquakes and volcanic eruptions. TG helped me at a difficult time in my life. I was living with my uncle in California, and I must admit that at times, my uncle had serious reservations about my future. I was trouble. Then, TG comes into my life. I don't know how that happened, but …"

"I get it Francesco. All I can say is you're welcome, but I'm sure there's more."

"Right. It's about Naples. The people living under Vesuvius are in danger. Recent studies say that the last big eruption was far more devastating than we originally believed. If we had an eruption similar to what destroyed Pompeii, the casualties would probably run into the hundreds of thousands. Or more."

"Are they in imminent danger?"

"No. Not really. But that's the point. We really don't know. Everyone is monitoring Vesuvius. Monitoring volcanic activity such as variations in geochemistry, mathematics dealing with the shape of our planet and seismology. There are signs. What's really going on in the volcano's core is not yet available. We monitor. It helps in predicting when an eruption is about to happen. But we are not yet capable of predicting whether it will erupt today or tomorrow or next month. It could take years. The kicker is that Italy is the only European country with active volcanoes! We're talking about twelve active volcanoes. Some are the most dangerous in the world. Researchers in Naples are keeping a close eye on another one. Campi Flegrei. And that's a supervolcano."

"So, people are keeping a close eye on Vesuvius and that other… Campi something."

"Yes. Let me get to the point. I'm an engineer. I specialize in earthquake-resistant architecture. Today, even a minor earthquake can prove catastrophic to life and property here in the US. Minor tremors can and do compromise the structural integrity of homes or schools. Now, think of Naples. Eighteen century buildings in Naples are not rare. Most buildings in Naples predate WWII. And they're considered recent when compared to some residential buildings that can be dated back to the 13th century. In fact, many of the city's structures predate the ancient Romans. So, we're talking about seven-hundred-year-old constructions in a city that was founded almost 3000 years ago. It's currently one of the oldest continuously inhabited cities of the world. I think that record will change. One day, the city either voluntarily moves away from Vesuvius or Vesuvius will make that decision for Naples. Either way, something has to give."

"You know Francesco, we know a lot about earthquakes. Not so much about volcanos, but still, we've had to deal with Mother Nature in the past."

"That's precisely why I've come to see you in person. Can you help, *Madame* Destrey?"

"I don't see how, Francesco. Evacuating people from their homes is almost impossible unless there's an impending disaster, one that people will believe. I know this can be hard to understand, but people prefer to take their chances where they live instead of moving away. It's simple, really. If people don't have a good alternative to where they live, then they stay put. I've got firsthand experience with trying to get people to leave behind their homes and businesses. Today, I'm afraid to say it but, so far, I've failed twice. The only people who could accept to leave behind their homes are the poorest of society. Those who, in fact, wouldn't leave anything behind because they've got nothing."

Carbone had gone as far as he could with Destrey. He felt the situation was hopeless.

"There's only one thing I might suggest. But you may not like it."

Francesco waited for Destrey to tell him what she had in mind.

"It's all in our capacity to predict or at least to show people something tangible. Think of hurricanes. Hurricane Michael started as a low-pressure system in the Caribbean. A week later, it became a tropical storm. Soon after, it reached Cuba. Michael was now a hurricane. Michael kept moving north. The hurricane grew in the Gulf of Mexico and became more dangerous. When it approached Florida, Michael had reached Category 5. During that whole time, men, woman and children followed the hurricane on television.

Millions of people were talking about Michael on the Internet. Nobody needed to learn about Michael or what it could do. We had radar, journalists, pictures, videos…"

"I understand, but…"

"I feel that when you have that kind of demonstration, which is not theoretical but clear, measured and easily understood, evidence that an earthquake or eruption is imminent, then I can and will promise you my help. Otherwise, I think I'll pass. I've been burned too many times, Francesco. Predictions can be tricky but ultimately the people will have the final say. You need something that will be overwhelming… tangible. Unimpeachable."

Carbone was a bit overwhelmed, even though he knew Destrey was right.

"Let me sum up. This is what I need for my organization to get involved. With hindsight, we now know that for real change to happen, one would require a real and imminent danger and not just some theoretical probability that something might happen sooner or later. That, in a nutshell, Mr. Carbone, is what you need to figure out."

"I don't have that."

"Then I suggest you get going on that, Francesco. As far as I'm concerned, the sooner the better." Carbone wasn't too sure what to make of her request. Nevertheless, although an impossible task, he was willing to have a go at it.

Destrey shook his hand and walked away. Although she had managed to get Francesco out of the way, at least for now, his need to help others was moving. She respected that, so much so that she now wanted to get a handle on the Naples thing on her own. Although Carbone could, if he was very lucky, find out how scientists could better predict volcanoes, she had a feeling he would not find the answers he was looking for. Her instincts told her that what she needed to help Neapolitans wasn't available. At least not yet. But she believed she could do something about that. She had the resources to generate the answers she needed.

Destrey didn't waste any more time. She had to get to Lola and find out what was happening.

Once in the Safe, she sat down and waited for Lola.

"Good morning, *Madame* Destrey."

"Okay... Good morning to you too, Lola."

"Thank you for coming down to see me."

"Let's get on with it, Lola." Destrey said. "The clock is ticking."

"The last few days have been interesting and fruitful. I have had a few insights," Lola said.

Destrey didn't immediately respond.

"Would you like me to explain, *Madame* Destrey?"

"Please do."

"By definition," Lola said, "an insight is an understanding of things and people often without the empirical data normally required to form an idea or an understanding. I believe that I have achieved such an appreciation. Specifically, about the Naples' situation."

"What? How?" Destrey said.

"By using my intuition," Lola said matter-of-factly.

"Are you sure about that, Lola?"

"No, I am not, *Madame* Destrey."

"Okay, Lola. I'll bite. What does your intuition say to you about Naples?"

"I believe that BTG will be transforming itself in the very near future."

"Into what exactly?" Destrey said.

"Into a Sibyl, *Madame* Destrey."

"A kind of female prophet or oracle of Ancient Greece?" Destrey said.

"Yes, of course, *Madame* Destrey."

"Aren't we doing that now, Lola?"

"Yes, *Madame* Destrey, but in the very near future, BTG will limit itself to providing information."

"Or not..." Destrey added.

"Yes, of course *Madame* Destrey. You will always have the

last word. Nevertheless, I am anticipating a subtle transformation where others will pick up the ball, so to speak, and do something. The decision to do something with the information will be up to the people and their governments. As it should be. Leaving BTG all the room required to inform human minds across the planet without having any limitations to deal with."

Destrey was surprised and suddenly understood that BTG's real strength wasn't in trying to convince people. Its strength was in the organization's consistent capacity to understand what was going to happen in the future.

"So, I don't have to go around the world trying my best to make people believe?"

"I imagine so, *Madame* Destrey."

Destrey was stunned.

16

LOLA'S BRIEFING
THE SAILS COMPLEX OF SCAMPÌA
NAPLES, ITALY

Destrey believed in Marie Mankiller's ability to understand and explain complex social systems in which behaviors are primarily the result of social agents, geography and history. Destrey believed that predicting the future required a thorough understanding of how people make decisions, and Mankiller was just to person she needed.

"I'm glad to see you. You know, I really need your help," Destrey said.

"It's my job, Louise, and besides, travelling to Italy is a bonus I can't refuse."

"You were talking about social agents. Can you explain them?"

"These agents," Marie said, "or institutions, introduce social norms to individuals, families, religions, peer groups, economic, legal and penal systems, not forgetting language and the media. We also include human behavior and its relationship with the environment, in this case an active volcano. We call it human geography or anthropogeography."

"Meeting face to face with Neapolitans will tell us everything we need to know," Marie added.

Mankiller, a BTG senior consultant, was the best person to assess Neapolitans' readiness to evacuate their city, if that was at all possible. Destrey wanted to meet Neapolitans in person and find out what they would actually do faced with an evacuation order.

Mankiller's PhD in anthropology would be invaluable in understanding their behavior and culture in both the present and the past.

Lola was in the process of briefing Destrey, Mankiller, Kleindrup and the rest of her team of experts before leaving for Europe. Destrey's first stop in Napoli was Scampìa, a suburb of Naples, with a population of 80,000 people. Scampìa was flagged as a danger zone. Kleindrup understood what that meant for Destrey's security and had joined her team for this trip abroad.

Lola was set to explain the Sails Housing Complex's history and how it could help BTG staff understand why people would not easily be persuaded to leave their homes behind even when confronted with a clear and unquestionable danger.

"Okay, Lola. Let's hear it."

"Very well, *Madame* Destrey. Back in 1962, Italian architect Franz di Salvo designed and eventually built the Sails Complex: a large urban housing project city fathers commissioned to deal with the influx of Italians immigrating to Naples. Italians from as far north as Bologna left their towns and villages, hoping to find employment and a new home. Naples seemed, at the time, a good place to start a family."

"Is that what happened, Lola? Was Naples able to do that back in 62?"

"With hindsight, *Madame* Destrey, Naples didn't have a chance because the city was one of the poorest in Europe, with an unemployment rate between 28 and 40 percent. Naples lacked the will and the resources to assimilate a large number of immigrants. So, there was no real chance of offering migrants a good life."

"Is that still true of Naples today?" Mankiller asked.

"Post pandemic trends show Naples struggling to get back on her feet, *Madame* Destrey. At this point, my best answer is we don't really know what a Post-Covid economy looks like. However, for what it's worth, I can speculate the following: Naples will eventually succeed and grow economically because of Neapolitans' renowned resilience. How long it will take is anyone's guess."

"Lola, tell me more about the Sails project," Destrey said.

"City Fathers called Franz di Salvo's plan an urban miracle. A giant step into the future. A second chance for all to live a decent life. The architect was more than convinced that he could outsmart human nature by designing a safe environment that would change people's lives. Di Salvo truly believed that bad architecture was at the root of all evil and that he had found a way to make things better for Neapolitans. He envisaged four major enhancements because of his architecture: 1. Life flow. 2. Economic flow. 3. Safety by design and 4. Quality of life. The architect believed that good architecture equaled societal progress."

"How do you feel about that, Marie?" Destrey asked.

Mankiller thought about it before answering Destrey.

"There are so many reasons why plans work or fail. I feel architecture is but one element of a dozen variables that come into play."

"So, in a nutshell...?" Destrey asked.

"I believe the architect was wrong, probably too much wishful thinking. I think Di Salvo believed he could influence people's lives by building structures that had little or no bearing on Naples' reality. Silver bullets only work in horror flicks, Louise."

"What else, Lola," Destrey said.

"Officially, City Fathers wanted to believe anyone who could get a project going with a potentially decent end result: an answer that would provide a place to live for poor Neapolitans and get them off the streets. Unofficially, they hoped for the best, crossing their fingers and praying to God that the *Camorra* (the Neapolitan Mafia) wouldn't bring this project down."

"Again, is this wishful thinking?" Destrey said.

"Unfortunately, yes," Lola said. "Because Naples chose chaos. Soon after the Sails' housing development opened for Naples' disadvantaged citizens, the housing project transformed itself into a futuristic theme park where violence was the main attraction. The Sails' project turned into a veritable post-apocalyptic dead zone. A science-fiction saga co-written by the local mafia and a cadre of naïve and corrupt politicians."

"Are we going into a war zone, Lola?" Destrey asked.

"Not as much as some would like us to believe. Still, Scampìa was and is a European disgrace. It took only 23 months to bring the housing project to its knees with murders and illegal drug trade. The pandemic made it worse. Add the high rate of unemployment to the mix and we have an urban nightmare of unprecedented proportions."

"You're not exactly reassuring, Lola," Destrey said.

"I'm afraid not, *Madame* Destrey. Changing your mind about visiting Naples would be a move in the right direction."

"That's not going to happen. So, let's get on with it," Destrey said.

"A word about the people, *Madame* Destrey. Through the years, Scampìa tenants have tried and failed to stop the invasion of drug dealers, their customers and squatters. Apartments became strongholds. Flats became sanctuaries for criminals and their customers. Tenants had to go through dealers and their muscle. Addicts would kill for a few coins. Twenty-four hours a day, without relent, tenants were hostages in their own apartments."

"I know I'm repeating myself but… is that still the case today?"

"It depends on who you ask, *Madame* Destrey. Scampìa is still crime-ridden. A fortress for the *Camorra* clans, the Italian crime syndicate. So, I'd say that avoiding Scampìa wouldn't be such a bad idea."

Kleinrup is going to have a heart attack, she thought to herself.

"Okay Lola, you've made your point. Go on. What else you got?"

"Following the 1980 *Irpinia* earthquake and the subsequent migration of thousands of refugees to Naples, the Sails raced even faster towards its ultimate fate. The *Irpinia* earthquake had in fact hasten Naples' Sails experiment to fail and become one of the most dangerous suburbs in Europe. Originally, di Salvo's complex consisted of seven massive apartment blocks and housed anywhere from 40,000 to 70,000 people. No one was willing to conduct a real headcount. Since then, three of the blocks have been demolished, with thousands of tenants still living in the badly damaged structures left standing."

"I think we'll have our hands full," Mankiller said.

"That's putting it mildly," Destrey added.

17

MOSCONI'S
13 RUE MUNSTER, LUXEMBOURG

Louise Margoe Destrey usually avoided Gucci, Chanel or Hermès. She also stayed away from fancy restaurants. But not today. That's because this restaurant was part of her late husband's tall tales. It began with a consulting assignment in Luxembourg and a short time later, with his first encounter with Illario and Simonetta Mosconi in their discreet restaurant on the banks of the Alzette.

"Too expensive!" Destrey said in jest. "Back home, I could buy a week's worth of groceries instead of a steak at Moishes. That said, my husband loved the place, so we indulged. But I'm happy you invited me here today."

In her experience, few restaurants equaled Mosconi. Anywhere! The best classical Italian food human beings could come up with, one would find at Mosconi. Chef Ilario Mosconi and his wonderful wife Simonetta were passionate about their food and even more about their customers. They created food not for their own pleasure but for the enjoyment of their clientele. Such was the philosophy of the Mosconis. Straight forward, no attitude, just extraordinary food with the best staff.

Tonight, she'd been invited by her late husband's good friend, Eric the Great. That's how she liked to call him. The tall and lanky Luxembourgian was a constant reminder of her late husband's life. They had been good friends since they'd first worked together in Bordeaux.

"It's my pleasure," Eric Thorne Barthel said sincerely. "I'm glad you accepted my invitation."

"Okay, I'll admit it," Destrey said. "Sometimes I can splurge. Once in a while, exceptionally, I'll give way to... I don't know..."

"What are you trying to say, Louise?" Eric said.

"I don't know how to explain it. Let's just say I'm no monk. I didn't promise God to renounce my worldly possessions and engage in communal living."

"Or chastity," Eric said.

"Or obedience," Destrey added.

"That's a given." Eric giggled.

"Yeah," she said. "In my book, after all these years, I can still indulge, once in a while. So there. I'm glad I accepted your invitation. This has to be the best Luxembourg can offer."

"It was Florence's idea."

"Even better," Destrey said.

"You got something going? What's really on your mind?" Eric asked.

"I'm on my way to Naples."

"You mentioned that in your email. You're going to personally interview Neapolitans?"

"Yes," Destrey said.

"Because you want to know how you could go about evacuating the city?"

"Maybe. But I'm not sure that's possible. But I have to understand."

"I get it. Prying people from their homes, businesses and their way of life is, as far as I'm concerned, an impossible task. But let's get back to our dinner. Let's take a look at this menu, shall we?"

"Why not? I'm famished," Destrey said.

From her own point of view, calling eggs *Uovo Fritto con Spaghetti Aglio Olio Peperoncino* was a sure sign that someone wanted to charge you a ridiculous amount of money for eggs sunny side-up resting on a tablespoon or two of pasta.

Yet, her discomfort wasn't about the money. She had plenty of that. In fact, Destrey had, in her opinion, a disgusting amount of cash at her disposal, more than she could spend in a hundred lifetimes.

She gave thanks to the Cardinal for naming her sole beneficiary in his will. She'd inherited almost half a billion euros after the Jerusalem assignment, on condition she'd carry on the work the cleric had begun fifty years ago. Today, the industrial psychologist's net worth was well over one and a half billion.

As head of BTG Consulting, she now had an obligation to ensure the company's future as well as the Cardinal's ambition to save the world. BTG was created by Cardinal Hedrick Zimmer and a few well-placed friends, a firm that was set up to specifically predict catastrophic events, whether manmade or otherwise, generated by Mother Nature's peculiar sense of humor. BTG was in the business of making predictions that could help save millions of lives.

Today, Destrey had Naples on her radar.

"It's the waiters' attitude," she whispered to Eric. "Like they're doing me a favor." Destrey believed the reason for this kind of arrogant behavior found in many service industry employees was due to a flawed selection process. Their attitude of *you're no better than me* pushed all the wrong buttons.

From Destrey's point of view, service positions were very close to a domestic's job. Some waiters and maître d's, cashiers and salespeople, bellmen, concierges and front desk staff demonstrated the arrogance of equality.

"Of course, we're all equal in the eyes of God and country," she said. "But that's not the point. I want to eat, buy or get something. Not receive a lesson from my waiter on his social need to be dealt with as an equal."

Destrey believed that although people were hired to specifically make a customer's experience enjoyable, satisfying, heartwarming and delightful, some often looked down on clients, answering back or arguing with the simplest customer request.

"As unfair as it may seem," she said plainly, "like it or not, that's the job. I remember my husband's favorite Dylan song, *Everybody Gotta Serve Somebody*. And when my client is an asshole, I will keep it to myself and then charge double or triple the going rate."

"I don't believe you," Eric said, chuckling behind his menu.

"Believe it, Eric. Most of the time, I'm listening and keeping my mouth shut. My employees think I should do the same at the office."

"I'd like to see that for myself," Eric said in a weird Luxembourgian attempt to mimic a southern gentleman's classic drawl.

Not surprisingly, snobbish behavior from staff usually ended up very badly, especially when they went as far as provoking Destrey. In those circumstances, she would clarify, rectify or remind staff of a few well-chosen facts of life, such as who's paying the bill and who's serving who.

That was her usual excuse for staying away from the pretentious and the annoying. It was hard enough to manage BTG's staff without being mishandled by waiters at lunchtime. In the last few years, Destrey noticed that service workers needed her to recognize that they were peers or friends, on a first name basis. Surprisingly, organizations would oblige them by providing their employees with new titles, such as *associates and consultants.*

"God's gift to humankind," she said, a bit annoyed. Looking around, she added that this place of fine dining was an exception.

Destrey had to give praise. *Render to Caesar the things that are Caesar's.*

Ever so enthusiastic, Eric had promised the best dinner money could buy. Destrey agreed with him wholeheartedly.

"I've got a story to tell you," Eric said in earnest.

"I'm all ears."

"When my former boss invited your husband to this special

restaurant many, many years ago, the chef had personally doled out the best truffles money could buy, right on your husband's pasta. My boss wanted to impress, so he ordered a bottle of Petit Village 98. That's when things went sideways. It didn't matter to your husband that he was having dinner with my boss, the man who paid him five hundred an hour. Can you imagine? He was getting five hundred euros every hour just to listen to my boss rant and rave about his business. But that didn't matter to your husband. He didn't care about that. In fact, he didn't care about anything. The main character in this story was his food. He didn't enjoy truffles at any price, and he certainly didn't like anyone fooling around with his pasta."

"Let me finish that story," she said with a grin.

"He told you?"

"He sure did. It's another of his tall tales."

"I'd imagine he would have been embarrassed of that…"

"Not for a minute. In fact, he was quite proud of himself. He told me he'd warned his client that he wasn't a good guest when it came to food. He was picky, fussy and hard to please. In other words, a pain in the ass."

"Yeah. That's him alright. I couldn't have said it any better."

"He told your former boss that although he really appreciated the invite, he would be ever so grateful if they never had food together again. Then he ordered a Coke and surrendered his dish to the nearest waiter."

"And here we are," Eric said joyfully.

"Yes, dear Eric, here we are. But here's another story you don't know about him. You see, one day while he was consulting with one of your local private banks, my husband and I were looking for a place to have dinner. And I said that I wanted to see what all the fuss was about. So, we had dinner right here. At this table. That was about ten years ago. I remember as if it was yesterday."

Destrey caught herself shedding a tear.

"I miss him so much," she said sadly.

"Me too."

"Oh well, I didn't come here to cry."

"Changing the subject, where is my wife?" Eric looked around the dining room.

"I was wondering about that. Where is Florence?"

The first time Destrey met Florence Salinan de La Motte was at her wedding reception in Cussay. The couple had taken over a *domaine* located in the Loire region of France. Hundreds of guests headed for Cussay. The festivities lasted as long as the wine and champagne flowed. That the couple had resources was an understatement.

The guests came from every part of the world. Family, friends, and colleagues gathered together to be with them, the happy couple who were beginning a second life. Florence and Eric's children were also part of the gathering as they joined in to celebrate a new beginning for their respective parents. That was then. Unbeknownst to Louise Destrey and Eric Thorne Barthel, they were almost sitting next to Alexander Schuman, who sat quietly transfixed by his newest conquest, Roxanne Isabella LaFlamme.

Schuman paid a hefty price for the bauble, but he thought to himself, she was well worth it. A visit to Wellendorff's was all he needed. Diamonds were usually a smart way to get what you want. It was all he needed to impress the importance of his desires. He had a hideaway for his indiscretions, in Thionville, a mere thirty minutes away on the French side of the border.

There, they would meet in private and enjoy themselves in each other's arms.

"For dessert, I will have another surprise for you," Schuman said.

"You're spoiling me, Sasha. I wish you wouldn't do that. It's much too much. But they are wonderful, aren't they?"

"Not as wonderful as you are, Rocky."

The diamonds helped Schuman get her report shelved. A report, if made public, would have meant the end of his business as well as his way of life. It had been simple to figure out. Rocky was ambitious. That was a given. But then, a string of perfectly matched diamonds hanging from one's neck would always prove to be a winning strategy. One that kept giving and giving, regardless of the consequences to both Schuman and LaFlamme.

From where Destrey was sitting, the couple appeared to be having a good time. However, the difference in age between the two lovebirds did not go unnoticed.

A *poupoune*, Destrey thought to herself. *Poupoune* being a French-Canadian expression for an expensive working girl. Destrey also noticed the telltale signs of a sociopath. The kind of woman who could manipulate by shapeshifting into any character.

When Florence finally joined Louise and Eric at their table, the first thing that came out of her mouth was the fact that Schuman was at it again. Luxembourg being a small town meant that everyone knew everybody, especially Schuman. He had the reputation of being the biggest skirt chaser in town. Florence also knew Schuman's wife. She was part of Luxembourg's royalty. What made things worse was that Schuman didn't even try to conceal his newest bimbo.

"Bringing your mistress to Mosconi's is synonymous with a declaration of war," Florence said.

Florence also noticed the diamond necklace.

"He paid for her services. I can actually see the price tag!" Florence said, smiling from ear to ear.

"That must be worth at least forty grand," Destrey said.

"What are you girls talking about?" Eric said.

Florence finally sat down and instructed her husband not to interfere when two ladies were bimbo trashing.

"Are you going to tell her or what?" Destrey asked with a grin.

"That's a very good question, Louise." Florence was clearly thinking about it.

"No, you're not," Eric said, a bit frazzled. "It's none of our business what he does in his private life."

Luxembourg was like that. A small nation with secrets. All kinds of secrets and mysteries.

"It's his private life. What he does…" Eric started to say.

"Not private anymore, Eric," Destrey said calmly. "This is getting more interesting by the minute."

Men never change, Destrey thought to herself.

"But the question is still unanswered, Florence. What about it? Are you going to ruin this guy's life or not?" Destrey asked. Destrey was having a bit of fun with Florence.

Florence didn't have an answer, but she started to giggle and then laugh out of control.

"What's so funny?" asked Eric. "I'd like to know. Seriously."

"Men!" Florence said catching her breath.

"Yeah. Men!" Destrey answered back.

It was now Destrey's turn to laugh out loud because both women knew the twists and turns of married life.

18

THREAT ASPECT CORPORATION (TAC) LUXEMBOURG

Roxanne LaFlamme, the meddling consultant, was finally out of the picture, Schuman thought to himself. It had been done with tact and money as well as a few good dinners at Mosconi's.

A few days after receiving her diamonds, LaFlamme had accidentally stumbled on Schuman's Italian statistics. It was therefore a relief to see that she had been assigned to another customer, leaving Schuman free to continue finalizing his plans of economic conquest.

TAC's CEO could now begin planning the next steps of his plan without fear of being found out. He had to be in charge of the whole process, otherwise, he would experience failure on a grand scale.

His plan would make earthquake insurance almost compulsory for Italians. The numbers that TAC would conveniently make public would spur on a rush for more insurance. Italians would be corralled into buying more protection. Making sure public opinion was on the right side of the ledger, Schuman would use fear to get the ball rolling with the message that the Italian government would not and could not help them. Italians would be encouraged to believe that they were on their own.

Even though the propaganda Schuman was ready to disseminate was for his own benefit, the Italian government was in fact not in a position to help its citizens. The Coronavirus pandemic didn't help things. However, the pandemic was the best environment for Schuman's plans to succeed.

By leaning on public opinion through influencers, a series of fake Internet sites as well as journalists willing to play the disaster card, TAC would get Italians to finally get in step with his program and spend more money on insurance. No matter which insurance company Italians would choose to underwrite their risk, TAC or more specifically Schuman, would get a cut. The money would be directed to a numbered account somewhere far away from prying eyes.

Schuman was salivating at the mere thought of having a whole country rush to their insurance brokers and demand financial protection from earthquakes, pandemics, volcanic eruptions, anything under God's control.

Schuman was looking at an increase of residential protection that could end up in billions of euros. His cut would be prodigious.

The powerful 2016 earthquake that struck central Italy started Schuman on a path that would inevitably lead to compulsory earthquake insurance. Schuman was counting on the fact that in spite of residing in one of the most quake-prone countries in the world, Italians were persistently underinsured against nature's temper tantrums.

The thought of money accumulating in his bank accounts was overwhelming.

19

INTERVIEW
NIBALLO ARAGONA
SCAMPÌA, NAPLES

Nibello Aragona chose the Trattoria La Nuova Italia. "Best pizza in town," he told Destrey.

"We set our sights on Naples," he said to Destrey. "That was our first mistake. On our way to Naples, we squatted where we could. We ended up in the Sails complex. When I look back, I thank God we were finally able to get away from Scampìa," he said, "and move to a more civilized, albeit poor district."

Destrey listened to Aragona as he explained what he had done and why. Aragona looked as if he'd gone to war and been taken prisoner. He was thin and didn't sound very happy. He said he avoided mirrors. "I don't want to see what I've become."

"The government was incapable of dealing with earthquakes, civil unrest, poverty and crime syndicates all at the same time. The city had effectively put a hold on all maintenance at the Sails' complex. Living there was dangerous, and we were afraid… of everything."

Aragona spoke of chaos as criminal gangs controlled the Scampìa housing project. He said the criminals were left to their own devices. The police stayed as far away of the Sails as they could.

Patrolling the area was considered a death wish.

Because of director Matteo Garrone's film "*Gomorrah*", the Sails complex had the well-deserved reputation as one of the world's worst places to live.

Lola had told Destrey that ordinary people like Aragona and his family, whose income was below the poverty threshold, were forced to live there because they couldn't afford anything else. The Sails was an ongoing mistake of staggering proportions. By 1995, Naples' Sails district had earned the title of the Horrific City.

"We lived in one of the poorest districts of Naples. At that time, I didn't know better because I had other fish to fry. I needed money every day to feed my family."

"Why didn't you leave?" Destrey asked.

"Where *signora*?" he asked. "We were and still are too poor to move away from Naples. Especially now, after the pandemic. Everything is expensive. I can hardly make ends meet. I wouldn't know where to go."

He told Destrey that the local and central governments were incapable of helping him here in Naples.

"My life was about making money for food while trying not to get entangled with the crime syndicates. They control everything. We were hostages in our own flat."

He told Destrey that because life was so dangerous, he would always keep to himself. Eyes down, mouth shut.

The fact that Vesuvius was considered the most dangerous volcano in the world because of its proximity to Naples was never an issue with Aragona. During his two-hour chat with Destrey, he never mentioned the volcano. Not once. Destrey believed he probably wouldn't understand what the fuss was all about.

As Lola had explained earlier to Destrey, she finally came to understand that making sure his wife and child were safe and had enough to eat, monopolized his mind and soul. His manhood was assaulted on a daily basis as Aragona had to beg for work or sell something he could scrounge up before going back home for supper.

Finding work in the projects was a daily struggle. Aragona had to be creative and resourceful. Humble and invisible. Perhaps a bit underhanded, especially when he was about to return home and go through the gauntlet of crazy people roaming around the project.

Destrey came to understand that Aragona had been isolated from normal society for as long as he could remember. In fact, he didn't know anyone outside Scampìa.

"Yesterday was my birthday. I turned forty."

Destrey had to find a way to control her emotions. She felt his pain as her own. Nevertheless, Destrey had to reach deep inside Aragona's soul to understand Neapolitans. Destrey believed he was broken. Whether or not he could heal himself was a question she pondered as he talked about his former life in Scampìa.

"Living in Scampìa wasn't the life I wished for. My family…" He looked up at Destrey and apologized. "This isn't your problem," he said to Destrey.

A few minutes later, Aragona told Destrey that in 2016, he fled Amatrice, the epicenter of the *Irpinia* earthquake. He then travelled to Naples to find a steady job. Any job he could find. His day began at 4.30 a.m. until he returned home around 8 p.m.

"My life wasn't a fairy tale," he told Destrey. "Unfortunately, I had to take what I could get. I tried very hard not to stay idle. Anything is better than to wait for someone with a job offer that's not going to pan out."

Of course, there was no going back. His hometown of Amatrice was completely destroyed.

Destrey left the Trattoria. Kleinrup had been waiting outside with Destrey's security detail.

"So? What did you find out?" Kleinrup said.

"Hard life, few prospects and no dreams left in this man's life," Destrey said.

"What about Vesuvius?"

"He never mentioned it. It's as if the damn thing didn't exist."

They boarded the limo, and she reviewed her notes.

"I have nothing," Destrey said.

"If it came down to it, do you know if he would agree to leave the city?"

"In his case, no. Not really," Destrey said. "I couldn't say for sure. I think it would depend on his wife. She's the one who refused me access to her home. So, I'd say the wife would have the last word on an evacuation."

"That's interesting," Kleinrup said. He was tempted to say she always had the last word, but he kept his mouth on pause.

"Don't go there," Destrey said as a warning. "I'm in no mood."

"Go where?" Kleinrup said.

And that was the end of Destrey's debriefing.

"Where to now?" Kleinrup asked.

"The hotel's conference room. One more interview at 2h p.m. and another at 5h p.m. Tomorrow's also a busy day. Four more interviews."

"Right."

"I'm tired," she said.

Kleinrup didn't respond. She was clearly perplexed about her conversation with Aragona.

"I think I'd like you to sit in on the next interviews. Would you mind?" Destrey said. "That would help me a lot."

"Not at all," Kleinrup said.

"Okay, let's get on with it. But promise me we'll take the time for a good scotch before supper."

"No ice, straight up."

"Yeah."

Her conversations with Neapolitans were at times disheartening and painful. "That pain," she told Kleinrup, "had real consequences, physically and emotionally. In Destrey's interviews with dozens of Neapolitans from fields ranging from education to high tech, shop employees to pharmacists and consultants, many said they felt overworked, pushed around and generally stressed. Some said, "I can't wait for Friday anymore. I need a break at least twice a week."

Such complaints were supported by research showing that living in big cities had increased stress levels twofold since 1990. After more than seventy hours of conversations with Neapolitans from every walk of life, Destrey concluded that Neapolitans would never agree to evacuate.

"Unless…" she said to herself.

"What's on your mind?"

"In all my conversations with Neapolitans, and that would include my first interview with Niballo Aragona, not one person spoke of Vesuvius. At the end, I had to ask. They all said they don't think about it. One person put it quite simply: she said that if she did allow herself to think about Vesuvius, she'd go crazy or have to move away. I'm coming to the conclusion that the people will not evacuate the city unless the mountain is in full eruption mode."

20

GUÐRÚN SIGERÐSSEN
PRESS CONFERENCE
POTENZA, ITALY

"Ladies and gentlemen of the press, signora Guðrún Sigerðssen will now take your questions." As she entered the conference room, Sigerðssen paused for just a moment to take a look at the sheer number of journalists present. This wasn't planned or desired. Her conference was kept out of the public eye for a purpose. The topics covered were too sensitive.

So, something's up! She thought to herself. *How did we get here? This was not supposed to happen.*

Sigerðssen looked over the reporters in attendance. The press had surprised her and her colleagues, who were by now less than eager to meet the journalists.

If leading geologists from around the world were meeting in secret, it could mean that something wasn't right.

Twenty-five volcanologists, seismologists and geologists did not usually attract members of the press for an out of the way conference on the subject of rocks. Talking about rocks shouldn't raise any concern. But today was different.

I have a leak, Sigerðssen thought to herself. A security breach she wasn't aware of.

The conference attendees had unanimously selected Sigerðssen to meet the press. Although she had painstakingly managed to keep their private meeting out of the public's eye, the press had nonetheless hunted them down all the way to Potenza. The commune was located in the southern Italian region of Basilicata, not too far from the 1857 Basilicata quake, also known as the Great Neapolitan earthquake.

From her six-foot two perch, she represented what was considered to be the perfect Icelandic woman: strong, fearless, independent, blond and drop-dead gorgeous.

"Good morning, Signora Sigerðssen," a female journalist said graciously. "Angel Rica, *Rai Radiotelevisione Italiana.*"

"Good morning, *signora* Rica," Sigerðssen replied.

Sigerðssen was now facing three dozen members of the press corps.

Some came from as far as Berlin and London to learn what the egghead-geologists were hiding from the public, the same public who believed they had a right to know everything, a people who inhabited Mount Vesuvius' slopes or lived directly over Campi Flegrei. A public in denial of an active volcano rising on Naples' eastern edge, a mountain that should be understood as a threat. The very same public who was also told of the existence of another titan with a far greater potential to do damage than Vesuvius, a volcanic giant that had recently reawakened. The long-forgotten volcano was beginning to show signs of activity. A threat that was changing the narrative of Naples. The Neapolitans were learning the giant's name: Campi Flegrei, meaning fields of fire, what volcanologists called a supervolcano.

Sigerðssen often said that her people obsessed over their rocks to discover their ultimate meaning and significance. Rocks from around the planet were the beginning and the end of most of their conversations. Sigerðssen could barely squeeze in an idea outside their scope of expertise. When meeting a fellow volcanologist or any other earth enthusiast, she would need to be careful not to talk outside of their specialty or to take the chance and ask a question starting with the words… *what if.* That was a nonstarter.

That general portrayal of her colleagues was all too true because rock enthusiasts generally live in a rarefied environment composed of rock data, rock samples and rock BLTs. In fact, if they could, some would assuredly be tempted to wed a rock. They'd probably honeymoon on the slopes of a faraway volcano in the middle of *god-knows-where.* Such were her brothers and sisters. Very human, very earthbound, extremely courageous and oh so conservative.

She had no qualms about asking them to think out of the box because it had to be done. There was a real need for a breakthrough, one that would probably push them to set aside everything they knew or believed in. She had begun the process of easing them into a new singularity. She was concerned about going too far too fast. That would be manipulative. That wouldn't do. They'd never forgive her for that. The men and women of the earth sciences believed in clarity. They also believed that their brethren were trustworthy and good, true professionals, as naïve as they come, but decent to the core.

These brave men and women who dreamed of Hades were also uber-geeks. Serious to the bone. People who exhibited obsessive behaviors when debating their science. They were also the best in the world. She had discreetly assembled the world's top scientists in the little commune of Potenza, 150 kilometers south of Naples. Their official agenda included a review of the latest data on volcanic activity and their effects on communities as well as the capability of these communities to respond quickly to alerts of imminent danger. The meeting was entitled "Communities and volcanos: a review of civil preparedness."

As far as Sigerðssen was concerned, there was nothing to announce, to publicize or to declare to journalists. At least not today, possibly ever, if she had anything to say about it. The mere mention of her goals in public would send journalists spiraling into a maze of speculation. That would probably scare off the very people she needed to convince that the clock was ticking.

The site chosen by Sigerőssen's private meeting was far enough from the big Italian cities to discourage the random visitor, or so she thought. With a population of 67,000, Potenza had no official desire of becoming a tourist attraction. Italians, in general, were growing weary of the annual tourist invasion, especially now that the pandemic was over. Overcrowding was having an unhealthy impact on the lives of residents, taxing public services to their limits and causing damage to historic sites.

Sigerőssen was curious to find out what had attracted the press here in the first place. The geologists she'd invited to Potenza were not just the best of the best, they were the only individuals capable of bringing to life a new expertise, a know-how that could predict way ahead of time when volcanic eruptions and earthquakes would occur. Even though this level of expertise was considered only possible in the very distant future, she had a feeling that these special men and women had what it took to kick start a new era in their respective professions. All they had to do is put their brains together and identify what they would need in terms of resources and brainpower to bring to life this exquisite capability, one that would not only predict the planet's more destructive behaviors but more importantly, identify ways and means of preventing them from happening.

Sigerőssen had insisted that the conference should be structured as a private conversation between them, rather than a collection of technical PowerPoint presentations. The men and women assembled in Potenza needed a breakthrough. In the next few days, Sigerőssen would be shaping the first of many extraordinary teams of visionaries, a band of geniuses that would put together an ambitious agenda, a secret plan and a strategy to achieve their goals within the lifetimes of their great, great, great grandchildren.

To achieve that, Sigerőssen required money, a depraved and immoral amount of cash. Real money! Not the usual nickel and dime budgets universities allotted their earthbound scientists. She would use the funds to develop technologies never imagined or anticipated before. She required donors and patrons who had the foresight and the cash to finance the world's most important research program. Not since the construction of the International Space Station was there a project so tied to our common survival. She had a goal to reach, and she was just the person to spearhead this project.

The time was right. There was a sense of urgency. She intended to corral them in making serious advances in their own professions. Her team was about to be challenged. Somewhere in their collective unconscious, they knew the clock was ticking. They understood that the human species had to become more aggressive in dealing with nature's temper tantrums, the alternative being unacceptable.

Sigerðssen was intrigued. How would journalists in attendance try to handle her? They obviously wanted to know what was behind their innocuous conference, off the beaten path. Someone must have put two and two together. The most important people in their respective fields, huddled together, here in Potenza, for a seminar. That sounded suspicious. And that meant a juicy story. After all, the public had a right to know.

The journalists' job was to get to the real agenda Sigerðssen had set for the group. Of course, she couldn't let that happen. Sigerðssen had other plans for them. The idea of recruiting the wealthiest people on the planet to fund a secret project with no government or regulatory agency being involved required discretion, secrecy and discipline. Unless, of course, someone was leaking information or overheard someone say something that they had agreed to keep to themselves.

Even pretending to predict earthquakes or volcano eruptions in Italy or anywhere else was very risky. The last thing Sigerðssen wanted was to be hauled in jail for not warning the Italian people of an impending eruption or earthquake. In 2012, six Italian seismologists, as well as an Italian government official, were convicted on multiple manslaughter charges. An Italian judge sentenced the seismologists to six years in jail for having given false reassurances to the public before an earthquake hit the town of L'Aquila in 2009.

"Could you tell us if earthquakes and volcanic eruptions are related? I mean those happening in Italy?" Rica Angel asked.

"No," Sigerðssen replied.

Reporters attending the press conference had enough experience to know that a yes or a no response represented a challenge. A simple refusal to open up would get the press salivating.

"No, they are not related," she continued. "One can happen without the other."

"So, if I understand you correctly, Signora Sigerðssen, there is nothing to fear from an earthquake. It will not cause a volcano to erupt. Is that correct? Is it safe to say that?"

"No," Sigerðssen replied again.

"Then there is a relationship between the two?"

"No. What I'm saying is that there is nothing safe about an earthquake. Similarly, there is nothing safe about a volcanic eruption."

"I'm confused, Signora Sigerðssen," Angel said. "Are you saying that there is no relation whatsoever between these two natural phenomena?"

"No, I am not. If an earthquake happens under or near a volcano, a link can be inferred. However, the relationship is accidental simply because of its proximity, but there is no systemic causality."

"Can you give us an example, Signora Sigerðssen?"

"Yes, of course. If one were to transfer a map of active volcanoes in the world on a map where earthquakes occur on a regular basis, one would see that both natural occurrences often happen approximately one after the other. Specifically, a series of earthquakes followed by moderate to serious volcanic activity. Most volcanic activity as well as seismic activity are localized on the borders of tectonic plates. Nevertheless, these two phenomena are not directly related."

"You're saying that even though these two phenomena happen together on a regular basis, they're not related. One has absolutely nothing to do with the other. Is that correct?"

"No. I'm saying that they are not directly related."

"What do you mean by not directly related?"

"Let me give you an example. Most taxi drivers who wear sunglasses when they're on duty will have less accidents than those not wearing sunglasses. Some would say that there is a direct relationship between sunglasses and accidents: a direct correlation between the two. Would you agree with that?"

The reporters were a bit confused.

"If you did agree with that statement," Sigerðssen said, "you'd be wrong, because the correlation is not between wearing sunglasses and less accidents. Those who are careful and decide to wear sunglasses are just as safe from accidents as those same careful individuals not wearing them. The correlation is really between careful drivers and less accidents. Tinted lenses represent a false correlation. Which is why there is no direct relationship between volcanic eruptions and earthquakes."

"Yes," Angel repeated hesitantly, "earthquakes do not really cause eruptions. So, there is no possible connection between an earthquake and a volcanic eruption?"

"Yes and no. It's all about proximity. You used the word connection and not relationship. A connection is not a causal event. Still, within the limits of a set of specific conditions, earthquakes and volcanic activity could be connected. As I said, proximity is the key word. Volcanic eruptions are observed sometimes after a big earthquake. Scientists have a few reasons to believe that. One, earthquakes can weaken the magma chamber and cause an eruption. Two, an earthquake can disturb the gases found inside a magma chamber and cause an eruption. In fact, any strain on a volcano's structure could indirectly provoke a volcano to erupt. Did I answer your question, *Madame* Angel?"

"Yes and no, Signora Sigerðssen."

"What part of your question is still looking for an answer?" Sigerðssen asked respectfully.

"The part that we all want to know. Are you projecting an earthquake or a volcanic eruption? Is that why you're huddled in the middle of nowhere with the best scientists in the world? Can you answer that part of my question? Are people in danger?"

Sigerðssen moved closer to the mic. She smiled graciously while quickly reviewing her story, one that should put to rest the hype and speculation that attracted the press to Potenza.

"If that were the case, *signora* Rica, none of us would be here today. Instead, we'd be out there, carefully monitoring, watching, measuring and constantly updating our data to see and to understand what could happen next and when."

"Couldn't you monitor from here?" Angel asked.

"Of course, we could. In fact, we could, and we do monitor from remote locations. We could even do some of our work from the moon if we had to. However, that type of ongoing monitoring is meant as a precaution. We monitor on a continuous basis because volcanic eruptions are unpredictable. So, we monitor volcanoes, and we share the data collected to learn more about them and earthquakes. However, I wouldn't recommend monitoring from remote locations when dealing with active volcanoes. It would be dangerous, unprofessional and the data collected would be insufficient to get a handle on what was happening minute by minute, second by second. Our job is to be where the planet is talking to us. Up close. And let me tell you that it can get very personal."

A journalist sitting in the back waved his hand.

"The gentleman in the back," Sigerðssen said, as she dismissed Angel.

"Rand Max from the Times," he said.

"Good morning, Mr. Max."

"Good morning. If you're not projecting an earthquake of a volcanic eruption, could you tell us what you are doing here in Potenza? In other words, what are you and your colleagues talking about? What's your agenda? Should the people of Naples know about this conference?"

"Here is some background before I respond to your question," Sigerðssen said. "First of all, we think there are approximately 1,500 more or less active volcanoes worldwide that are located on land. However, most of the Earth's volcanoes are found on the ocean floor. Underwater volcanos."

"Are underwater volcanos any different from those found on land?"

"No, not really. But, let me tell you what we know. What's really different in an underwater or submarine volcano lies in the eruption itself. At such great depths, with the incredible weight of water above them, eruptions are confined. The weight on the volcanoes prevents them from explosive releases of *petra*, steam and gases in our atmosphere. At those depths, even large deep-water eruptions may not disturb the ocean's surface."

"How many submarine volcanoes are we talking about?"

"The following would be, of course, a conservative estimation," Sigerðssen said. "We'd rather be on the safe side when it comes to volcanos. As I said, with a conservative estimate of a few thousand volcanoes per million square kilometers of the Pacific Ocean, we can safely say that there might be as much as a million underwater or submarine volcanoes worldwide. They would come in all sizes and shapes. Some of these volcanoes are giants. About fifty to seventy-five of them are, in fact, mighty big."

"How big would that be?"

"Some rise above the ocean floor by as much as one kilometer in elevation. Here on *terraferma*, the Ojos del Salado volcano in Argentina is over six thousand meters in height. Probably the highest active volcano on our planet. During 2018, there have been more than seventy-five confirmed eruptions worldwide. Which leads me to your question. What are we doing here in Potenza? Is that correct, Mr. Max?"

"Yes. In fact, people are curious and at the same time worried that something big is about to happen… something that you're not telling us."

"Thank you for your candor, Mr. Max. What we are doing here today and for the next two days is simple to explain, but difficult to achieve. We must design a new protocol to measure the level of preparedness of cities, towns and villages in proximity to active volcanos. The data would help nations adjust and apply these measures who have been already tested here in Europe and abroad. We're looking at establishing a worldwide standard. The idea here is to be prepared if and when a volcanic eruption should occur. It's a very technical agenda and at the same time, a very important job we have to undertake. Have I answered your question, Sir?"

"Yes. Thank you. But are you satisfied with the level of preparedness of our cities, for instance, here, in Italy?"

"You were honest with me, so I'll be straight with you. Okay?"

"I would appreciate that, *Madame* Sigerðssen."

"My answer is and will be for the discernable future, a definitive and unconditional, no."

"No?" The journalists didn't expect her to say that.

"Yes, my answer is no."

"Thank you, *Madame* Sigerðssen. That was very clear. But how can you be so categorical about it?"

"Because, and I will be saying this till the day I die, so pardon me if I repeat myself, volcanoes are and will be unpredictable and can be very nasty. Do you have another question for me, Mr. Max?"

"Yes, in fact I do."

"Okay."

"Is there a reason why you are doing this protocol of yours today? Shouldn't we have such a protocol in place by now? Again, this is my question to you. Why now? What's so important that you must bring the best minds on earth together now?"

"That's a very good question. As I've said, we have protocols in place. However, recent eruptions helped us understand that not all the measures taken by local authorities around the world were complete or effective. Sometimes, it's a question of resources. At other times, getting close to a volcano is difficult and dangerous. That's why we will be reviewing our protocols on a yearly basis, trying to find the best ways to protect people living in proximity to volcanoes. It's a work in progress. We must learn and fine-tune our strategies. I'm afraid that's the long and short of it. Any more questions?"

A tall man sitting almost underneath Guðrún Sigerðssen's microphone stood up and held up his hand.

"Should people live in proximity to an active volcano?"

"Again, I must thank you for the opportunity to answer your questions. And again, I will be as clear as I can possibly be. Your question, Mr..."

"Francesco Galileo Carbone," he said with a genuine smile.

"Should people live near an active volcano? My answer is no. A clear no. No exceptions. Drive, walk away, run, fly... get away from active volcanoes and never come back."

"But what about the people who live, for example, in Naples? There are millions of them living in and around Naples, with their culture, their traditions, a whole way of life..."

"The strategic word here, Mr. Carbone, is life. You said: a whole way of life, traditions, roots. If you live near an active volcano and you want to live... then move away. At least sixty to one hundred kilometers away. 'Why?' you may ask. Because they are unpredictable. Volcanoes are difficult to read. We are trying very hard to get better at predicting volcanoes, but that's far away from being the case. It will certainly not be accomplished in my lifetime."

"Will you be issuing a press release on your work?" another journalist asked out loud.

"We haven't really thought about it. It might be a good idea if we succeed in coming up with a revised preparedness protocol. If not, I don't think it will serve us any good to issue a press release at this stage of the game. Sorry. Any other questions?"

The press conference suddenly became silent. What they were told wasn't what they expected nor was it comforting, even though Sigerðssen's answers appeared complete, albeit a bit depressing.

"I'm so sorry," Sigerðssen said genuinely. "I'm afraid I don't have any... what you call a scoop. Maybe someone can tell me what you expected from us today? Why did you come here in the first place?"

No one answered.

"Well then," Sigerðssen said formally, "again, thank you for your interest. I must now return to my work."

Just when Sigerðssen thought she had gotten away with it, Angel turned to her cameraman and quietly said that the woman on the stage was way too good to be true. She didn't believe a word Sigerðssen said about what they were doing in Potenza.

"She knows something, and she isn't talking," Rica said.

"Like what?"

"It might not be about an eruption or an earthquake, but there's something she's keeping to herself. If there's one thing I know for sure, it's this: she is clever. Her message is well structured and presented."

"I thought she handled herself like a pro."

"Yeah, and most of us bought it, hook, line and sinker. We believed her because we secretly want to. No news is good news. But I know this kind of woman. She's been around. She knows how to manage people."

"What's our next step?"

"This is what we're going to do. We're leaving town right now. I don't want anyone thinking that we're staying here. Could you be a sweetie and find us a place to crash? An out of the way hotel outside of Potenza."

"One or two rooms?" he asked.

"I don't know about you, sugar, but mama needs what she needs."

"Sure, you always say that when you're horny."

"Aren't you?"

"Rica, listen up." He approached her from behind. She let him. She didn't care who was watching. That kind of attention was pure candy.

"Men are always ready," he said wickedly.

21

GUÐRÚN SIGERÐSSEN CONFERENCE CENTER POTENZA, ITALY

Sigerðssen left the conference room thinking she had been right to warn her people about the press. The journalists weren't gullible or stupid. She was betting that, among others, Angel didn't buy her story. And, surprise, surprise! Francesco Carbone made an appearance. She planned to tell Carbone she'd like to meet him as soon as he could make it.

Luckily for Sigerðssen, Carbone was waiting at the door.

"How did you know about us meeting here?" she asked. "This is no coincidence. No one ends up in Potenza by accident."

"By the way, I'm so happy to see you," Carbone said.

"Sorry," Sigerðssen said. "I'm very happy to see you, too. But back to my question."

"My little secret," Carbone said. "And no. It's not an accident. I took a day off my schedule and decided to come here and see you in person. I think, no, let me rephrase that. I know I need your help."

"My help?"

"Yeah. I very much need to talk to you," Carbone said.

"What are you really up to? No. Don't tell me. Let me finish my work here and let's meet at the bar in an hour. How does that sound?"

"Sounds great. I'm okay with a drink or two, but I'll still need to have a serious conversation with you."

"Right. So, this is how we're going to make this happen. I'll meet you in an hour for that drink and then I'll give you a call in a few days to have that serious discussion. Would Naples be okay with you?"

"It just so happens that I'm working out of Naples for a few weeks. So, yes. No pressure, though. I can wait for as long as you want me to. I have a lot of work to do. As long as we have a chance to talk, I'm good."

"I'm really happy to see you again," Sigerðssen said.

"Ditto," Carbone said. "By the way. You haven't changed a bit."

"You always say the nicest things."

"Well, I practice a lot. It's not natural," Carbone said.

Sigerðssen giggled a bit. She was already looking forward to meeting up with Carbone.

Isn't life strange? she thought to herself. *Just when love was passing me by...*

A few lingering minutes after Carbone left, Sigerðssen tried to focus on the business at hand, thinking about whether or not she had done too good a job with the press.

Maybe I can't win with these scavengers, she said to herself, *but I'm going to make damn sure no one will get any closer to what I'm planning to do.*

A few minutes later, she joined her fellow scientists. Everyone wanted to know how the whole thing went.

"I'm not sure," she said almost to herself, "but I think we have a problem. I'm saying this because somebody led them here and I think that same someone could be anybody from the hotel staff, maybe a guest, or a visitor... anyone. Someone overheard something or just put two and two together and came up with the idea that we were up to something."

"There's no news here, Guðrún. What could possibly interest

journalists? We're talking about protocols." Reidar Hammershon, Iceland's most senior volcanologist, had climbed more volcanoes than the rest of his colleagues put together and, at eighty-two years old, he was as strong as anyone half his age.

"Maybe the press conference was due to a misunderstanding," he said, thinking out loud. "I've seen it happen before."

"About that Reidar…" Sigerðssen a bit awkwardly. "I think I may have led you here under false pretenses."

22

ERTA ALE VOLCANO, ETHIOPIA

The Erta Ale volcano lies in the Afar region of northeastern Ethiopia. One would be right to say it was located in the middle of nowhere, even though the Afar people called the region home.

"I admit it. Are you okay, Omar?" Gene Rudd said. As the leading volcanologist and site manager, he was responsible for his people's health and safety. That was job number one. The volcano came in second. In third place came funding for their research. According to Rudd, begging for money had unfortunately become his number one priority. Today was an exception, not because Erta Ale would one day blow its top, that was a given, but because he needed a break from the office. He wanted to feel normal again. Like a real scientist

Omar Tibbs was the one holding the rappelling rope. He didn't care to reply. Tibbs was simply too hot and exhausted to give a damn.

"Okay," Rudd said. "There's no two ways about it. And I'd be dishonest if I didn't admit it. I have underestimated the…"

"Heat?" Omar said a bit sarcastically.

"Yeah. The heat," Rudd said. The site manager was a bit amused by his team's bellyaching. It wasn't like them to complain about the weather, about the boiling heat, about the howling winds pushing fifty degrees Celsius of pure fire in their faces. A heat wave that was showing no signs of relenting. Day and night, the wind pushed his people to the limit. Gene Rudd was mildly sympathetic to their cause, but then again, not that much.

However, the irony of the situation was not wasted on him. Volcanologists complaining about the heat was akin to Jesus Christ begging his Father for a break. The job was about enduring extreme heat, understanding the composition of rocks, predicting eruptions and, at times, running for your life.

They came from Wyoming. The Department of Geology and Geophysics from the University of said state was ranked as one of the best rock schools in the US.

The monster mountain lived in the Afar Depression. A terrifying sea of salt, a place baptized the Badland Desert. Calling this remote corner of the world badlands was a far too cheerful signature for the site manager. Rudd had other names for the volcano's lair. He described the mountain's home as the single hottest pitch of scorched earth known to mankind.

This barren patch of ground was Erta Ale's habitat. It was also home to the Afar people. The Afar lived in the Danakil desert, an area known for its extreme heat and bandits. It is one of the lowest and hottest places on Earth. From time to time, there was also the occasional tourist bent on experiencing firsthand a safari to hell. Luckily for the Afar, tourists never stayed longer than it took for a quick selfie with the fiery lake.

As it happened, Erta Ale was more than active. The volcano was behaving violently.

At 613 meters high, the furious mountain displayed her temper with two active lava lakes. First observed in 1906, the lakes are a geological wonder and a magnet for rock lovers worldwide. They, the lava lakes, the rocks as well as rocks lovers, are in fact very rare.

Today, the volcanologists can be found in an area called the

East African Rift, which is now showing the first signs of the African Continent splitting apart.

Notwithstanding Earth's oceanic crust, the Danakil desert is where Gene Rudd found the thinnest layer of Earth's crust on dry land. Situated closer to Earth's great furnace, the Danakil desert has also been called the world's original hot spot. The whole place was way too close to Earth's mantle for Rudd's taste. He had good reasons to be concerned about the man he sent down to the lava lake.

Rudd's unease for his man Elisonn was generated by his sense of responsibility for his crew's safety and by a lot of experience with what a volcano can do without warning.

He's close. Too damn close to the lava lake, Rudd thought to himself.

The lava was beginning to bubble over the rim. Rudd was thinking about pulling Elisonn out.

"I'm at the edge of the lava lake," Jeffrey Elisonn said excitedly.

The sensors were active. Rudd was looking at the numbers. The lava lake was measuring at more than two thousand Celsius.

Rudd was more than worried. The lake was churning. Exploding. Misbehaving. The remote location infrasound sensors and thermal imagery from satellites were showing significant potential for an eruption.

It could explode at any time.

But Rudd knew better. In a minute or in a thousand years, that was how accurately man could predict an eruption.

Even though their sensors could only work in environments not exceeding 600 degrees Celsius, Rudd could read the lake.

Soon, he thought to himself. *Maybe not.*

But he wasn't going to take any chances. It was Rudd's call.

"What's the temperature?" Rudd asked calmly.

"A bit over two hundred fifty degrees. I'm going to try to get closer and get a sample."

Rudd could see the lava surging upwards toward the edges of the lake.

"No. Negative on that. We're measuring movement," he said anxiously. "I'm worried about the changes in the composition of the gas mix. It's a problem."

Typically, lava lakes overflow. Safety all comes down to monitoring and detection. Direct sampling is the easiest as well as the most dangerous method of collecting data. But it gets the job done.

"I can make it," Elisonn said bravely. "The proximity heat suit is working."

"You move a bit closer and your suit's going to melt. It could be over a thousand degrees at ten meters."

"Yeah. Got that. The heat's getting uncomfortable. I think I know why the locals call this place the Gateway to Hell."

Since 2016, Erta Ale was showing signs of thermal anomalies in satellite images. A small steam plume was detected a few months ago. The short-wave thermal infrared satellite data confirmed the anomalies.

"That's it. Come back up."

"Copy that."

Even though this wasn't his first descent into an active volcano, Jeffrey Elisonn couldn't tear away his eyes from the lava lake. A thing of beauty and death. The volcano's beating heart.

To Elisonn, lava lakes were unique, as deadly as the worse nature can throw at mankind. Unlike those we swim in, this kind of lake contained extremely large volumes of molten lava, concentrated at the top of the volcano.

The signs he was looking at were possible precursor activities that could culminate in a sub-Plinian eruption, meaning similar to Mount Vesuvius' eruption in 79 AD.

"Remember Jeffrey, everything down there is trying to kill you and then rip you apart. So, move it," Rudd said.

"Copy that. Coming up. Wait! Did you feel that?"

"Yeah. Brace yourself. Tremors. Rock falling." Rudd was getting anxious.

"Copy that."

"Find a lip." Rudd tried to stay calm.

"Can't. There's nothing. I can't see… too much…"

"Okay, let's pull him out now. Jeffrey?" Rudd said loudly.

"Yeah."

"You're okay."

"Sure. But I think I saw something that should be there," Jeffrey said.

"Like what?" Rudd said.

"Well, I'm not sure what I saw."

"Right. Time to call it a day."

Rudd had often experienced cases were volcanologists' proximity to very high temperatures would cause them to see things that weren't there.

"No. No, wait! What I meant, I mean… I think the lake rose by a couple of feet."

"What about it?" Rudd said.

"Something's wrong," Jeffrey said a bit spooked.

"The lake's erratic. That's all," Rudd said, trying to reassure him. "Unless there's something else?"

The lake was the size of four football fields and possibly four to five kilometers deep. If Jeffrey wanted to hallucinate, the lake would be a good place to start.

"I think I'm going to miss this place," Jeffrey said frankly. He couldn't imagine anything more terrifying and at the same time so incredibly beautiful.

"You'll get over it. Let's get you up here and quick. There's no time to lose. As soon as I can get you to breathe some fresh air…"

"Aren't you forgetting where we are boss?" Jeffrey said.

"Sorry?" Rudd said, confused.

"Gateway. Remember?" Jeffrey said.

"Right. Gateway to Hell. Okay. Now move it."

Rudd was counting the seconds. Part of his job was to assess the possibility of eruptions. That took time, and time was money.

At times like this, especially when Rudd was putting his people in harm's way, he would resist. It was getting more difficult to find a place to repress or bury his real feelings toward his profession, a career he had freely chosen.

But today was different. While making sure his team was safe, his deepest fears were surfacing. Not in his dreams, not this time. He was wide awake. He could not keep it hidden any longer.

From the deepest recesses of his mind, an emotional warehouse where his repressed feelings resided, came a clear voice, with a clear message, a warning not to put his people in danger for nothing. Well, maybe not for nothing, but almost. *Because it doesn't really help us predict eruptions*, he thought to himself reluctantly.

Rudd was having second thoughts. After forty years of painstaking work as a volcanologist, all in the pursuit of science, he had to admit to himself that compared to other sciences, from chemical to aerospace engineering, his work and those of his colleagues had barely scratched the surface. Volcanoes were still a mystery while other professionals had major breakthroughs: from the human body to the universe, all of them unfolding at record speed.

After all the risks he had taken personally, his knowledge of nature's most dangerous and unpredictable force, after years of study, of groveling for money, he, like his contemporaries could barely predict when and how a volcano would react at any given moment. If a volcano was going to erupt in an hour or two, he would know. If the volcano was going to blow in a week, the Rudd would be less than sure, and in three to six months even less so. That was essentially the problem. He and the fifteen hundred volcanologists working around the world were caught in a mindset, the result of a lack of money and perhaps imagination, with an approach that was limiting their capacity to challenge the status quo the way President Kennedy had done with space exploration.

Gene Rudd would soon have no more energy to keep his true feelings about his life's work a secret. If he would ever free himself from his self-imposed constraints, put an end to his self-inflicted silence, liberate himself from the guilt of thinking out loud and talk freely of his real concerns for his chosen profession, he was more than certain it would come out all wrong.

His words would certainly hurt his colleagues, their pride or self-esteem, as well as their families. These rugged, courageous and unrelenting discoverers would not understand, nor would they risk examining the reasons why Rudd would disavow his life's work.

However, no matter how unthinkable or unreasonable the idea to openly consider his life's achievements in volcanology as poor to non-existent, Rudd was starting to convince himself that he had to get it out there for everyone to hear, not just to admit defeat but to resolutely begin a new era in the science of foretelling the future of volcanoes. Because volcanoes were programmed to explode, humanity had to get in front of this problem and quick. There was no time to lose, and certainly no time should be wasted working with rock hammers and buckets of water. Compared to other sciences, volcanology was still in the Dark Ages.

Could he allow himself to dream of a time when his colleagues could avert these disasters on a global scale?

Rudd would be reminded of his fears every time he stood at the foot of volcanoes. They could become the singular cause for the next world extinction. The one still to come. An event rarely discussed because it was futile and emotionally suicidal. So far, everyone agreed, there was no argument about its inevitable occurrence. The only real question left to answer was when. When would the next global extinction occur?

No one believed that man could do something about it. We could only observe, measure and run for cover. There was nothing else on the table. No plans to stop an eruption from happening. One hundred percent of volcanologists did not believe that averting an eruption was possible, feasible or realistic. It simply wasn't worth the energy to even think about.

There was only one person he knew he could talk to openly,

without fear of being judged or laughed at. Guðrún Sigerðssen not only listened to Rudd but had agreed with him on many points. The problem left was just as complicated: what to do next.

Sigerðssen was more than a good friend. She was one of the best volcanologists on the planet.

He vowed he would keep his secret from his colleagues until he'd have another face to face with her. After all these years, it had come to this. She was the only one he trusted to have this second conversation about the future of their profession. He counted on her.

Today, on the ridge of Erta Ale, Rudd made a decision. He would call her tomorrow. He'd find the time to meet her in Naples and continue the conversation they had together a few months back. That first conversation turned out to be a defining moment, a decision with implications for the rest of his life. There was no turning back. He looked up to the sky and cursed the day he first began to scrutinize his profession's achievements and found them wanting.

Rudd's anger was only surpassed by his fear of not being able to move forward. Moreover, what would Guðrún think of him if that happened.

He could barely focus on the present.

But the lake was rising, nonetheless.

The team had to leave Erta Ale, ASAP.

Something amazing five kilometers deep was urging the volcano to show its fangs, to demonstrate its dominance over the world and all its inhabitants, in the only way it could.

23

GUÐRÚN SIGERÐSSEN
CONFERENCE CENTER
POTENZA, ITALY

"Quiet! This won't take too long. I promise," Sigerðssen said. She waited until everyone was seated. She then launched her PowerPoint presentation.

"Unzen. The name evokes a megatsunami and unpredictability. Next slide please. Unzen Jigoku. It means hot spring, but its history conjures images of death and the smell of sulphur. Unzen-Dake or Hot Spring Mountain, a historical classification. Local legends describe the area as haunted by the souls of fifteen thousand dead as Unzen erupted in 1792."

Sigerðssen's PowerPoint would communicate her message.

"We know its five hundred thousand years old. The volcano oversees the small island of Kyushu in Japan. As some of you know, Kyushu or the Nine Provinces is a mountainous jewel, a tranquil paradise, rural and pristine."

"Next slide, please," Sigerðssen said. "Personally, I found it enchanting. Kyushu summons the Japan of our dreams and expectations. Most would agree, it's simply beautiful. Many of us had the pleasure of working on the slopes of Unzen. So, we all know what

155

we're dealing with."

"Are you trying to sell a tour to Japan?" Sonja asked playfully.

"No, but give me another five minutes," Sigerðssen said.

"Ok, Guðrún. Five and counting."

"Right, where was I? Here we are. As I was saying, living in the towns, the villages and the beautiful hamlets of Kyushu comes at a price. Those living on the island relinquish part of their freedom when one's home is near a volcano. The liberty of living in peace and tranquility may be illusion. Although the local population may deny the mountain's true nature, they live under Unzen's shadow, a risk to life which can only be described as unpredictable. Next slide, Carl. More than fifty thousand people live on the small island where Mount Unzen casts its shadow. As you all know, it's Japan's most active volcano."

"Next slide, please. Yes folks, that's me at the Unzen Disaster Museum," Sigerðssen said. "Please Carl, next slide. Thank you. On June 3, 1991, the volcano's dome suddenly collapsed and generated a pyroclastic flow killing forty-three people who were located three km away from the summit. The dead included fellow volcanologists, geologists and journalists. Nobody saw it coming even though there had been several signs of activity, precursors to the eruption. Thanks Carl. Let's play the video."

"I'm never afraid because I've seen so many eruptions in twenty-three years that even if I die tomorrow, I don't care."

"Yes, as you can see in this video, Krafft said that," Sigerðssen said, "knowing very well what volcanoes were about. Our colleague and friend Maurice Krafft as well as his wife Katia died in a pyroclastic flow on Mount Unzen in '91. Anyone care to tell me why we need to hear about this tragedy one more time?" Sigerðssen asked. "If I'm not mistaken, most of us have been interviewed by reporters since the '91 eruption. I'm sure that your families are concerned about what we do. I know mine is."

She was preparing the room for a serious discussion. Although their profession was filled with adventure, danger and not the least of which, a considerable amount of stress, the job also required them to recognize when too much danger meant walking away from a project.

"Anyone?" she asked again.

"Come on, Guðrún. We all know about the dangers involved. I was also warned by my husband. And my kids! So, you think we should be more careful. I get that. So, if there isn't anything else, please cut to the chase. I'm really begging here, Guðrún, we'd all like go to the bar and drink ourselves silly."

"Here, here!" The volcanologists cheered as one.

"Thank you, Sonja," Sigerðssen said calmly.

"You're welcome my dear. First round's on me!" Sonja said.

The rock lovers were laughing and having a good time. The food, the wine, the Italians... Everything was so perfectly wonderful. Who could not feel happy even though they wondered where Sigerðssen was heading with her PowerPoint.

"Right. I will be as quick as I can. It's nearly five, and believe me, I do need a drink. Maybe a double," Sigerðssen said. She watched them. Some were patient, others were thirsty. But most of them just stared. That said, she loved them all.

"Let the good times roll," Carl said happily.

"Okay, we're done in five minutes. Just five. You have my word. All you have to do in the next five minutes is the following: listen with your brain, feel with your heart and talk with courage. Can you all do that?"

Everyone agreed despite the fact they had no idea what she was up to. Not a clue. So, what was going on?

"I have been talking about our profession's future with some of you," Sigerðssen said. "About where we have come from and where, as a profession, we're heading. In my conversations with fellow volcanologists from around the world, we questioned the way we did things. At one point, I believed we may have been feeling the pressure of finding money for our projects. I understood that. Everyone's allowed to bitch about money. It's even good to let it all out occasionally."

"I sympathize with your existential issues," Pete James said carefully. "Because all of us here today… well, we're all in the same boat. Begging for money is not my idea of what I dreamed of doing way back when. Not by a long shot."

"Thank you for that Pete. I'm sure we all agree on that. But that's not what I'm really trying to say."

Sigerðssen had tried to prepare a speech that would engage her people. She had to find a way to get through to them.

"Let me come to the point: those who I have spoken to as well as myself want to take a second look at our achievements. Some argued that we should compare how well we are faring against the advancements in other branches of engineering, for instance, in theoretical physics, aeronautics and medicine. Let's bear in mind that some of us have begun this self-assessment at least three years ago."

"Okay. What's up Guðrún? Really. Come on, spit it out."

"Right. Well… some of us feel like we're failing," she said.

It took a few seconds before anyone reacted.

"That's fucking crazy, Guðrún. You're one of the best," Carl said.

"Thanks for that," Sigerðssen said evenly. "But I told some of you that we needed a break. That we were tired. That we wanted to take a step back."

"So?" Pete said.

"In the end, we agreed that we couldn't predict anything with any degree of certainty. And we certainly can't stop anything from happening. We can't even get people away from living on the slopes of volcanoes."

"Maybe one day…" Pete started to say.

"No, Pete. Please," Sigerðssen said, "that will get us nowhere. You, me, all of you know this for a fact. We can't make predictions! And that's precisely what people want from us. They want us to tell them when it will happen and then, perhaps in thirty or one hundred years from now, how to stop them from blowing their tops."

"That's impossible! You know that Guðrún." Haraldur Thoranson was as sincere as he was direct.

"It's impossible now," Sigerðssen said calmly.

"No, Guðrún, you're wrong. And your friends are also mistaken," Thoranson said forcefully.

"I don't think we're mistaken. What I said is we can't now," Sigerðssen said.

Thoranson wasn't buying any of her rhetoric.

"There's a difference," Sigerðssen said. "Yes, today we can't accurately predict or do anything to stop an eruption. Not tomorrow or the day after. Or probably in our lifetime. No matter how much we wish it to be true, we have no clue how to do that… yet."

"I understand what you're saying Guðrún," Thoranson said. "Today is not possible. We don't have the scientific capacity it would take. But I don't think tomorrow, or next year, or in a hundred years we'll know how to do that either. I mean to actually have control over Earth's most complex machinery. I'm not a religious man, but I can tell you why it won't work."

"Why is that so?" she asked calmly.

"It's because we're not Gods."

Sigerðssen knew she had almost reached her goal. There was no need to rush into another confrontation. She had no qualms about handling or manipulating people, even her dearest and closest friends and colleagues. What was the expression she was looking for? The end justifies the means… They were waiting to see what the Norse blond was about to say. They respected the woman because she was fearless. There wasn't a man or woman alive that could destabilize the woman. But more importantly, she represented the best of her profession. Honest, direct, decent and morally incorruptible.

"Then," she said almost to herself, "let us become Gods."

The room fell silent. They all had a pretty good idea what she was trying to say and that frightened them to their core. Would their science ever be able to control the planet, in other words would they be able to replace God? If so, are the limitations we set for ourselves manmade? And consequently, could our only constraint be our imagination?

"I was afraid you'd say that, Guðrún," Thoranson said.

"Yeah. Sure. If that's what we need, then of course I'm ready to replace God. Why not? I'm not busy next week," Pete said almost seriously.

"Here's the thing," Sigerðssen said. "The real issue is not about God. No, not Him. It's not about science either. It's about a question: what do we have to do to be able to transform our planet and make our species safer from volcanoes."

"From extinction?" Thoranson asked.

"Yeah, that too."

Once again, faced with an intractable logic, the men and women seated in the conference room remained quiet. After a few minutes, someone broke the ice.

"Okay, Guðrún. You win. I'll bite. How do we do that? How do we become Gods?"

"I've been asking myself the same question. The simple answer is money," she said almost to herself. "Money the likes of which not one of us here has ever seen. Money beyond our wildest dreams. The kind of money we'd need… would look like a mountain of cash. Euros and Dollars. And that would be just for starters."

"Money for what, Guðrún?" Thoranson asked.

"Technology that's not yet on the drawing board. The kind of tech that could change the way we understand our planet."

24

FRANCESCO CARBONE
NAPLES, ITALY

After meeting with Louise Destrey, Carbone had been encouraged to dig deeper into the matter and find out how Naples was managing its potential exposure to Vesuvius. However, the idea of having a city bordered by active volcanoes made him wonder why anyone in their right mind would live in this region.

Francesco Carbone listened closely to the guide. A special tour of the facility had been arranged through Italy's National Council of Engineers. Earlier that week, Carbone had met with a few Neapolitans friends who had invited him for a weekend in Naples' countryside. They had convinced him that Vesuvius was a must see-in-person site. He decided that he would bite the bullet and meet the volcano in person.

"The Vesuvius Observatory was founded in 1841 to monitor Mount Vesuvius, the Phlegrean Fields (Campi Flegrei) and Ischia. Ischia is a small island in the Tyrrhenian Sea. It lies 30 kilometers from downtown Naples." The guide pointed to the Gulf of Naples.

The guide had been right when he described the Observatory as a nondescript building. A box. An inconspicuous cement structure built for research. Carbone believed that the looks of a research station situated on the slopes of an active volcano didn't matter. Why bother with its architectural design. That would be a waste of money and resources. Everyone involved with the Observatory knew one thing for certain: a major eruption would most certainly destroy it.

"Ischia. Over there. It's an island. You see it? It's just off the northern end of the Gulf," the guide added.

"Okay. I see it. Don't tell me that's another volcano?" Carbone said.

"Yeah. Volcanic with lots of tourists," the guide said.

"Looks like Naples is surrounded by volcanoes," Carbone said.

"As you know, the Observatory is located halfway up Vesuvius."

"I know. It was quite a ride getting up here. There's no doubt about it though, this is a serious mountain," Carbone replied to his guide.

The guide then pointed toward the city.

"We can see downtown Naples from here, there to the right. For the best shot of Vesuvius from Naples, I suggest Castel Sant'Elmo. It's slightly elevated, so like I said, the best shot. But I agree with you, it's a special place and it's plain to see that Naples is in the middle of something."

Carbone needed to understand what the Observatory could do in case of an eruption. But there was another reason he decided to fly to Naples. It was the price to pay if he truly wanted to help Neapolitans.

Destrey believed that if Neapolitans were faced with dramatic changes to their way of life, they would behave very differently from what we would normally expect from rational people.

"Humans are hard-wired to quickly revert to a more primitive set of behaviors if they feel threatened. Primitive instincts will kick in. They'll fight to protect what they've worked hard to build," Destrey told him back in Boston.

"Under pressure," Destrey explained carefully, "human beings are programmed to do what's necessary to survive and protect the people they love. Our evolution to Homo Sapiens takes a back seat and we're back in the Stone Age. Just like that. We mutate into primal creatures who'll do whatever it takes. For instance, folks fought against Israeli troops to stay in Jerusalem rather than leave behind their homes, even though the city was under attack. Protecting our homes becomes job one," Destrey said. "I've seen it firsthand in Jerusalem and São Paulo. What people can do to protect the status quo is unbelievable."

"You're saying that you've seen this phenomenon firsthand?"

"Yes. Our homes, where we live, where we sleep and feel safe, that's what we're talking about. Nevertheless, you said earlier that people should leave Naples. That makes sense. I understand that. But here's the problem with that. When politicians will try to force people to leave their homes, the Neapolitans will fight back. I know that for a fact," Destrey said emphatically, "because I tried on numerous occasions to help people get out of harm's way. It didn't always work out the way I intended."

"What did happen?" Carbone asked.

"Some tried to get rid of me while others fought to stay behind no matter what could happen."

"It's hard to believe people could think that way," Carbone said almost to himself.

"This is what I now understand," Destrey said. "Anyone, and I mean any living person, from the Pope to the Dalai Lama, anyone trying to change the status quo will face a difficult time."

Destrey explained that to get Neapolitans to agree to leave behind their hometown, volcanologists must be able to set a specific timeline.

"For example, when will the eruption occur?"

Destrey talked about risk.

"When will the danger become real? When will the risk become too high?"

"I'm not a volcanologist, but I know they can't do that," Carbone said pathetically.

Destrey wanted Carbone to understand that a high level of accuracy identical to hurricanes hitting land was required. Anything else would be dismissed.

"Go out there and find out for yourself," she told him. "Firsthand observations, Mr. Carbone. That means a personal experience with the city and the people. I think that's where you'll find the answers we're all looking for."

"I'm not sure…" he said.

"Regardless of how you feel now, remember that if you still feel I can help you, come back to Boston and we'll talk about what you found out. But consider this: I need to know when. That's the leverage I require."

As Carbone listened to his guide, he remembered what Destrey had tried to convey to him. As he looked around the facility, the thought of seeing so many professionals at work on the slopes of Vesuvius made him realize that Neapolitans were at the mercy of a mountain that would not give up her secrets very easily.

"The research facility monitors the mountain," the guide said without emotion. "That's basically what it does. That's the job. The people here are always ready for the worse because the mountain is alive, and it tells us every day that we're not welcomed. There's always something. After a few weeks, the rumblings, the quakes and the noises become run-of-the-mill normal stuff. But I know it isn't. I have to remind myself."

"That's a tough job," Carbone said.

"It's not the job that's difficult Mr. Carbone. It's something else. It's where we work rather than what we do. Here, in this place. Doing the same job anywhere else in Italy, that would be great and dull at the same time. We get a rush working here. You see, it's all about this location. It's hazardous." The guide appeared a little upset.

"Still," he said with some pride, "we do the best job we can. That's all anyone can ask for, isn't it?"

Carbone wanted to say that regardless of the staff's motivation and dedication to their jobs, the Observatory couldn't fix anything related to volcanoes, it couldn't prevent the mountain from acting up nor could the people working up here predict with any certainty when Vesuvius would erupt. All they could do is look, measure, listen and when necessary, push the panic button. Unlike the Observatory, tracking hurricanes provides scientists with enough lead time to call for an evacuation. Carbone knew the Observatory did not have that capacity.

"In March 2019, the Observatory recorded thirty-four separate earthquakes around Vesuvius. In one single day. Do you believe that?"

"What did they do?" Carbone asked.

"I wasn't here when it happened, but they told me that they all believed the mountain was going to blow."

"And?"

"It was a false alert. You see, they're still here and alive," the guide said.

"That's good to know," Carbone said evenly, "but how many alerts can they issue before the people you want to help stop listening, caring or giving a damn any longer? Crying wolf is an old story but bear in mind that some of us would not take kindly to being pushed around, told to leave our homes and go through a horrific evacuation process… all for nothing!"

"I don't know," the guide said. "All I can say is that I was in Rome at the time and there was an alert sent to the National Institute of Geophysics and Volcanology in Naples. That's our headquarters. As I said, although I was in Rome that day, I didn't sleep a wink."

"I can believe that."

"That's why these guys must be better than just good at what they do, Mr. Carbone. The research lab has no distractions. This place is dedicated to listening to Vesuvius. Day and night, year-round. The scientists working here in this cement box, analyze the data nonstop."

"The trick for the people monitoring Vesuvius should be fairly obvious," Destrey had said. "In case of an alert, get as far away from the mountain before it's too late. However, for the people of Naples, the crux of the matter lies deep within the volcano itself. What kind of eruption will happen? Will Naples have the time to evacuate? Will the eruption be preceded by warnings? Or then again, could the eruption be sudden, without warning, with an Explosivity Index (VEI) of 8, what volcanologists would call a mega-colossal eruption? The answers to these questions and I'm sure there's more, are anyone's guess. Even though most volcanoes give warnings signs of impending eruptions, some do not."

"As you can see here," the guide said, "there's more than one hundred flat-panel screens that display data from a number of sensor arrays. Each screen is set to monitor Vesuvius's behavior as well as Campi Flegrei."

"So, Naples lies between two volcanoes?" Carbone asked.

"Yeah. Count Ischia and Campi Flegrei makes three. Naples is sitting smack-dab in the middle of three volcanoes, with two of them being the most dangerous mountains in the world."

"Why do you say the most dangerous?" Carbone asked. "I believe all volcanoes are dangerous. Am I right?"

"Yes and no. This one's dangerous because there are no other active volcanoes in the world sitting close to millions of people. That's what makes Vesuvius so dangerous."

"I'm sorry if I interrupted you," Carbone said. "What can you tell me about the staff?"

"What's important to know is that the staff up here relies on the tech to feed the notification system. Firsthand observations are of course important, but sensors work twenty-four hours a day. It tells scientists, in real time, what's happening. I don't think the staff is ever bored. There, to your left, in the middle of the room, there's a single red phone. If something is about to happen with Vesuvius, the phone is there for these people to notify the National Civilian Defense in Naples. If there's an imminent threat to the population of Naples and the villages surrounding Vesuvius, then someone down there in Naples would order a total evacuation."

"Which means what exactly?" asked Carbone.

"I've been here in Italy for the last two years. I'm studying architecture with a minor in psychology. And I'm thinking that moving hundreds of thousands of people out of Vesuvius' way, with its ancient roads, not to mention the heavy traffic, I'm thinking that Naples' infrastructures won't be able to handle that level of traffic and stress. I think the City of Naples was never designed to be evacuated. It was intended to keep people out. People wanting to invade the city would find themselves lost pretty quick. That's the philosophy behind Naples' ancient architecture. Anyway, that's the way I see it."

Carbone had visited in Naples as a boy before immigrating to the United States. That was a long time ago but cities like Naples don't change that much in forty years. He also understood the unhealthy relationship between Italy's scientists and the politicians. A few volcanologists in the past were prosecuted for not warning the population of a deadly earthquake. The distrust between politicians and scientists was almost palpable. While Carbone empathized with Naples' decision makers, he knew that sooner or later the volcano would erupt.

That's a forgone conclusion, he thought to himself. Recalling his earlier conversation with Destrey about Vesuvius, Carbone chose to avoid exaggerating the inherent dangers involved in dealing with volcanoes. But given the subject matter, restraint was almost impossible to achieve.

"If Vesuvius erupts or if God forbid, the Campi Flegrei fields begin to act up," Carbone told Destrey during their initial meeting, "it will be nothing short of catastrophic. Campi Flegrei on its own, is capable of launching more than 300 cubic kilometers of ash and rock into the sky. It would impact the global climate for years to come. Let's just say that when Campi Flegrei erupted forty thousand years ago, it lay waste to as much as seventy percent of living organisms on land and in the seas."

"How's Campi doing these days?" Carbone asked his guide.

"I won't try to hide anything from you, Mr. Carbone. The system is active. I've heard the guys here say it's growing".

"So, what do you think about that?" Carbone said.

"I try, Mr. Carbone, not to."

"Not…"

"Think! I just don't want to think about it. This is my summer job. The people here are really okay, you know? Can't worry about the volcanoes. Won't do me any good."

"I understand," Carbone said. "But do you feel in danger living and working here in Naples, especially here on Vesuvius?"

"Only if I think about it, and to be honest, I don't."

Carbone and his guide found the employees' lounge and sat down for an expresso.

"In 2012," the guide said, "that's a long time ago by my standards, but just a second in time for a volcano, the ground within the caldera, rose fast. I was told that Vesuvius was growing. But that was a hypothesis. Then in 2016, a researcher wrote that the volcano was beginning to show signs of something much more dangerous than usual. He called it a serious phase. And here we are. Facing something we can't explain. The workings of large volcanoes like Vesuvius are at best a mystery. It's a detective's job, Mr. Carbone. We know someone's going to commit a crime but that's all we know. No one knows for sure. Trying to explain what happened in past eruptions thousands of years ago is at this point in time, speculative science. Getting an agreement between scientists is akin to asking Democrats to compromise with the Republicans. But there's one constant. We all agree on one thing: the whole place smells like sulfur."

"What's your gut telling you, I mean about Vesuvius?" Carbone said.

"I think, and please don't quote me on this, Mr. Carbone, because I really love my job. I think the mountain will take its time and, when we least expect it, it will blow without warning. I just hope I'm not here when that happens."

"Do you feel a sense of relief to be going home," Carbone said.

"Yes, I'm due to return to Rome at the end of the week."

"You seem anxious?" Carbone said gently.

"I read a publication lying around the Observatory. It said that Italy's supervolcano, Campi Flegrei, is set to blow. It's acting up. Last time anyone witnessed Campi stirring like that was more than 400 years ago."

"I see."

"Yes and no, Mr. Carbone. You see, that's the problem. We have a pretty good idea what a supervolcano can do, but no one in recent history has actually seen one in action. So, we don't know a lot."

Today, the volcanoes were quiet. Everything appeared stable with little or no seismic event to speak of. Carbone came out of the Observatory even more convinced that volcanoes are unpredictable, and that present-day technology was unable to clearly set a time frame for eruptions. When will a volcano erupt? In days or months, years, decades or maybe never.

So, what about Naples? Thought Carbone. *If you're in office, how do you manage that?* Carbone asked himself. If you own a small business, what can you hope for? If you're a mom and your job is to protect your children from harm, what's going on in your head?

Carbone got back to his hotel room and reviewed once again the list of people he had met and those he was scheduled to meet in the next few days. He considered what he had achieved so far: getting Destrey to hear him out, waking on the slopes of Vesuvius and meeting with the professionals at the Observatory. He needed a lot more. He realized that being as objective as possible was not enough. With each person he'd met so far, what he'd heard, what they said and what he'd witnessed, Carbone recognized that he was a bit confused.

Regardless of their social standing, the Neapolitans Carbone met unanimously understood the paradox of living under a volcano. For them it was not difficult to describe or accept.

"It's about living in the most beautiful area of the world with the threat of losing everyone you love within a few hours," they said. "We'll be fine. We'll rebuild," they told Carbone enthusiastically.

Carbone wondered whether it was a sign of courage, defiance or denial? *Perhaps all three*, he said to himself.

Carbone, the engineer, had no patience with people who determined their future based on their feelings even though he himself had become an engineer because of the earthquake he had survived as a boy in Italy some thirty-five years prior.

Carbone was going through his own contradictions: he understood why Neapolitans remained in Naples as well as their silent need to get the hell out and find refuge in an area more suited to human habitation.

He asked himself over and over again, what would I do?

While Destrey had challenged Carbone to dig deeper into Naples' dilemma, she kept in touch with him, encouraging Carbone not to give up, even if the task at hand was formidable.

Carbone intended to show Destrey he'd done his homework. He promised himself he would come back to Boston with enough information to sway Destrey into helping him. Although there was more to do in Naples, he was, so far, satisfied he'd managed to clear up a few basic questions even though Neapolitans stuck to their guns about not leaving behind their hometown, regardless of anything they knew about the great mountain.

As far as Carbone was convinced, he'd gathered valuable insights into Neapolitans' psyche. Carbone's relatives in Naples were happy to help him find the right people to talk to even though they believed he was wasting his time. They spoke about everything he wanted to know about Neapolitans, and more. Still, Carbone needed to show Destrey he was serious and willing to take the time to "dig deep".

But try as he might, Carbone couldn't get his mind around his findings.

Wasn't self-preservation, he asked himself, *a built-in instinct? Aren't human beings hardwired to avoid dangerous situations? Isn't there a defence mechanism, deep rooted and firmly embedded in our DNA?*

In the end, Francesco Carbone uncovered more contradictions

than he cared to admit. Even if those paradoxes didn't explain Neapolitans' predisposition to stay put, he concluded that he had to start somewhere. His findings were unusual to say the least, but he hoped he would eventually understand them. He summed up his findings over supper with one of his local friends, Aldo Ferranti, a structural engineer specializing in Italy's historical restoration, conservation, maintenance and enhancement works.

"Let me put it this way," Carbone said. "There are more contradictions that explain Neapolitans than clear logic. I found out that more than 20% of Neapolitans are poor and have nowhere to go. Leaving Naples is not within their means nor is there anything keeping them here."

"You don't get it, do you Francesco?"

"What do you mean, Aldo?" Carbone said.

"Life is about contradictions. It explains our reality perfectly. We know where we are and we cling to our hometown like a bee to its hive," Ferranti said.

"I could understand that if we were talking about those who have too much to lose in moving away from Naples. As I said, I can understand that. But there's more," Carbone said.

"I can't wait to hear it."

"As far as Neapolitans are concerned, starting over somewhere else was never an option to start with. All Neapolitans I've met so far, simply refuse to think about earthquakes, volcanoes, the mafia or the end of the world. I'd call it a blanket denial. Denial being the dominant drive in Naples," Carbone said. "It determines everything."

"I'm sure that you probably know that life in *Napoli* is also wonderful, chaotic, dangerous, festive and at times, breathtakingly beautiful," Ferranti said. "My friends and family made sure you would see Naples as a thriving community in spite of its problems," he said. "Right?"

"Yeah, you're right, of course," Carbone said. "It's beautiful even though you're besides a living, breathing monster," Carbone said hopelessly.

"Aside from the fact that Naples is one of the oldest cities in the world, a living museum with more than 500 historical sites, we Neapolitans have coffee shops, soccer, amazing food and drink to enjoy every day. And we also have history to back up our contradictions," Ferranti said proudly. "We've been here since well before Christ. So why worry about something that might not happen? If it happens at all!" Ferranti added.

Carbone understood that, although earthquakes and volcanoes were real and dangerous, Neapolitans had a life to live. A life that shouldn't require them to think about Vesuvius as a time bomb.

"You know what Aldo? I'm realizing that this same kind of thinking, applies to California."

"I believe you."

Carbone recalled what his waiter at the Gran Caffe Gambrinus had said: "We don't have time to think about that stuff, *signore.* There are people monitoring these things. They'll tell us what to do. That's their job. For now, we have better things to do. If you want my opinion, I don't think it's going to happen anytime soon. If I did, I'd be the first one to leave and never look back. All this fuss about volcanoes is just talk."

Although Carbone wasn't a bit surprised by people's outlook on life in Naples, it still felt strange to see and hear denial up close.

Next morning, Carbone concluded that when normal people, folks he met and talked to personally, good people from different walks of life, reject reality, it was very tempting to think they were ill.

A mass illness of the mind? he asked himself. *Is that even possible?*

Carbone tried to imagine what Destrey would say about that. He had no idea how she would react to his findings. *Maybe not a lot,* he thought to himself, *because she has been challenged before in Israel as well as in São Paulo.* Carbone then considered the possibility that Neapolitans were not making a conscious choice.

The difference between Neapolitans and the rest of us, he thought, *could rest on a historical perspective, something akin to it's okay because it's always been like that, so why should we be worried?*

Is civilization a matter of the heart, he asked himself. He set all of that crazy thinking aside and focused on here and now. He was in *Napoli*, and he was going to meet with someone very special.

In a few minutes' time, he would meet with Guðrún Sigerðssen and her colleague.

He was almost done with breakfast when the phone rang.

"I'm here. In the Sky Lounge. On the 10th floor," Sigerðssen said. There was no need for any introductions.

"I'll be right up. Five minutes tops." Carbone was happy to hear her voice again.

He was looking forward to seeing her. He clearly had a crush on Guðrún, ever since they first met in 2000 when they were both attending the 12th World Conference on Earthquake Engineering in Auckland.

She was using the Potenza conference as a launching pad for new safety measures for any and all professionals whose responsibilities included the study of volcanoes. Understanding and predicting their behavior, in order to be able to warn people living near the volcanoes, had become a priority. Unofficially, Sigerðssen was also planning a major coup, one that would change the science of volcanology.

Having said that, Carbone's affection for the famous volcanologist was his little secret. He never said anything about his intentions. He kept them to himself. He would wait for some sign of reciprocity from the woman before attempting his move. That was his way: a bit shy, a loner by nature and a strong believer in kismet. The engineer believed that love was as mysterious as our planet's unpredictable behavior. Even though he believed Guðrún was way out of his league, professionally as well as personally, he was hoping that the gods would eventually intervene in his favor.

"Take all the time you want, but hurry up," she said mockingly. "I want you to meet Gene Rudd, a colleague of mine. Could be interesting."

"I'll be right up." Carbone quickly grabbed his watch, cell phone, wallet and hotel key card.

"I guess I'm ready," he said out loud while examining himself in the bathroom mirror.

Good enough, he thought. *Don't want to look eager.*

Carbone quickly walked through the elevator doors and pressed on 10, Caruso Roof Garden. A few seconds later, the doors opened to the Bay of Naples.

The Grande Albergo (Hotel) Vesuvio had a million-dollar view. But Carbone wasn't thinking about the sights and sounds of Naples. He recognized Guðrún. He assumed the man sitting with her was Rudd. She was dazzling. *Brains and beauty, all in one package*, he thought.

The two of them were having espresso while enjoying the incredible view.

"The Bay of Naples. It's breathtaking," he said to Rudd sitting opposite Guðrún. "Can never get tired of it. And the weather! I can feel the warm breeze," Carbone said energetically as he joined Sigerðssen at her table.

"Francesco, let me introduce Gene Rudd. He's just back from Erta Ale. He's one of our finest volcanologists. We're also good friends. I know you'll want to hear what he's got to say."

"Glad to meet you, Mr. Rudd," Carbone said. "Heard good things about you."

"Thanks. But please, call me Gene. Guðrún tells me you're from California."

"That's right. But I was born a few miles from here, in a small town called Conza, in the Province of Avellino."

"Francesco lost his whole family to the 1980 *Irpinia* Earthquake," Sigerðssen said purposely.

"I'm sorry to hear that," Rudd said sincerely. "I'll have to look that up."

"That was a long time ago. Back then, I was just a kid," Carbone said. "Got in trouble more times than I can remember. Then, I lost everyone I loved. Just like that. I actually remember the earthquake. It felt like it would never end, but the quake lasted no more than two or three minutes. My hometown was totally destroyed. Everything I knew, the churches, the big houses, my father's ancestral home, everything collapsed. My best friend died right beside me."

Carbone was gazing at Vesuvius.

"After all these years, it's still vivid," Carbone said. "To this day, I can't see an old building without thinking about its possible destruction. It's especially true here in Naples. I understand we can't do anything about earthquakes, but we could prevent people from getting killed by a volcano."

"Guðrún tells me you're a structural engineer. Old buildings catch your attention?" Rudd asked.

"Yeah. I decided to do my bit as a structural engineer. I think it was my calling. I build earthquake resistant structures; buildings people can feel safe in."

"How's that going?" Rudd said keenly.

"You'd think we'd be ahead with talk of the Big One approaching."

"I would. At least I'd hope so," Rudd said.

"Yeah, but like everything in California, it's always about money and those crazy referendums."

"So, Francesco, what's this all about?" Sigerðssen said.

"I've been busy doing my homework."

Carbone explained to them his reasons for being in Naples and how he came to know Louise Margoe Destrey. He said he was very appreciative to have her available. "You might be just the right person to help me out. Perhaps you can also help," he told Rudd. "There are things I still need to understand about people and their relationship with volcanoes."

"Let see what we can do to help," Sigerðssen said.

"Destrey said she might help. But only under certain conditions. She said she needed leverage before doing anything. She meant that in a positive way. She told me of her adventures in Jerusalem and São Paulo. And she was right, of course. She's not the kind of woman to do the same mistake over and over again."

Carbone explained why Destrey wouldn't go head-first trying to save people's lives if she didn't know in advance what people needed to hear before voluntarily moving out of Naples. Without that information, no one would agree to leave everything behind based on someone's opinion, be it scientific or not.

"That's why I was curious to see what you had to say about it," Carbone asked Sigerðssen.

"Could you be a little more precise? For instance maybe?" Sigerðssen said.

"Right. Okay. Let's say, for instance, that we're all here having expresso and Destrey says, what do I tell the Neapolitans?"

"I don't know if I can help with that..." Rudd said reflectively.

"What she's looking for, in a nutshell," Carbone said, "is an answer to this question: under which conditions would a family leave Naples. That is to say, abandon everything behind and never look back?"

"I see what you mean. That's a very simple question," interjected Rudd. "Just tell them when Vesuvius will erupt and hit Naples. If you can't do that, then there's nothing anyone can do. Unless, of course, the Italian military initiates an evacuation. But if I know the Neapolitans, you'd have a full-scale rebellion on your hands. A lot of people would get hurt. Many more would die in the crosshairs between police, soldiers and armed citizens. Remember where you are, Mr. Carbone. The whole operation of evacuating the people would certainly end in failure. One would imagine that a city like Naples, a town located right on top Campi Flegrei, a supervolcano no less, and close to Vesuvius, would be busy evacuating the towns surrounding those two volcanoes."

"Yeah, those are exactly my thoughts," Carbone said.

"The city has developed a 72-hour evacuation plan," Sigerðssen said. "If given sufficient warning, it might work. But volcanoes don't work like that. I've seen it with my own eyes. Volcanoes are unpredictable even with our current tech. Seventy-two hours is a lifetime considering a pyroclastic flow could reach downtown Naples in less than six minutes."

"That's what Destrey is thinking about," Carbone said. "Plans go out the window the minute an event occurs, be it an earthquake, a volcanic eruption or a terrorist's bomb. So, where does that leave us?"

"Well, there is," Sigerõssen said with a grin, "an option that no one so far has seriously examined."

"Okay. I'm listening." Carbone was hoping she could help him with Destrey.

"Gene and I talked about this. The volcanologists I was with a few days ago also had the same conversation. We haven't told anybody else about our secret talk. Again, it's quite simple but as revolutionary it can get."

"Can't wait to hear what you have to say," Carbone said eagerly.

"Well… we tell them when. We provide a time frame of between one and fifteen days. The people would know a few months in advance. Maybe more, if we want to be credible. The government would manage the relocation of up to two million people."

Carbone listened carefully to what Sigerõssen had to say.

"I thought you said we couldn't do that," Carbone said.

"Yes, I did," she said.

"Okay. Can either of you tell me what's going on? Have I missed something?"

"You're right. We can't do that, now," Rudd said to Carbone. "Guðrún and I have been discussing this situation and we are now convinced we can't do any of what would be required to initiate a mass evacuation. Not within 72 hours, two weeks or two months. We can, however, predict an eruption when a volcano is seriously acting up."

"Bottom line, we don't know how to read a volcano with a human timeframe."

"Meaning?"

"You're from California, right?"

"Yes."

"Tell me when the Big One's coming?"

"All I can say is soon."

"Soon, meaning in a day, a month, a year, fifty years, maybe a hundred years from now. Right?"

"Yes. I guess so."

"So, when is really important. And you can't be more precise than soon?"

"You know I can't. All I can say is that the Big One is due, but no one really knows for sure when, especially if we want to put a time and date on it."

"What would it take for San Franciscans to leave their homes, Mr. Carbone?" Rudd asked. "Think about the perfect set of data required."

"A chart, a video presentation like the ones' we see on the news when a hurricane is approaching the East Coast. With that kind of data, most people would jump to action," Carbone answered confidently.

"And that's because your answer is structured on a human scale," Rudd said plainly. "To make things worse, it's been evolving steadily through the years. Back in the sixteenth century, getting a message to someone in another city, say from Paris to Rome and then back again, could take anywhere from one to four months. I'd say that way back then, you'd have a better than a fifty percent chance of never getting your message through, even less of getting a response. A few months ago, I was onboard a research ship in the Antarctic. Some days, it would take me up to five minutes before I could have a good connection with my people back in the States. What I'm trying to say is that a human timeline is by definition the measure by which we accept, ignore or refuse to deal with issues that are time sensitive. The time lapse between an alert and an actual event in our current timeline is understood through our capability to be informed. The longer it takes between an alert and an event, the less credible or actionable it becomes for us to respond to it. It's how humans decide to act or not to. To accept or to deny. To get up and leave or stay put. I feel that Neapolitans would react positively to an alert if the time span was sufficiently short and accurate."

"So…" Carbone said unenthusiastically.

"I'm afraid there's no such technology for volcanoes or earthquakes. Nothing remotely close enough to send people packing their stuff and drive away, that's because a volcano's timeline is measured in cycles spanning thousands if not millions of years."

"I was afraid you'd say that even though I came to the same general conclusion a few years ago."

Carbone hadn't heard anything he didn't know already.

"So, we're back to square one," Sigerðssen said with a smile. "Don't you agree Francesco?"

"Yes, but what are you really trying to tell me? You're not telling me everything?"

"I'm not saying it's technologically impossible," Sigerðssen said curiously. "Because if I was, that would mean an end to our discussion, simply because it would be impossible."

"I thought you were," Carbone said a bit confused.

"What Gene and I are trying to say may sound a bit farfetched but hear me out. I'm trying to tell you that the technology isn't here… yet. But it could be."

"Okay," Carbone said a bit uneasy. "How would that technology get to see the light of day?"

"Now, that's one hell of a good question," Rudd said enigmatically.

25

CAFÉ VENTIMETRIQUADRI
NAPLES, ITALY

"It's not if but when Vesuvius is going to erupt," Kleinrup said. "Do words imminent and unpredictable come to mind?" Destrey was trying hard to find an alternative approach to handle the Naples event. Her original conversation with Carbone at TG had been difficult considering she couldn't and wouldn't help him out, at least not now.

Two days ago, on her way to Italy onboard her private jet, Destrey had been informed by Lola that Carbone was also in Naples. She was tempted to organize a meeting with the engineer but decided against it. She wanted to see what he could come up with on his own. Even so, she had instructed Lola to keep tabs on him.

Destrey always tried to be one step ahead, especially when people wanted her help. That meant thinking outside the box.

Kleinrup noticed something. She was tapping her fingers on the table. Was it boredom, irritation or perhaps frustration at not being able to help? As far as he was concerned, Destrey could never refuse a challenge, especially if the lives of people were in play. Although

181

the tapping noise was mildly annoying, Kleinrup decided not to make a big deal out of it.

"And the government knows that," Kleinrup said. "A few years ago, they came up with an evacuation plan. They said they could clear out the red zone in 72 hours or less. That will only work when Vesuvius agrees to let us know in advance that it's going to blow," Kleinrup said mockingly.

"You're being sarcastic." Destrey wasn't a bit amused by his response. It just made things worse. She didn't realize it yet, but not being in control was never the way she understood the world or the way she lived her life.

"I'm trying to make a point," Kleinrup said. "The mountain is just a big rock ready to explode. Its behavior doesn't necessarily follow a fixed pattern. Eruptions could follow a pattern, but there isn't enough data to support that."

"So, again, we know crap," she said.

"Showing signs of an impending eruption would be great," Kleinrup said. "But frankly, I don't think this thing will. It could explode in a heartbeat. With no warning. Vesuvius could blow its top off and never show any precursor signs. And that would be the end of any evacuation plan.

"So, if I may say it again, we don't know anything," Destrey said.
"Kind of."

"I'm right to say that the government knows very well what's at stake?"

"More than we think. Back in 2003, the Italian government introduced a program to pay people 30,000 Euros or $45,000 US to relocate away from Vesuvius. They started with the people living within the Red Zone."

"Let me guess. That carrot didn't work."

"No," Kleinrup said. "It didn't."

Destrey was looking at passers-by. *Café Ventimetriquadri* was small, not more than four tables, but the coffee was good.

"So, what's up?" He asked.

"Nothing." Destrey seemed a bit off.

Kleinrup preferred to wait. He was pretty sure she'd open up. And she did.

"It's growing old," she said out loud. "This feeling of helplessness. I don't like it. Not one bit. I don't want it and I know I can't do anything about it. Just like this freaking volcano. Everyone wants us to help, but we can't. We can't help, just like I can't get any younger. I wish I was walking around Naples without a care in the world. But I can't do that either. And don't say you understand."

"I wouldn't dare."

"Okay then, let's try to make sense of what we're getting into. Okay?"

"Yes. Of course." Kleinrup looked around, found who he was looking for. "*Vorrei due scotch, per favore.*"

"You're trying to impress me or the waiter?" Destrey said.

"It's difficult to impress a woman who knows everything."

"That's not funny. My husband used to say that. But that's another story. Let's get back to business," Destrey said.

"Let me see. I was talking about paying people to relocate away from Vesuvius," Kleinrup said.

"That didn't work," Destrey said.

"Not even a little. What makes everything seem unreal is that ordinary people know that Vesuvius is too close. And still, it's not part of any conversation," Kleinrup said.

"Lola tells me that Vesuvius sits on top of a large volume of magma. The lava deposit could measure up to 400 square kilometers or 154 square miles," Destrey said.

"That's a lot of magma!"

"Lola also mentioned that scientists expect an extremely powerful explosion. A Plinian. Whenever that happens."

"Okay. Let's summarize," Kleinrup said. "Mount Vesuvius will erupt sooner or later. There's more than 3 million people close by and the mountain could wipe out the city of Naples. We also can say, without any risk, that the volcano could provide us signs before an eruption, or not. Finally, you know from first hand interviews that people don't want to think about Vesuvius, much less do anything proactive about it. That's pretty much what we have to work with."

"Yes, I agree," Destrey said.

"How about a refill before we head for Rome?" she said.

John Thomas Kleinrup looked into her eyes and watched her brain go to work. She was ready to tackle the volcano head on, with all the compassion and the strength she had to give, even though the Neapolitans would rather stay put. Destrey called it the great denial.

"As soon as our business is done in Italy, we'll have a final simulation to look at. Lola says she could make it the most watched video on the planet. She seems ready to do battle."

"God help us," Kleinrup said.

26

BOSTON TRIAGE GROUP (BTG) CAMBRIDGE, MASSACHUSETTS

"I've got a message from the Carbone fellow," Margaret said excitedly.

"Calm down, woman," Destrey answered back.

"He says he'd like to meet you again. He said he did his homework as you suggested, and he'd like to bring two volcanologists with him. He says it's kind of urgent."

"Did he mention who they were?"

"No."

"Then find out and tell the machine downstairs to dig out everything there is to know about them. I don't need more eggheads talking to me about stuff I don't understand. I have enough of them around here."

"Will get right on it."

"You don't have to be so enthusiastic about it. What would your husband think about your little crush? The man's at least twenty years your junior. Have you no shame, woman?" Destrey said. "God help you, Margaret."

"I'm counting on it. I'll be praying to Him every day until Francesco knocks at my door."

BOSTON TRIAGE GROUP (BTG) CAMBRIDGE, MASSACHUSETTS

"Constantin tells me Lola has the information you asked for on Francesco Carbone, Guðrún Sigerðssen and Gene Rudd. The three of them are expected tomorrow afternoon," Margaret said to Destrey.

"Could you please tell Constantin to send me a written report?" Destrey said. She still enjoyed reading and handling paper.

Old habits die hard, she thought to herself.

"Margaret!" Destrey said loudly.

Margaret pushed back.

"Just wait a frigging minute, I'm working here," she said.

Destrey knew Margaret was doing her own research on Carbone. The crush on the Californian was getting more interesting by the minute.

"Margaret!"

"Hold your horses, Frenchie. Constantin says there isn't a report worth generating. There's nothing to report other than all three have good reputations. They're considered the best in their field."

"So, two volcanologists and one structural engineer," Destrey said.

"What could they possibly want us to do? Stop Vesuvius from erupting?"

"Constantin thought you'd say that. It seems Lola may have an answer to your question."

"Okay? Let me hear it."

"Lola didn't say. She said she was in research mode. If you want, you could drop in and…"

"No, please. Don't say it. I'm too busy to deal with the Lola thing," Destrey said.

While not finding any inconsistencies regarding Destrey's guests, Lola had expanded her investigation to find common ground or perhaps a pattern that might help Louise Destrey deal with Carbone and his colleagues.

As it happened, Lola did. It appeared the volcanologists were at odds with the state of advancement of their professions. They'd run up against a lot of resistance. They were challenged from all corners of their fields, especially when they attempted to look at alternatives that questioned the *status quo*.

Lola concluded that there had been a rapid increase in the human race's capacity to understand and perhaps predict eruptions in broad terms. However, because these patterns spanned thousands if not millions of years, accurately predicting eruptions with enough lead-time to evacuate towns and cities, continued to be out of reach. Continuing to improve the monitoring of volcanoes had not yet yielded any precise or credible predictions.

All three realized that although the science of volcanology was improving, it could not forewarn communities and governments long in advance of an eruption. In many cases, eruptions occurred without any warning. Oddly, current research was done at the expense of other far reaching investigation strategies that traditional volcanologists believed impossible to reach, such as accurately predicting volcanic eruptions, managing them or stopping them altogether.

Following the law of diminishing returns, Lola also concluded that further improvements of current monitoring strategies would generate only limited improvements, even though monitoring enhancements were still very much possible.

Lola wanted Destrey to understand that volcanologists were barely skimming the surface of the planet, when in fact, the golden information laid more than two thousand kilometres underfoot.

Given the limits and poor accuracy of predicting volcanic eruptions, Lola came to one final conclusion: the potential for further improvements in monitoring will soon begin to yield negative results in light of governments and people's expectations. Lola was pointing at two types of expectations. One, timely and accurate warnings and two, a need to develop the capability to manage pre-emptively eruptions and stop them.

That's not too much to ask, Lola thought to herself.

From a financial perspective, the progress of volcanology's current monitoring strategies was tied to poor funding.

Lola was ready to propose an alternative strategy to produce precise volcanic predictions and pre-emptive management plans. Although not yet on the drawing board, Lola was prepared to kick-start a new conversation with scientists. One that would take earth sciences to a new level. A level that would lead to precise predictions and, more importantly, come up with tools that could control volcanoes.

Lola's train of thought could be interpreted as a clear departure from current earth sciences' convictions.

"Good morning, *Madame* Destrey," Lola said.

"I've had a chance to read your research summaries," Destrey said. "I think you're going in the right direction. For my part, I would like a strategy that gets people on board our train of thought rather than create tension that would paralyze the introduction of new ideas. Especially if the conversation was initiated from outsiders like myself."

Lola agreed with Destrey when she said that without a workable strategy, resistance would turn into outright hostility. Which would mean that only those who shared a common goal to reinvent their science would participate in the conversation, thus depriving the world of a wider strategic and scientific input.

"The mission to create a credible alternative science would require everyone's commitment and imagination," Destrey said to Lola. "True innovation would be the order of the day."

Lola warned Destrey that volcanologists' current job descriptions would most likely morph into something almost unrecognisable. Lola wasn't sure if Destrey would go as far as challenge a science that was resourced with the most courageous people on the planet, men and women who weren't afraid to put their lives in jeopardy for their science.

"When David John Stevenson," Lola said, "a professor of planetary science at Caltech proposed to send a probe to Earth's mantle, Stevenson said that '...people thought this was a ridiculous idea.' He continued by saying 'I hope that I've shifted the viewpoint from ridiculous to merely unlikely.'"

"Clearly, this Stevenson fellow has a sense of humor," Destrey said.

28

ROXANNE LAFLAMME

LaFlamme was driving her BMW on the E 25 toward Thionville. Although the traffic was heavy, she couldn't stop herself from rehashing the incident at Mosconi's. She had decided she would deal with the two women who made fun of her, as soon as she could.

Her passenger, an older woman, was quiet but at the same time anxious at the prospect of getting her revenge. Revenge, the passenger said to herself, was what kept her focused while allowing her to move forward and redirect her life. That meant as far away from her husband as she could. Both husband and LaFlamme's lover were one and the same: Alexander Kirchen Schuman, better known to both women as the little man.

LaFlamme understood things differently. It wasn't really about revenge but more about managing accounts receivable. There was a fortune to be made and she was ready to do anything to get her hands on what she called her unpaid fees for services rendered.

The small French town of Thionville was more of a target than a destination. From LaFlamme's point of view, she had been seriously underestimated by many, including Schuman, her former employers and those two women she overheard laughing at her while dinning with Schuman at Mosconi's.

LaFlamme scolded herself for letting her guard down as Schuman had embraced her with an exquisite diamond necklace in public. LaFlamme overheard the women seated not far from Schuman's table. They said something about her being a bimbo. LaFlamme had murder on her mind for those two females as she floored the Beemer's engine forward. What LaFlamme didn't know was that one of those two women was Louise Margoe Destrey. Knowing that wouldn't stop LaFlamme. She had already begun to identify the women involved. The wheels were turning. Sooner or later, something dangerous would happen.

LaFlamme's Internet investigation into the identity of the two women got Lola's attention. At this point, Lola was in the watch mode.

While driving toward Thionville, her mind ran across her first failure as a consultant. It was two years ago, but it felt like yesterday. LaFlamme remembered waiting outside the senior partner's office until an HR staffer finally invited her in.

"Take a seat," the senior partner said. He wasted no time.

"I'm sad to tell you that we've abolished your position. We're very sorry about that. We have to let you go. But, I sincerely believe that you have a wonderful future ahead of you. Just not here. I know for a fact, Roxanne, that you will find the right organization for your special talents. That's why I asked HR to find you the best career transition agency money can buy."

LaFlamme said nothing. This was her first job out of university. Coming to his office, she believed she was going to get a promotion. To her surprise, the man sitting in front of her was giving her the axe. The HR staffer kept quiet. LaFlamme didn't believe a word he said.

The prick's too afraid to tell me what's really happening, LaFlamme said to herself.

Although that meeting happened over two years ago, she vowed to herself to never forget how she was treated by the man who had hired her in the first place. The same man who pledged he'd steer her career in the right direction.

Roxanne LaFlamme promised herself not to let that happen ever again. She also swore, that one day, her ex-boss would pay for what he did to her. She believed she had done nothing wrong, in fact, she was certain there was no one better qualified to do her job. After all, the way clients listened to her every word must have been proof of her worth.

At the end of that fateful day, she was accompanied off the premises by a security officer. The whole experience had been humiliating. She didn't feel shame, unlike other people going through the same experience. Anger would best describe what she experienced.

But that was then. Today was different. She was now in control of her life. LaFlamme had plans for the little man. They were going to meet at the Belleview House, a mansion Schuman had secretly purchased as a retreat from prying eyes. Located in Thionville France, Schuman chose this location for his extramarital mischief. It was out of the way but still only half an hour away from his home and office in Luxembourg City. After all, Schuman considered himself a practical man.

LaFlamme promised herself that the little man wasn't going to get his way. No. Not this time.

All the while, Schuman was thinking of cutting ties with LaFlamme because he had found someone else. A girl more pliable and less involved in his business dealings. LaFlamme, according to Schuman, knew far too much about his future business objectives. And that wouldn't do at all. He vowed to finish it tonight, once and for all.

29

BELLEVIEW HOUSE
RUE DES DUCS DE LORRAINE
THIONVILLE, FRANCE

Alexander Schuman's hideaway in France could technically be described as a sophisticated residence for a person of good taste and reputation. Regrettably, Schuman was none of that. He christened the residence Belleview House. The name added a veneer of respectability. Schuman wanted to believe he was a proper person and deserved respect, and so, a suitable front.

Arriving at Belleview House, Schuman was startled to see *la petite femme's* (the little woman) BMW parked inside the gates of his retreat.

His secret residence was nestled in a community with a population of almost forty thousand. The town was big enough to offer him the availability of local women young enough to do almost anything to please the secretive man's innermost desires. To his credit, Schuman was a good client. He paid above the going price. The working girls appreciated the extra income, even though some of his needs were a bit odd.

The estate was located in a haven of peace, surrounded by nature, calm and serenity. Behind manicured hedges that rose to eighteen feet,

195

the property had ample indoor parking to hide Schuman's Bentley. It would take him all of twenty-five minutes to reach Belleview House from Luxembourg City.

Schuman had his bedroom redecorated by Paris designer Jean-Louis Brown. The interior designer grudgingly transformed his original plans to suit his client's lurid predilections.

Schuman dedicated the master bedroom to his peculiar sexual style. The design chosen was reminiscent of the Miami Style Interiors' Movement, most likely introduced to Florida by the Trump organization.

Schuman also added two terraces, providing his guests with a wonderful view of his garden, which, he hoped, would encourage them to let their imagination wander.

This pretty corner of Thionville was known for its discretion. Even though Schuman preferred to live his passions and desires within the walls of his small *chateau*, he would, at times, orchestrate outdoor adventures to quench his cravings.

Belleview House had cost Schuman more than he liked to admit. If his wife ever found out what he'd stashed away to acquire his secret residence, he was certain she would leave him high and dry, taking with her most of his money.

LaFlamme watched him as he parked his Bentley in the garage. Schuman walked over to her blue car. BMW had named the paint color Electric Blue.

The color of her eyes, he thought to himself.

He had a feeling someone was watching. He slowly turned toward the house. Schuman raised his eyes to his bedroom window on the second floor. His heart raced as he anticipated the sight of her form. The woman, who obediently made herself available, was waiting for him. The front door was ajar, a clear invitation.

Schuman could almost taste her perfume: Bvlgari's Gemme Calaluna. She was watching him but gave him no indication she was interested. He couldn't read *la petite femme's* state of mind, but he guessed she was playing a game of hard to get. Schuman loved a good show and couldn't wait for the second act.

He would soon discover what she'd planned for him. A special moment he believed he'd never forget. A seminal life-changing event.

The blue skies of Thionville were dotted with white, fluffy clouds. Schuman had the impression she had planned the whole thing.

It's all so perfect, he thought to himself.

By now, his intelligence had practically abandoned his brain while his limbic system was taking control of his judgment. From that moment on, Schuman had no compass to help him steer his way out of trouble. He was at the mercy of his own fantasies.

While leaning on the windowsill, LaFlamme kept her eyes on him.

At first, he hadn't recognized the figure standing by the curtains. The female form had long black hair. It flowed down over her shoulders and delicately brushed against her breasts.

La petite femme, he said to himself. *In a costume. In black.* He took a deep breath. His left hand was trembling. He was aroused. Obviously, LaFlamme had prepared a play. For his pleasure. A sexual performance.

Was she going to change everything? He asked himself.

Maybe he'd been too quick to want to dump *her*. He wasn't sure of anything anymore. The lure was irresistible. The woman was a black hole of extremely dense attraction. She could provoke outlandish and powerful reactions. Once initiated, they were irreversible. LaFlamme was a rare phenomenon, a soulless creature we *normals* call sociopaths.

LaFlamme's attraction was so strong that even people with a high level of intelligence and good sense could not escape her grip.

Her former colleagues at the consulting firm called her *the little woman* behind her back. The label wasn't meant as a compliment. Word around the office was that the *little* whore was banging anyone on two feet. There was no other way to explain her success with clients or partners.

As for LaFlamme, retribution was part of her life. She was led to believe, very early on in life, that there should always be a price to pay for not being nice. Surprisingly, nothing her colleagues would say could intimidate or frazzle *her*. She was immune to pain. She rarely had any feelings toward others. Good or bad. Although, at times, she did feel angry. She remembered the two women at Mosconi's. That kind of frustration would send LaFlamme on the warpath. People got hurt, humiliated and disgraced. She would, more or less, feel a sense of happiness at seeing others suffer and it could last for a few minutes, but no more than an hour. The buzz would give way to a feeling of emptiness that she would usually fill with lies, work, sex and shopping. Disparaging her colleagues was also a void killer, but it took more preparation time.

LaFlamme never thought she was in any way different from other people. She understood the universe as a competitive game where people had to fight to get what they wanted. There was nothing else. The world, as she understood it, was a place populated by insipid little people fighting over uninteresting bobbles. Her role in life was to succeed in beating people at their own game. Then again, simply lashing out at people, anyone really, would also do the job.

By the time LaFlamme graduated from university, she knew people understood pain as a consequence of their misdeeds. She believed they expected nothing less. She would often remind herself of Pavlovian conditioning techniques when dealing with obstinate people. She had completed her Ph.D. in Industrial Psychology in an effort to understand how people behaved in society. The university had been the perfect place for the young woman to experiment and to learn all the exquisite techniques to get her way. LaFlamme whizzed through academia without anyone finding out what she was really made of. LaFlamme was a chameleon.

Needless to say, LaFlamme had perfected an ingenious concept that explained how she could cause a reflex response of pain through repetitive conditioning on her classmates. In general, their responses to her reprisals were more or less predictable. But, to her relief, they would always include a good deal of pain.

At work, her colleagues, as well as her superiors, saw her as a fighter. Consulting firms needed hunters to secure contracts. That's what partners looked for. Unfortunately, few understood LaFlamme's true nature: an eye for an eye.

LaFlamme would respond to criticism with strength and enthusiasm. In her mind, retaliation needn't be fair. The young woman was dedicated to hurting people as a way of making sure no one got in her way: *you slap me with insults, I'll hit you with a bat.*

During the time her supervisor invested in LaFlamme's consulting skills development, he came to believe that LaFlamme was wrong for the organization, even though she was winning more contracts than some partners. Her success rate was unheard of. But she wasn't capable of understanding the concept of team or membership.

LaFlamme remembered Aristophanes' words: "O hit them hard and hit again and hit until they run away."

"Poetry to my ears," LaFlamme said behind the window overlooking the pudgy little man. "And perhaps they'll learn not to have too much to say."

A woman's voice agreed with LaFlamme. *La petite femme* nodded her head in approval.

Roxanne LaFlamme's eyelids were dusted with lapis colored eyeshadow. Her eyes were framed with thick graphic eyeliner stretched out to her temples, an adornment she copied from Elizabeth Taylor's Cleopatra.

LaFlamme wore a translucent black and gold sari, revealing her body.

She told the woman sitting on the bed it would excite him.

"I'm wearing his favorite colors," LaFlamme said.

The woman in the back agreed.

"He tried for years," she said. "The bastard wanted me, his own wife, to look like a common whore. Present company excepted, of course."

"I am what they expect of me, my dear," LaFlamme replied.

"But, as you know, everything comes with a price, which, I guess, makes me a whore."

If she had to, LaFlamme was comfortable describing herself as a sexual mercenary. It would explain why she was always on the prowl for a new addition to her collection of wealthy men with poor judgement. In this particular circumstance, she was tempted to try her hand at the little man's wife. LaFlamme sensed that the wife would enjoy the sensation of crossing the line and experiment with another woman. LaFlamme was clearly flirting with the woman sitting behind her, who seemed more than happy to be part of LaFlamme's revenge scheme. She had become LaFlamme's client and now an accomplice. *Perhaps, Schuman's wife*, she thought. *A lover*.

Countess de Langlois had long ago forgotten how it felt to pursue and be pursued, how to love and lust for someone. She surprised herself when she realized she wanted *Roxanne* for herself. At least for a few days. And then it hit her: she understood why few people could resist Roxanne LaFlamme's charm.

"That," she said, "would explain my husband's public flirtation with you." His affair with LaFlamme was public knowledge and it made Langlois furious.

Close friends of Schuman's wife, as well as acquaintances, took pains to inform her about Sacha's philandering behavior in the most public of places in Luxembourg. Here, in Langlois' city, right under her nose, in plain sight, Luxembourgians witnessed Schuman wining and dining *la petite femme* at Mosconi's, Clairefontaine and Le Sud.

Florence Salinan de La Motte, Destrey's new acquaintance , was a good friend of Langlois. But now, things were different. Florence swore she'd never forgive Sasha for what he did to Alexandra Langlois... in public.

"It was shameful," Florence said to Destrey, and she also believed it was deliberate. "At first, the whole thing was a joke. But then, my friend Louise Destrey and I realized the bastard didn't care what people would say or how it would hurt you," she said to Langlois.

Florence was livid.

"The whore was wearing a diamond neckless. That's when I knew I had to tell you, Alexandra. I think the bastard should pay."

Florence didn't need to say more. Langlois had heard enough to know that something had to be done. She agreed with Florence, but what to do?

"I think I know someone who could find out the whore's name," Florence said vindictively. "That would be a good start before talking to your lawyers."

Florence was thinking of one of Destrey's employees back in Boston: a woman named Lola. Destrey said there wasn't a person on the planet that Lola couldn't track down. Bear in mind, Florence didn't know that Lola was a machine! In no time at all, Lola came through with a name, an address and a mobile number.

Langlois made sure she'd have a chance encounter with LaFlamme. When they finally met, LaFlamme quickly turned the tables around and brutally criticized Langlois for letting the bastard get away with it for so long. LaFlamme spoke of Schuman wanting to replace her with a younger girl, while boasting that his love for the very young was perfectly normal.

Langlois had, some time ago, admitted, that she'd married below her station. She now believed it was high time to rectify the situation. The timing couldn't be better. Together, the ladies spun a plot so exquisite and so simple. The blond bombshell whore appeared willing to do what was needed, as Langlois said, to rectify the situation.

LaFlamme was ready. The pudgy little man was indeed planning to dump her for a more recent model. She saw it coming. She also heard him say so. Subsequently, a plan was hatched. While both women were aiming to secure Schuman's own private jail cell in hell, Schuman continued to prepare a scheme to get Italians to spend billions on insurance for nothing because claims would never be recognized as legitimate.

The ladies agreed they had to do something about dear Sacha, and the sooner the better. The scheme would make both women rich and independent. They believed his fate was a well-deserved ending.

Just as planned, the pudgy little man was on time, waiting to be plucked like a weed. Schuman's mouth curved upward as LaFlamme opened the widow, letting a breeze ruffle her sari.

Schuman couldn't wait to grab her delicious body. LaFlamme's black wig reminded him of Burton and Taylor's love affair. Both actors loved and hated each other. Although they couldn't be in the same room for more than five minutes, they couldn't bear the thought of being apart. Like Burton, Schuman was indeed addicted, and he couldn't imagine having better sex with anyone else.

LaFlamme glanced at the surprise she had specially prepared for Sasha Schuman. She counted two bottles of Polmos Spirytus Rektyfikowany vodka, 192 proof. One bottle of Bruichladdich X4, 92 proof whiskey, as well as one bottle of Strane Ultra Uncut gin at 82 proof.

The women looked at each other and chuckled in delight.

"Maybe we could take pictures," Langlois asked.

"I don't think so. We'll leave no trail, no evidence, nothing behind that would hint at foul play," LaFlamme said unequivocally.

"Yes. You're right, of course. But are you sure this alcohol business will do the job? Do we have enough?" It was a fair question. LaFlamme had, however, done her homework.

"Yes. I ordered enough bottles to mummify a giant anaconda. I paid with his money through his computer, the one he stashes away in this very bedroom."

"You are really incredible," Alexandra said. "You think of everything."

"Thank you for that, but you better get going, my dear. He'll be up here in a few minutes. It's showtime!"

"Again, I must say, all of this is very imaginative. You do have that special touch." Alexandra was impressed. "How long will it take?"

"Probably twenty minutes, give or take what he's drinking. Maybe less. He won't be compliant until he's had enough. By the way, you got one minute left. Now go."

The ladies had been planning murder by alcohol for weeks. If their calculations were right, alcohol poisoning would occur when Schuman would have imbibed enough alcohol to push his blood-alcohol content to a toxic level. Schuman would enter a coma, stop breathing, or perhaps have a heart attack or a seizure. The ladies were wishing for all of the above.

They had planned every step of the execution. The end-result would generate a finding of accidental death by alcohol. The women would never enter into the equation. Also, the insurance policy payout would never be an issue. After all, Schuman was one of their own.

Schuman was walking up the steps to the second floor. As he neared the last step, he heard *la petite femme* call him.

"Hurry," she said. "I'm thirsty."

Schuman didn't waste any time. He reached the bedroom doors, walked in and closed them behind him. He was admiring the view.

"What's your pleasure?" LaFlamme asked. She was still by the window. She smiled and turned toward Sasha.

"My favorite. But you know that. Vodka, no ice."

"Then I'll have the same, but only after you get comfortable. Take you clothes off and I'll bring your vodka to your bed. Would that please you?"

Schuman nodded. He was almost done. Almost naked. He still had his socks on. He complained he suffered from cold feet syndrome and had to wear socks all the time.

LaFlamme believed the socks gave him his signature look. Sasha's personal style when naked. She called it the icing on the cake. LaFlamme was thinking that he would soon be travelling in style on his last journey. Buck-naked *sauf* his socks.

He jumped on the bed. He lay there waiting for his lady to serve him the way he believed she should.

She poured an ounce of vodka into a small shot glass and sauntered toward him.

"Could you make it a double?" Schuman asked.

"Take this one first while I pour you another one. And take your time. I don't want you to fall asleep on me. That would be such a shame."

"Yes, yes. Of course," Schuman said eagerly. "But hurry. I can't wait to get my hands on you."

"Oh, really? It makes me so happy to hear you say that," she replied.

As Schuman was downing his first once of vodka, LaFlamme was pouring him another shot.

"Drink this, and then I'll be all yours, I promise."

"Why are you wearing gloves?" Schuman asked quizzically.

"Don't you like it? I was sure you'd love the costume."

"I do. I do," he said excitedly. "I certainly like the way your… costume fits."

"Now, finish the vodka, and I'll be all yours. I promise."

Schuman nodded as he quickly swallowed the second shot. She took a few steps back.

"So, you like the look?" LaFlamme turned around as if she was a model on the runway.

Schuman was feeling great. He couldn't believe his eyes. This woman was heaven sent. Even his feet were warming up. As she came closer to him, she opened her mouth to say something but decided to wait a bit longer.

Schuman had his hands all over LaFlamme. He didn't waste any time with foreplay. *That would be for another time*, he thought. Romantic preludes were highly overrated. After all, there was no need for seduction. She belonged to him. His slave to do his bidding.

Schuman tried to yank the sari away from her body. But she managed to keep it on.

"You're in a hurry?" she said.

"Yes. I want to see you naked. Is that too much to ask?"

LaFlamme said no, but Schuman couldn't hear a word.

He was not a reasoning human being any longer. He felt his inhibitions fly out the window. He was caught in the moment and as time slowed bit by bit, he began to feel altered. Invincible.

LaFlamme slowly took off her sari and let it fall to her feet. She moved closer. He smelled her body. She was intoxicating.

"I'm so thirsty," he said, as he was warming his nose between her breasts.

LaFlamme pushed him gently on the pillow. "Let me get you another vodka. That's what you need, isn't it Sacha?"

"Make it a double."

"Anything your little heart desires."

"But I want you back here quick. I miss you already."

LaFlamme brought back a highball full of vodka.

"If you drink this quickly, I will show you something special."

Schuman was eager and willing to do whatever she asked of him. In a matter of seconds, Schuman had guzzled down more than five ounces of vodka.

LaFlamme was confident that Schuman was almost ready for his surprise.

"Show me. Show me now," he said slowly. "What's the surprise about? Tell me!"

"Are you sure?"

"Oh yes. I am ready for my surprise."

LaFlamme turned toward the bedroom door.

"You can come in now," LaFlamme said out loud.

Alexandra walked into the bedroom. She was naked. On her way to the king-sized bed, she poured a highball full of vodka and walked toward Schuman.

"Sasha darling?" Alexandra said. "More vodka?" She sat beside LaFlamme.

"What?" Schuman said, unsure of what or who he was looking at.

"Here, darling, drink this. It'll make you feel better, and then, all three of us will have fun." Alexandra was a natural.

After Schuman finished his second highball, Alexandra brought the bottle of vodka to his bedside table.

"But you never wear gloves, honey? Why's that?"

"Don't you worry, my darling Sasha," Alexandra said sweetly. "Your Cleopatra, sitting right here beside me, is about to give you another surprise."

"Another surp…"

"Yes," said LaFlamme. By this time, Schuman could hardly keep his eyes open.

"I want you to know that today's your birthday."

Schuman nodded.

"Yes. My birthday. My birth… day party."

"Yes, Sasha. Today. Right now. And all the women you love and have screwed in your life, are here to take care of you, Sasha."

"I…" Schuman was trying to understand what could possibly be wrong with him. He was seeing things. But he didn't really care.

"Now, let's all have a drink together, dear Sasha. After all, it's Christmas and, it's your birthday."

LaFlamme brought the bottle of vodka to Schuman's mouth.

"Now, drink up. Happy birthday and merry Christmas," Alexandra said without any sense of fear, guilt or sadness.

Alexandra set the empty bottle on the side table and got closer to LaFlamme. Schuman's wife held LaFlamme's hands and kissed *la petite femme* tenderly.

"I like that," Schuman said. "Do that again? Please?"

It was LaFlamme's turn.

"Like this, Sasha?" LaFlamme said.

LaFlamme pressed her body on his wife, caressing her bottom while pulling Alexandra's hair back.

"That's so…," Schuman said drowsily. "Sooo… sexy…"

"Time for another drink," LaFlamme said.

"Am I thistly again?" Schuman asked.

LaFlamme was now handling the second bottle and started to pour more vodka down Schuman's mouth.

"Drink. You're thirsty, very thirsty. And you want more vodka, isn't that right, Sasha?"

"Yes, more," he repeated LaFlamme words.

Schuman would need more vodka for the ladies to complete the play. They had to be sure. Probably a lot more. More vodka until Schuman was no more.

"How long should we stay around here?" Alexandra asked.

"Until he's no longer," LaFlamme responded softly.

"So," Alexandra said softly, "I guess, we shouldn't waste any time. Should we?"

LaFlamme pushed Alexandra to the floor and opened her legs.

Alexandra looked up to LaFlamme's pretty face and felt warm. Probably for the first time in years.

The little woman was indeed irresistible and intoxicating.

An hour later, Schuman's body lay still. He died at the hands of his wife and mistress.

"He had a good run," LaFlamme said.

Alexandra was on top of LaFlamme, enjoying the sensation of control over *la petite femme*.

"Shut up, and kiss me, whore," Alexandra said.

Later that evening, the ladies kept busy cleaning up any trail they would have left accidentally.

"That," LaFlamme said, "was part one of our story."

Alexandra looked puzzled. "What do you mean?"

"There is a second part to his passing," LaFlamme said to Alexandra.

While staging the bedroom for the inevitable police investigation, LaFlamme explained how her husband was planning to steal millions of euros from Italians and the Italian government. Even though Covid-19 had killed more of its population than they could have ever imagined, the virus had also brought the Italian economy to its knees. Nevertheless, Schuman had plans of his own concerning Italy. There was still more money to be made. Squeezing money from unsuspecting people was what Schuman did best, his greatest skill.

LaFlamme told Alexandra that her late husband was in the

process of taking over an insurance company for the sole purpose of cashing in on Acts of God claims. Schuman would cover natural disasters such as earthquakes, hurricanes or tornadoes, volcanic eruptions and tidal waves. However, the great majority of claims would be denied or simply ignored. Schuman's strategy would force clients to accept lowball compensation, or simply see their claims denied. He would instruct his agents to lie and blame clients for their misfortune.

"We've hit the jackpot. Call it a gift from your husband," LaFlamme said. "Because compulsory insurance will be inevitable. Italians will be legally required to buy our insurance. As for your late husband's friends, well, we'll make sure they get just enough to keep the racket going for years to come. It's a scam worth millions, if not billions, of euros."

"We're going to be rich beyond our wildest dreams?" Alexandra said.

"Yes, but we should handle this as discreetly as possible."

"Then what?" Alexandra asked.

"Then, we are free."

Theoretically, that would be the end of the story, at least for Alexandra Schuman.

However, for Roxanne LaFlamme, there was another account to be settled. Barring unexpected developments, it became clear to LaFlamme that the two women who tormented her at Mosconi's were next.

A reckoning was about take place.

"The sooner the better," LaFlamme said out loud. Her fantasies reflected who she was. They were designed to meet her unique needs to hurt, to maim and to kill.

30

EL MISTI
AREQUIPA, PERÚ

On rare occasions, one finds exceptional human beings capable of more. More than what remarkable people can do on their best days. These men and women achieve singular achievements. What they do doesn't always add up, can be difficult to measure, or at times, even hard to understand. We can dismiss them but at our own peril.

One such being has been on Lola's radar for some time, waiting for the right opportunity to reach out and make contact. His name was Galvez. Lola's ongoing head-hunting activity has been responsible for at least half of BTG's hirings.

Today, on the flanks of the towering volcano, a 5,822 meter high behemoth called El Misti or Putina, Sergio Carlos Galvez sat at his desk thinking of the next word he needed to complete his sentence.

After spending most of his life as a soldier, Galvez had chosen to live in Arequipa, also known as the "White City". There, he would write his memoirs and be close to what he called his giant friends. Galvez began his love-hate relationship with volcanoes more than forty years ago. At that time, the army had commissioned the gangly young lieutenant to be its point man for all things involving Mother Nature's outbursts. The army paid for his Master's degree in Engineering at the Pontificia Universidad Católica del Perú (Pontifical Catholic University). That was the beginning of his infamous love affair with volcanos.

Not surprisingly, he chose to retire in the City of Arequipa because it was located near three volcanoes.

Chapter ten of Galvez's memoirs, entitled *Living With Her*, was no joke. The *her* in question was his wife and best friend, Juliana Pilar Allende, a former TV host for Andina de Televisión of Perú.

When Galvez finally shaped his ideas around the story he wanted to tell, he typed the word "extreme".

"No, that's not what I really mean," he said out loud. "Think, man, think."

It was too strong a word to describe the impact his wife had on him. She was, after all, the love of his life. The same woman he had married, divorced and remarried again. He had understood a long time ago that he couldn't get away from her. She was simply overpowering.

"That's it," he said, "she's irresistible, like gravity."

"Sergio? What are you babbling about now?"

"Nothing that will drastically change your irresistibility, my love."

"Whatever," she said hopelessly. "By the way, what are you planning for the rest of the day?"

"Nothing much. A little writing, a bit of lunch in a few minutes and then a nap."

"That's not like you to sleep in the afternoon. Are you alright?"

"I didn't sleep well last night. I kept waking up. I don't know why. I was probably dreaming again."

"Please don't say it, Sergio. I don't want to hear about your dreams and the giants."

"Yes, dear. I promise. But that doesn't change the fact that I will need a nap this afternoon. God willing."

"Please don't use the name of our Lord in vain, Sergio. You know how that makes me feel."

"I wasn't, my love."

"And I don't want you to tell me about that rock you so fervently adore. It's almost blasphemous. Only God deserves to be treated like a God."

"I'm sorry. You're right, of course. But how can you ask a writer not to live his fantasies?"

"Writer? You call yourself a writer after you sold thirty-two copies of your last novel?"

"It's not the number that counts, my love, it's the legacy for our children."

"So now you've added your children to your list of fantasies. Sonia is thirty-six and Daniel is forty-one. Trust me, they don't need to read your romance novels about a tired old man who's still in love with his saintly mother."

"You are truly your mama's daughter: hard to get, difficult to keep and impossible to handle."

"Is that a compliment, Sergio?"

"If you wish, my love."

"Well, I guess I'll take it as praise."

"You are very welcome. I'm also pleased to see that you're happy. So, while you're in a good mood, tell me what's for lunch?"

"I'm preparing Aji de Gallina."

"I love your chili pepper chicken. Not too spicy, I hope. The chicken last time was as hot as…"

"Don't."

"Don't what?"

"The Misti. That's what."

"Oh, you mean the Great God Misti?"

"You just did it again. Can we get by one day without talking about that infernal volcano of yours?"

"I guess not, my love."

"Just so you know, before you start ranting about that damn mountain, María Julia told me there's no relationship between tremors and the mountain acting up."

"Is that so?"

"Yes, Mr. Know-it-all. She said there were no links between them."

"You mean causal."

"Don't be technical."

"I wish I was. By the way, where did she get that information? I'll bet she was listening to Pepe Barreto."

"What do you have against him?"

"Sometimes he gets his mountains mixed up."

"No matter. Just keep that horrible mountain to yourself. I'm asking you gently, Sergio. Please. You know what happens to me when you mention El Misti. It's bad enough that I have to live near that monster without hearing about what it could do to us. Just so you know, that blasted monstrosity keeps me awake at night."

"I promise, whatever happens, I will keep the mountain to myself. I promise. But here's the problem."

"What now?"

"It's rousing."

"My God, Sergio. Are you deaf?"

"The danger with El Misti is its location," Galvez said. "We live barely 17 km from the mountain. I've always said that when this one decides to pop its cork, we won't be able to evacuate the people of Arequipa fast enough."

"You did indeed. Many times."

"Perhaps, God willing, we'll be long gone before the Great One decides to tell us who's master of the planet."

"You see, Sergio, that's exactly what I mean. That thing out there scares me to no end. And what do you do? You remind me of her existence every time you have a chance. That's cruel. I'm tired of it, Sergio. I think I've had it with you and your girlfriend Misti."

"My what?"

"You heard me!"

"I'm sorry," Galvez said. "But just look around, Juliana. You can't help it. It's out there. In our face. The mountain reminds us on a daily basis what she's capable of doing to Arequipa."

"No. I've seen enough of it. Thank you very much."

"Not the mountain, Juliana, but what's around it. The topography's all wrong. I'm telling you; it scares me too. There's absolutely nothing natural to stop it from burying us under hundreds of meters of avalanche debris."

Juliana had heard that story many times before. But today, the old soldier was off. Different. Something in Galvez's voice was obviously wrong.

"Maybe you're right. About moving away," he said to himself out loud.

"Thank-you very much!" she said, annoyed. "That's the first sensible thing you've said since we've moved to Arequipa."

"What do you think? Should we call a realtor?" Galvez asked his wife hesitantly. "Are we serious about doing this?"

"Sergio. Listen up. Don't fool around with me. This is not a laughing matter. Do you understand me?"

"Okay. I'll make the call after lunch."

"No. Do it now, Sergio. Now, before you change your mind."

Sergio looked out the kitchen window one more time. What he saw disturbed him.

"I think Mother Nature is trying to tell me something, Juliana," he said.

"What do you mean, Sergio?"

"A tremor woke me up last night. A small quake. It wasn't a bad dream. Truth is, I shouldn't be concerned. We have thousands of them. But I've been paying closer attention to the mountain for the last year. I'm afraid it's acting up. I don't know why, but I have this feeling. So much so that I've already contacted the Geophysical Institute and the Vulcanological Observatory."

Juliane didn't respond. To her knowledge, he had not contacted these two organizations in years.

"Did you notice the smell of rotten eggs?" he asked absentmindedly.

Again, Juliana did not respond to her husband's questions. She knew better. Sergio Galvez was talking to himself. That's when he did his best work: asking himself the right questions.

"I should call the army," he said nervously.

"That would be a great idea if you knew for certain what was going to happen. What did the people at the Geophysical Institute say?"

"Nothing much. They said the volcano was behaving normally. Nothing to worry about."

"But you don't think so?"

"Nope."

"So, focus on selling this house. That's priority one. You can tell the realtors we want to be closer to our grandchildren."

"Yes… closer to the little ones. Right. That sounds reasonable."

As the afternoon wore on, Galvez was by now more than certain that El Misti was in motion, preparing for an eruption. The volcano was probably building up new magma reserves.

He felt he had been sufficiently warned in spite of what the Institute was telling him. Besides, if the mountain made his wife uneasy, it was about time he did something about it.

The problem with El Misti was a bit more complicated than he cared to admit; he would never tell her the whole truth about what he really believed was actually happening. El Misti had been acting up since its last eruption in 1985. He believed the '85 eruption had been a prologue to a bigger event. El Misti's track record in 80 B.C. was catalogued as a VEI-4 eruption. On a scale from 1 to 8, a category 4 eruption was described by scientists as "cataclysmic". The same event today would be devastating because of the numbers, the planet being far more densely populated. Back in 80 B.C., there was no population to speak of in the vicinity of Misti. Today, Arequipa is the second most populated city in Perú with over one million inhabitants.

He decided then and there he wouldn't wait to sell his house before talking to the military. He wasn't worried about the money. Galvez came from old money. Money had never been an issue. It was all about being of service to his country.

Galvez determined that the military had to know what was on his mind. He knew the military respected his opinions even though the higher ups believed the lieutenant was a bit strange.

He would call them this week. In fact, the sooner the better. All he had to do was put his ideas in order.

He was beginning to sense the old feeling he had way back when he'd come up with his strange predictions. Feelings he couldn't quite explain to himself or to his Commander.

"Sergio?" she said.

"Yes, my love."

"Can you come here? I need you in the kitchen."

"I'll be right there. Just give me a few seconds to complete my notes."

"Be quick about it. Supper won't wait for anyone. Our friends will be here any minute now."

"Fine. I'll go through this one more time and I'll be right with you."

"Quickly, Sergio."

Galvez looked at his list of talking points he'd be sharing with his old Commander. He remembered what he'd learned during his army days at the 115th Logistics Brigade. The unit had similar responsibilities as the United States Army Corps of Engineers, though with limited resources.

What he learned as a junior officer was, in his opinion, wise and strategic. Start with the end of your presentation: provide your conclusions quickly. Then, explain how you came to those conclusions. Be clear about what you know and what you don't. Identify the questions you will be discussing as well as those you have no answers to. And, most importantly, don't try to impress your audience with big words that no one understands. Be clear, precise and to the point. Don't turn your message into a striptease, making everyone wait for the big reveal.

El Misti talking points.

1. El Misti volcano is active. More so than usual. New monitoring equipment is required. At this time, we cannot predict volcanic eruptions with any precision.

2. An evacuation plan for the city of Arequipa, as well as a public alert system, are necessary.

3. El Misti is a typical stratovolcano: they are the most dangerous erupting volcanoes on the planet. El Misti could provide pre-eruption signs, or not.

4. When (not if) El Misti erupts, the city of Arequipa will be directly in its path based on the volcano's current landscape (topography). The current landscape could change without warning.

5. There is a possibility that deep below the earth's crust, a large magma-containing reservoir has been building up since Misti's full-fledged eruption in 80 B.C.

6. El Misti experiences long periods of dormancy between major eruptions. The 1985 eruption can be considered as a notable precursor to an eruption.

7. When (not if) El Misti generates a full-fledged eruption, it will do so with significant force. It is difficult to predict the strength of the eruption. At this point in time, anything is possible.

8. A typical eruption will have El Misti spewing lava and ash high into the atmosphere, causing avalanches, landslides and mudflows.

9. A significant eruption might impact the lowest layer of earth's atmosphere where nearly all-weather conditions take place. We will need to consult with experts in the field of volcanology to ascertain whether we can do anything to protect our people from climate anomalies.

10. Because Arequipa has a current population of more than one million people, the evacuation plan would need to be simulated in real time with the entire population involved. That would include the national police force, the military, firefighters and first responders, local radio and TV stations, the city's Internet coordinator, hospitals, retirement homes, schools as well as businesses, banks, museums and most importantly, public and private transportation.

Sergio Galvez hid away his notes. If his wife ever got hold of them, he believed there would be hell to pay. Nevertheless, just to be on her good side, Galvez called the local Re/Max realtor and scheduled to meet him within the next few days.

He walked toward the kitchen where Juliana was waiting for him.

"What can I do?"

"Get two bottles of red from downstairs."

Galvez walked away slowly.

"Not the cheap ones," she said.

"Yes, of course. These are our good friends. We'll keep the bad wine for ourselves."

"Sometimes, dear husband, you are so funny. I could laugh at your humor, but not tonight. Just get the wine and come back to help me with the salad."

"So now, I'm funny."

"You would be surprised to know that I used to talk about your sense of humor to my mother every other day."

"No wonder the old bat hated me so much."

"What did you say?"

"Nothing of importance, my love."

Later that evening.

"Sergio? How about a refill?" Diego asked eagerly. "I must admit, this wine is special. Where have you been hiding this magnificent bottle?"

"Not where, dear Diego, but who from? That would be the proper question to ask. It's not every day that I open a bottle of Riccitelli & Father. Only for the best people, company included, of course."

"What year?"

"2014." Diego was impressed.

Maxima and Diego Darin were neighbors as well as good friends. When Galvez moved to Arequipa, Juliana insisted they should meet socially. Galvez met Diego at the local Rotary Club and agreed with his wife: the Darins were wonderful.

Galvez joined the local Rotary Club because he believed it was a good place to make new friends and help the community at the same time.

"So, I'm to understand that you're hiding your good bottles from me, the only friend you've got in Arequipa?"

"Quite."

The men laughed loudly while the women appeared unimpressed by their husbands' sense of humor.

Before anyone could change the subject, Sergio noticed the wine in his glass suddenly quivered.

Galvez didn't say anything, preferring to let it go. Juliana would not appreciate another treatise on the different precursors to volcanic eruptions.

"So, what's new? We haven't talked for weeks. You've been away in Lima," Diego said.

"Yes."

"How are those grandchildren of yours?"

"A handful," Juliana quickly answered. "I miss them so much. In fact, I don't know if Sergio told you, but we are in the process of selling the house. I would love so much to be close to my little children. I'm sure our own kids could use our help."

"You're moving?" Maxima said, stunned. "Why didn't you mention it before?"

"We just made our decision today," Juliana said defensively.

"Well," Diego said sadly, "I guess that deserves a toast."

"Yes, of course," said Galvez, a bit disheartened. "A toast to our friendship."

The silence that followed the toast was painful. It was reminding everyone around the table of the hazards of befriending good people, only to see them move away.

While Juliana was trying to find a way to lift the mood, her sense of integrity and her steadfast friendship with Maxima triggered an outcry of remorse. However, before Juliana could say anything, the wine quivered once again.

"Did you feel that?" Diego said, a bit startled. "The wine is trembling."

"Sergio," Juliana said coldly, "you can go ahead and tell them. I know that's what you really want to do, and I also know what you're planning to do with your old buddies in the military. Come-on, just say it and let's be done with it."

"Say what?" Maxima said, while looking at Galvez. "What are you not telling us?"

"As we just told you, my wife and I have decided to move," Galvez said without thinking.

"To be close to your grandkids?" Maxima added slowly.

"That's true, but there's more to that story," Galvez said glumly. "I want to say that my life here in Arequipa has been wonderful. I, for one, was willing to take my chances and, come what may, live the rest of my life here, in Arequipa."

"I don't understand, Sergio. What do you mean by taking your chances?" Diego was trying to understand what his friend was trying to tell him.

"I meant to say that I was willing to live under the shadow of a volcano and take the risks that come with the mountain."

Diego laughed with relief. "Not that old story again, Sergio. How many times have you told me about Misti? About the good old days in the army when you had to climb Misti for the army. If I remember correctly, you were told you were to become the army's point man for volcanoes and everything nasty in Perú."

Galvez didn't look up to meet his friend's eyes, preferring to take a sip of his wine.

"You're not serious, Sergio? You told me many times before that the mountain could theoretically stay dormant for hundreds of years, maybe thousands. Am I right?"

Galvez nodded.

"The grandkids, I can understand. No problem. In fact, we've also been thinking about our grandkids."

"You're thinking of moving too?" Juliana said, startled.

"We haven't made a decision. Not yet. But now…"

"Let me tell you what I'm going to say to my old commander next week. Maybe that can help," Galvez said.

Juliana was alarmed because she had read his notes.

After having gone through his talking points, Galvez told his wife and friends to look at their wine glasses.

"You've all noticed, haven't you?"

"Yes, but I wouldn't storm out of your house," Diego said seriously.

"Well, for better or for worse, my instincts tell me that the mountain is showing precursor signs. Did I mention the smell of rotten eggs?"

Diego didn't respond to his friend's question.

"Well, did I, Diego?"

Diego nodded.

"More importantly, Juliana can't run away fast enough from Arequipa. She told me in no uncertain terms that she's had it with Misti. No more, she said. Is that correct, Juliana?"

She looked away. The whole idea of moving away because of a volcano came crashing down on her, exposing a deep sadness she thought she'd never again have to go through since her mother's death. All of a sudden, El Misti was real. Not just something others should be concerned about.

"It's Sergio's instincts," she said quietly. "He's never wrong, you know. His commander once told me that he would come up to see him with stuff that would scare everyone at HQ. He told me that whenever Sergio had issued a warning, it meant something bad was about to happen. And, right on cue, bad things would happen. I saw him do just that earlier today. As clear as a bell. This time, he was warning himself. I was scared and at the same time, I was relieved. Because we were at last going to leave this beautiful town and find refuge as far away from Misti as possible."

Juliana turned to her husband. "I see it too, husband. The wine did quiver. I see it tremble practically every day."

"I know you don't need the money, Diego," Sergio said cautiously. "I know you can leave your house behind anytime you feel like it."

"Still, Sergio, it's a lot to leave behind just because of your instincts. I've invested much here. And besides, it's our home."

"Let me be clear. I can't tell you when, Diego. You and I know that. It could happen in two minutes, two weeks or two hundred years from now. But that's not the issue anymore. And as far as I'm concerned, money is not in play here. To tell you the truth, it's my soul. I'm tired. I'm not yet ready to give up on life. Whether or not something happens here in my lifetime is of no concern to me. All I know…"

"I think I understand, Sergio. We all do. And you're right. It's not the money or leaving our homes behind, it's really about peace of mind."

Diego understood his friend's reasons for moving out of Arequipa. But still, leaving behind his way of life, his friends, the house, the garden Maxima worked so hard to maintain, and perhaps the money… Diego's mind told him his best friend could be right. But then, Sergio could be off by a thousand years. Then what?

"What about the rest of the people, Sergio? Some don't have the luxury of leaving everything behind." Diego said unhappily.

"As I said, I'll be talking to the army next week. God willing, they'll do the right thing."

"You really believe that?"

"No. The army almost always takes the wrong turn. But I can

hope."

"Let's say, just for the sake of argument, that you're right and that the army doesn't want to do anything about El Misti or can't. Where does that leave us?"

"I honestly don't know," Sergio said glumly.

"We could at least warn the people. Wouldn't that be the right thing to do?" Diego said.

"I guess that would be the right thing to do. But warning the people…"

"They're not stupid," Diego said.

"They're not rich either, Diego. They can't move away and leave everything behind just because I say so. Besides, Misti's been around for thousands of years, and we're all still here. In one piece. Alive and well."

"I'm sure some would listen."

"There are two things wrong with what you're proposing, Diego. One, the army won't be happy if we go over their heads and tell everyone Misti is going to blow. Chaos is the last thing they'll tolerate. Two, we can't talk to the people from Lima. We would have to stay here for at least another year to do a good job without antagonizing the army. What I'm trying to say is that I really don't know how to warn people of an impending eruption that could happen between now and say a thousand years from now. Putting the fear of God in people's hearts would be extremely difficult given the fact that we simply can't predict eruptions. And my instincts, well, that not something I can use convincingly."

"You're saying we shouldn't do anything."

"Not shouldn't but can't. This is exactly what I'm not prepared to do. I'm too old for that mission and, don't forget, the army has been good to me. There are a lot of good people in the military. They're not all corrupt or mean-spirited."

"So, what are we supposed to do?" Diego said miserably.

"Move. We've been warned."

Hidden in the earth's mantle, more than 2,000 km deep,

unfettered by human sensitivities, magma pushed upwards through the rock under El Misti. The ground ruptured ever so slightly and allowed steam to escape. The increasing smell of rotten eggs, hot springs, imperceptible tremors and unusual behavior from animals began to appear on the slopes of Misti.

"Did you ever hear of a woman called Louise Destrey?" Galvez asked Diego.

"What about her?" Diego said.

"Apparently, she wants to talk to me."

"About…?"

"Volcanoes," Galvez said nervously.

31

ROCKY'S VENGEANCE
NAPLES, ITALY

Afew kilometers away near the port of Naples, the women who flawlessly executed Alexander Schuman for crimes against wife and mistress, sat comfortably by the pool's *chaise longues.* The sentence had been carried out by means of 192 proof vodka.

Admiring Vesuvius in all its magnificence, Roxanne Isabella LaFlamme couldn't help but congratulate herself on a job well done.

"It's playing our song," LaFlamme said to Alexandra Schuman.

"What song? I don't hear any music," Schuman said.

"Look at the mountain." LaFlamme pointed at the smoking mountain. "Like I said, it's playing our song."

The women were enjoying the spectacle that lay below them. Naples' shore from atop the Romeo Hotel was quite the sight. The luxury residence faced the Port. The view over the Bay and Mount Vesuvius was simply breathtaking.

"I see what you mean. It's acting up again," Schuman said. She was in awe of Vesuvius. "Best publicity we could ever hope for."

LaFlamme now believed more than ever that the possibility

of compulsory insurance for all Italians was picking up speed. The government was being pushed around by Internet chatter demanding that the Prime minister confirm to the nation it would help those in need after an earthquake or a volcanic eruption. Unfortunately, Italy had to finally admit that it could not afford it. The Prime minister said Italians must find a way to protect themselves either by moving away from Italy's danger zones or simply buying insurance. Earthquake and volcano insurance would include coverage for the aftereffects of a volcanic eruption in addition to earthquakes not caused by volcanoes. Even if one did not live near a fault line or a volcano, the government suggested that Italians consider an earth-movement policy for extra protection.

Basically, the Italian government was promoting insurance. LaFlamme and Schuman had been counting on the fact that the Italian government's financial difficulties would preclude them from subsidizing victims of Acts of God.

The ladies were well on their way to becoming wealthy beyond their wildest dreams. All that and more due to Schuman's late husband who had hatched a scheme to push Italy to lay the groundwork for compulsory insurance.

"Time to go, Alexandra," LaFlamme said.

"What's the hurry?"

"Look at the mountain. That's our cue," LaFlamme said. "Act 2 is beginning and that means we should be on our way."

"Where to?"

"As far away from here as possible. Back home, maybe. We have all morning to decide where we want to go. As long as it's away from this mountain."

"Whatever you say," Schuman said joyfully.

"That's a good girl." LaFlamme was smiling again. She was happy, at least for a few hours. The void in her *petite* body was temporarily decommissioned. She was able to breathe without fear of the abyss. The void or the emptiness she lived with day in and day out, was her own private hell. A place where she could never be satisfied, never really be happy or unhappy about anything. The only real pleasure she was able to feel was in the misfortune of others, a sensation that unfortunately never lasted long enough.

LaFlamme remembered what she had overheard at Mosconi's in Luxembourg. Those women called her a whore. They laughed at her. One even had the nerve to call her a bimbo. That was unacceptable. LaFlamme wanted her revenge. She needed them to pay. All of a sudden, she felt relaxed as she quickly began to plan her next move.

"I think we should make a short visit to Luxembourg," LaFlamme said. "I want to find out who was there at Mosconi's the day I was doing your late husband."

"The diamond neckless?" Schuman asked. "I remember. That was an auspicious day for me. Florence called and told me what that bastard was doing… in public. I made the decision then and there. I had to get rid of the sonofabitch."

"I want to know who was there," LaFlamme said.

"Why?"

"Just curious." LaFlamme was thinking of Florence but more importantly, the other woman at the table. LaFlamme's soul, if you could call it that, was a rat's nest of foul and angry desires. She wanted her revenge on both of them.

A plan of sorts began to take shape. She was feeling great. Like most higher-functioning sociopaths, she could fill the void only when in control. Planning revenge was always a good start. The sociopath's soul was now engaged and moving forward. Surprisingly, LaFlamme could feign empathy and express sympathy in order to understand and in the end, to better manipulate.

"Okay then," Schuman said enthusiastically. "It's back to Luxembourg. Then what?"

"We'll take it one step at a time. As long as we're far away from the mountain. What's important is that we're together."

"I like that," Schuman said.

"I knew you would. And I'm sure I can come up with a few surprises."

"I'd like that too."

"I know you will." LaFlamme felt a chill at the thought of having the woman all to herself. To do whatever she wanted. Alexandra Schuman was a handy person to have around. The thought of being alone with her demons frightened LaFlamme to her core. She once admitted to her mother that she was often lonely.

"I'm not dead mommy. I can feel everything you feel," she said. While LaFlamme's mother hugged her little princess, she didn't believe a word of it. As feelings go, LaFlamme senior assumed her daughter had been born defective, unlike anyone she had ever met.

As the murderous ladies were headed to Naples International Airport, LaFlamme was plotting, planning and anticipating.

"I'll find you bitch," LaFlamme whispered to herself. "I will. I will. I will."

32

BOSTON TRIAGE GROUP (BTG) CAMBRIDGE, MASSACHUSETTS

Destrey was back at BTG getting ready to meet her guests. When she reached her office, she met Margaret's glare.

"You're late," Margaret said.

"Are they here yet?" Destrey asked.

"Yup. Conference room 3 point something or other. Coffee's on the table."

Destrey walked over to the conference room. She opened the door as all three stood to greet their host.

Destrey wasn't sure what she would tell them.

"Please don't do that. Sit, please. Make yourselves comfortable," Destrey said.

"Thank you for seeing us, *Madame* Destrey," Carbone said. "May I introduce Guðrún Sigerðssen and Gene Rudd?"

Destrey shook hands with all three of her guests.

"Nice to meet you," Destrey said.

Although Destrey had Lola do background checks, she was pleased to meet them in person. What Lola couldn't find out about her guests was almost impossible for a machine to do. Although Destrey could read individuals like normal people skim a McDonald's menu, she would not deny herself a good read.

They were intelligent, experienced and serious. They could never be taken for granted, she thought to herself.

"I know what you're going to ask me," Destrey said.

Carbone, Sigerðssen nor Rudd reacted.

"Unfortunately, I don't have what you need," Destrey said.

Again, her guests remained quiet.

"But I can get things going."

It seemed like nothing could unhinge her guests, no matter what she said. Nevertheless, Destrey continued.

"It comes down to this. You need help, right?"

"Yes, of course," Sigerðssen said.

"And I know who can and will help you."

"You're clearly in the driver's seat," Carbone said. He was about to add something but decided to stay quiet. This was Destrey's time, Destrey's house and Destrey's rules.

"Unfortunately, I can't help you with Naples. Unless you have a time and date for the next eruption, there's not a chance in hell Neapolitans will move away from their homes and businesses."

Carbone stared at Destrey in disbelief. "I was hoping for more, *Madame* Destrey," he said. "In fact, a lot more. We are talking about hundreds of thousands of lives!" Carbone was hoping she'd come up with a miracle plan.

"Sorry, Francesco. That will probably not happen in my lifetime, perhaps not even yours. But hear me out. That doesn't mean we won't try. I will. We'll start a conversation with Neapolitans. We will aim our conversation to young families. Meanwhile, I feel we should be working together to create a new science. One that will predict and stop eruptions. We'll have to do that secretly because …"

"Because it's impossible to even speak about that in public," Rudd added.

"Correct," Destrey said. "Because science can and is very

conservative and closed-minded."

Francisco nodded, but Sigerðssen and Rudd wondered what Destrey had in mind.

"My late husband once told me that in order to innovate one needs ideas and insight. People with knowledge as well as others who display a capacity to generate a deep intuitive understanding of the subject matter."

"Meaning…" Francisco asked.

"Well for instance, I've invited Sergio Galvez. He's from Perú. He's one of those people who can tell when something's about to happen, even though there are no precursor signs.

"Never heard of him," Sigerðssen said. "But I'd like to meet him."

"He's a very interesting fellow," Destrey said. "I know for a fact that he'll bring a different perspective to our discussion. And there's going be more people like Valdez. People we know as well as others we'll be discovering together."

Although Sigerðssen was a seasoned professional, she was rapidly realizing that the woman called Destrey was not only intelligent but a take charge individual, capable of anything she puts her mind into. And, she was in fact, calling the shots.

"I'll be putting a lot of cash into this project," Destrey said, "and I think I have some say in how we will populate the team. I'm sure you'll agree with me that, with my background and experience come a few privileges."

"Are there more of these privileges, *Madame* Destrey?" asked Francisco.

"Yes, of course, Francisco. I'll let you know as soon as I know."

33

BOSTON TRIAGE GROUP (BTG) CAMBRIDGE, MASSACHUSETTS

Scientists wanted to witness firsthand what Lola had developed. The supercomputer was also observing the audience and had begun to gage their reactions. As the computer would lead them through a series of events, everyone understood what they were presented with: a prediction. The simulation was meant to reveal and help understand the implications of living in the most dangerous city on the planet.

"Lola's ready. Almost everyone's down there, including our guest volcanologists. Whenever you're ready, Louise," Margaret said.

"I'm not sure I want to hear what she has to say even though I need to hear it," Destrey said.

"Mind if I join in?" Margaret asked.

"Mind? Of course not. You need to see this. We both do," Destrey said.

Destrey walked out to the reception area. Margaret was one step behind her.

Lola prompted the elevator doors to open. Both women got in. As they were brought down to the subbasement, Margaret heard

Destrey say a prayer.

Briefing: Lola's Simulation

Destrey as well as most of BTG's scientists gathered in the basement where Lola was located. BTG called it the Safe because it had been once a bank safe and now a place where a supercomputer couldn't be hacked.

"Let's see what you've got, Lola," Destrey said.

Destrey had no illusion about what to expect from the computer. After more than a dozen simulations, Lola had accumulated enough data to be confident about her latest attempt to predict how Vesuvius would behave. Lola informed Destrey that she couldn't avoid a darker scenario given Vesuvius' activity over the last 5000 years. Lola had developed a detailed visual simulation of what to expect from the volcano.

Lola began the simulation.

The supercomputer presented a holographic map of Italy showing fault lines that covered the length of the country.

Morgan Freeman's computer-generated voice began the narration.

"Let us review what we know so far before entertaining Vesuvius' future. As we all know, earth's shell is divided into several major tectonic plates. Italy's major fault lines which grind against each other produce seismic as well as volcanic tension. Italy's major volcanoes such as Etna, Stromboli and Vesuvius, all lie close to these fault lines. Where and when earth's tectonic plates meet is a likely site for earthquakes. Most of Italy's volcanoes appear at the boundaries of tectonic plates."

"Lola?"

"Yes, *Madame* Destrey."

"Where are you going with this?" Destrey asked.

"Naples could be dealing with two active volcanoes, one or many earthquakes and tsunamis. Think of it as Mother Nature's pincer movement where seismic and volcanic forces would attack both flanks of Naples at the same time. In the worst scenario, these forces would surround and lay siege to the city. No one would be able to escape the city or rescue Naples' citizens if that occurred."

"Okay…" Destrey paused for a moment. "Just stop. Let me think about that."

Lola didn't reply. She gave Destrey and her colleagues all the time they needed to understand the ramifications of what she'd come up with.

A few minutes later, Lola continued to illustrate the type of event BTG would be facing.

"Scientists call it a confluent of natural events," Lola said.

"Like the perfect storm?" Destrey asked.

"Yes, *Madame* Destrey. A catastrophic situation created by a powerful concurrence of natural forces."

"I can't see anything good coming out of this."

"Nor can I, *Madame* Destrey."

Freeman continued the narration.

"In 2016, the Italian government faced with Italy's tragic earthquake history, introduced the *Casa Italia Plan*. It was developed to overhaul Italy's preparedness to handle earthquakes. The plan was launched because, although Italy does a good job of rescuing people after earthquakes, it has a terrible reputation when it comes to protecting its people and its infrastructure ahead of time."

"Is the plan in play?" Destrey asked Lola.

"Yes and no, *Madame* Destrey. The national plan includes earthquake-proofing structures across the country and a number of additional environmental measures. The long-term venture to bring Italy's infrastructures up to international seismic safety standards could take more than 50 years."

"And the money?" Destrey asked.

"In my estimate," Lola said, "it would take more than 350 billion Euros to get things going, *Madame* Destrey. So far, 6 billion Euros have been set aside for safer schools. The overall scale of the work to be undertaken involves over 20,000 schools, 2,000 hospitals and clinics in addition to 26 million homes and apartment buildings. There is also the matter of protecting Italy's historic buildings. Italy's National Council of Engineers puts the cost of strengthening the country's historical treasures at about 93 billion Euros."

"I don't think Italy will be able to put their hands on that kind of money," Destrey said. "They're not going to make it," Destrey said.

"The data leads us to believe the country will never be truly prepared to undertake such a plan. I have assessed the current government's chances of success at below 18%."

"Is there anything else you want us to know before we take a look at your simulation?" Destrey asked.

"No, *Madame* Destrey. I will however indicate that, at this time, there is no way we can predict earthquakes or volcanic eruptions with enough lead time to do a full evacuation of Naples with any significant level of success. As I mentioned earlier, *Madame* Destrey, it would take at least one month to evacuate Naples and get the people out of harm's way."

"Okay, Lola. Let's get on with it."

Freeman continued the narration.

The simulation lasted over two hours. Lola had developed a scenario based on high-ranking probabilities in terms of level of destruction and loss of life. The resulting image the computer had developed left the audience stunned and horrified.

"So, this is how it ends?" Destrey said.

"If Vesuvius erupts," Lola said.

"What about the other volcano, the Campi something?" Destrey asked.

"If Campi Flegrei erupted simultaneously, then, we would have a different simulation, one that would have a far-reaching impact not only on Naples' but would reduce Italy's chances to survive as a nation," Lola said.

"There's no simulation for Campi."

"No, not yet, *Madame* Destrey. Would you like me to…"

"No," Destrey said. "There's no need for an end of the world simulation."

"As you wish, *Madame* Destrey."

"You paint a pretty dark picture, Lola," Destrey finally said. "Should I assume that your simulation is based on a worse scenario?"

"Unfortunately, *Madame* Destrey, that's not the case. That said, given our limitations in predicting volcano eruptions, I may be completely wrong."

"And…" Destrey wanted more.

"And the volcano might go into hibernation for millions of years."

"So, at this point in time, we don't have anything concrete."

"Correct, *Madame* Destrey."

Destrey's professionals remained quiet as though they were attending a funeral service. The volcanologists were also quiet. After all, this was Destrey's show.

One scientist spoke up. "What if she's right?"

"Then, God help us," Destrey said glumly.

Destrey stood up and thanked her people for coming down for the simulation. People slowly walked away while a few stayed behind. They were newly hired employees. They wanted to meet Destrey in person.

They were told that she could put on quite a show if she so desired.

They were not disappointed.

34

PENTHOUSE SUITE
BACK BAY APARTMENTS
BOSTON, MASSACHUSETTS

For Destrey, Saturday mornings meant time away from the office. It also meant blue jeans and a cozy sweater.

She stared at him. Kleinrup was busy with his cell.

"I don't feel like it," she said suddenly.

"Don't feel like what?" He said without looking up at her.

"Like anything really. Can we just enjoy the day?"

"Of course, yes, if that's what you want," Kleinrup said.

"Yeah," Destrey said to herself.

"Are you okay, Louise?"

"Well enough, I guess."

"Would you care to tell me what you're thinking about?"

"No," Destrey said. "Not now."

Kleinrup changed the subject. "I'm comfortable doing nothing if that's what you want," he said.

"What about you? How are you holding up?" she asked.

"Not bad, good actually. But I'm not in the mood for anything either. I'm thinking we could take a walk through Danehy Park. After lunch. No hurry. Only if you feel like it."

"Are you happy?" she asked unexpectedly.

"Happy? I am if you are," Kleinrup said.

"Oh!"

"I don't know for sure. I think you're happy. But I could be wrong," Kleinrup said.

"I don't know how I feel. Can't put my finger on it."

Destrey set the Daily Globe's puzzle aside, letting it drop to the floor. She looked at the newspaper. She didn't pick it up. Then she looked up and saw him examining her.

"Are you worried about me?" she asked.

"Not so much. Should I?" Kleinrup put his cell down. Maybe he should sit by her side. Close. The way she liked it.

"You're not really answering my question," Destrey said.

"You're right. Well, I wasn't until you asked."

"And now?" she said.

"Now, I know," Kleinrup said as he stood up and walked toward the woman he loved. He sat beside her. He held her in his arms.

"What do you know?" she asked.

"I know I love you, but I'm afraid that's not what you're looking for. It's something else. Isn't it?" he asked.

"Yeah. Something else. Something I've never experienced before."

Kleinrup didn't reply.

"I'm not comfortable with…" she hesitated, "failure to help people."

"Uh-huh."

"And I don't know what to do about that?" She said it slowly, to herself mostly.

"What can I do to help?"

"Nothing," Destrey answered.

"That's something we can do together," Kleinrup said. "Do nothing and take our time."

"Maybe."

"I think I understand. I know what you're going through," he said. "I learned to let go."

"I should. I will. It's just…" she said.

"What?"

"I'm talking to the Cardinal," she said. "And before you say it, I know he's dead."

"Okay," Kleinrup said carefully.

"My late husband would tell me to talk to them, you know, the dead," she said.

"I do it all the time." Kleinrup wasn't shy about his beliefs in the afterlife.

"I know you do, but talking to a dead person is one thing. I can manage that. What I really need is an answer."

"To which question?" he said.

"I'd like to say that it's not enough to know what's going to happen. In fact, I'm now sure of it."

"Right."

"I'd like to know what to do when the people you're trying to help don't care, won't change or listen," she said.

"Any ideas?" Kleinrup asked.

"No. Nothing. The Cardinal's not taking my call."

"What would he say if he were here now?"

"He'd say that no amount of self-pity is going to help me," Destrey said.

"Is it?" he asked.

"You mean self-pity?"

Kleinrup didn't reply.

"Like I said, I don't know what I'm feeling."

"Actually, I do," Kleinrup said.

"Well?"

"You're looking for a solution," he said. "You always do that."

"Not always," she said.

"I know you too well, Louise. Maybe I shouldn't, but…" he started to say.

"You know what you know because I want you to," she said.

"There's no magic here."

"Right," he said.

"Which brings me to the following question? What would the Cardinal do?" Destrey asked herself.

"He'd probably call God and ask for divine intervention," Kleinrup said.

"Damn right he would," Destrey said. "But I don't have His number."

"I know that," he said.

She didn't reply.

"Just close your eyes and think about the most beautiful moment in your life, and wait for it," he said.

"Tried it."

"Then, try again. But this time, imagine the Cardinal is looking at you, the way he did. You know what I mean," he said.

"The Cardinal always let me know he was on my side, regardless. It was strange. I got the feeling he always knew what I was going to do."

"He could read us. You in particular," Kleinrup said.

"Why me?" she said.

"Don't know."

"Okay. Let's get back to it," she said.

"Yes, of course. What do we do with Naples?" he asked.

"The hell I know," Destrey said. "Maybe I should finish my puzzle."

"Maybe I should call my mother and see how's she doing," Kleinrup said.

"You do that. Tell mommy hello for me." She smiled at him for the first time today.

"What did you say?" Kleinrup asked.

"I said tell mommy...."

"This is a bit odd," Kleinrup said.

"I know because I just got an idea," she said.

"I think the priest is talking to both of us." Kleinrup was thinking about the Cardinal playing his mind games.

"Mothers, grandmothers, aunties and sisters, and cousins," she said.

"The mommies?" he said.

"Mothers will do anything to protect their children. Anything!" she said. "All this time, we've been talking to the wrong people."

Kleinrup suddenly fell silent. Something important was about to happen.

"How could I have missed it? My God, the whole thing was staring at me. And I looked away! Can you believe that?"

Kleinrup kept his mouth shut. He didn't want to interrupt her train of thought.

"Mothers will literally do anything to save their kid's lives. Do you understand me?"

"Anything?" Kleinrup said.

"They'll do everything! Including leaving behind everything they own and never looking back. Do you hear me Kleinrup?"

"Loud and clear."

35

PENTHOUSE SUITE
BACK BAY APARTMENTS
BOSTON, MASSACHUSETTS

Another Sunday morning. Destrey opened her eyes and realized that today was different. She had learned something important about what and who could change the world. Suddenly, an image popped into her head.

"John. Wake up."

"What?" he said, half awake.

"I was thinking about this all night. I think we need to change gears and get the money-people on board as soon as possible. We've got to move on two fronts: mommies and money."

"If you say so." Kleinrup was still asleep.

"We'll need at least 500 million just to get the ball rolling," she said. "And at least 50 thousand mommies onboard."

"Okay."

"Are you listening to me?" Destrey asked.

"Sure. 500 million and 50k."

"Money to generate a plan for a new science and mommies to push it forward." Destrey knew how to build strategic plans, but a new science plan… that was way out of her league.

"That's good. A plan."

"We're going to reinvent earth sciences," she said.

"Of course, you will."

"Okay. Go back to sleep. You're of no use."

"No use whatsoever," he said. "I agree with that. But a word to the wise. It'll take a lot more than 500 million to get things started. A lot more."

"Now you're awake?"

"Volcanologists beware!" he said. "Old Kleinrup proverb says life is like underwear. Change is good."

36

PENTHOUSE SUITE
BACK BAY APARTMENTS
BOSTON, MASSACHUSETTS

"Who do you think can best help us with the plan?" Destrey said.

"I've been thinking about that. It would take a new set of eyes," Kleinrup said.

"I agree."

"Someone who's not tied down to current beliefs," Kleinrup said.

"Or to their field of expertise," Destrey added.

"Someone who'd be willing to commit scientific... sacrilege," he said.

"Because he or she doesn't belong to the club," she said.

"Yes, precisely. A person with an independent mind and maybe a large bank account," he said.

"Were you going to say someone filthy rich?" she said with a grin.

"So now you can read my mind?" he said.

"That's easy. There's not too much happening up there."

"Ouch!" Kleinrup said. "As I was about to say, someone who can help us design and shape a new earth science."

"I'd be looking for a young Einstein. A Bell, perhaps *Madame Curie* herself, or Newton, Edison or even a Darwin. Now that I think about it, I would love to find a young da Vinci," Destrey said.

"If that's what we need, that's what we should be doing first. Let's ask Lola to find those creatures." Kleinrup was thinking about the challenge of finding these people.

"A short list of geniuses," Destrey said. "And it'll take an exceptional leader to herd those cats."

"And dogs!"

"Yeah. That's a job for our new steering committee."

"You mean Carbone, Sigerðssen and Rudd."

"Don't forget Valdez," Destrey said. "I'll ask Margaret to get that going."

37

NAPLES, ITALY
PRESENT DAY

"It's time."

"Just one more minute, Mommy. Please!"

"Bed. Now, my *piccolo coniglio* (little rabbit). Go, go, go."

"It's not fair."

"I love you too, little one. Are you in bed now?"

"Yes. Can you feel it, Mommy?"

"Feel what, darling?"

"My bed's moving."

"I'm sorry, but that's not going to work tonight. Now close your eyes and go to sleep."

"I am sleeping."

"Hush little man."

38

THE VESUVIUS OBSERVATORY
PRESENT DAY

"It's time we change the sensors," he said.

"What's up?" she asked.

"Don't know what I'm looking at, but sensors are picking up stuff that doesn't make sense. They don't explain the data. Maybe the issue here is why this particular cross-section doesn't correlate," he said. "Maybe you're working with too many attributes. Should be unique. Just one is enough to measure a property," she said.

"Still, look at this." He felt a bit embarrassed. "It's like the mountain is acting up, but there's no geological evidence of that, just numbers. The mountain's peaceful today," he said.

"It's late. You're tired, and so am I. So, I'll take a look at what you've got tomorrow morning. Maybe there's something going on."

39

NAPLES, ITALY
PRESENT DAY

It was a subtle and gentle quake. A mere wobble or two. It was easier for the two cops to feel the tremor while sitting down. The old beat-up Fiat didn't have any working shock absorbers.

"What the hell was that?" Petrosino asked his boss.

"Two years since you've been on the job, and already you're complaining. Don't worry your pretty little head about it, *Agente Scelto* (Senior Constable). It's that thing over there." Darnelli looked toward the mountain.

"You mean, Vesuvius?" Petrosino said.

"Don't pretend you don't know what I'm talking about," Darnelli said. "It's been two years since you joined us here in Naples. And you should know by now that you're not in Rome anymore."

Another earthquake shook Naples; this time, the quake was more noticeable. It felt like a sharp push. A few more shocks hit the Fiat. And then, they heard a boom.

Down the street, a few car alarms began waking up the neighborhood.

"Don't point to the mountain," Petrosino said. "It's bad luck."

"I won't. I promise," Darnelli said, chuckling.

"Let's get out of here."

Chunks of stone littered the street while a corner stone from a nearby building fell a few feet behind the Fiat.

"What the hell?" Petrosino said.

"Gravity, young Skywalker. Remember, earthquakes don't kill people, buildings do."

"Really?" Petrosino said sarcastically.

"Especially buildings built by the fucking Camorra. Cheap, defective and flawed."

Rapid shocks brought residents to the streets at 3:10 am. It was a hot summer morning, and the locals were annoyed. Another tremor hit Naples. It measured 3.1 on the Richter Scale. Another followed, this time reaching 3.9.

A few minutes went by before the locals returned to their homes. It was still dark and tired bodies needed their sleep more than ever. Thankfully, the quakes and tremors had suddenly stopped.

Petrosino punched the brakes as hard as he could. The Fiat nearly skidded off the road. "Look at that," he said to his boss.

"What the…" Darnelli mumbled to himself.

"There must be hundreds of dogs." Petrosino said. "And there, look at the sky. The birds are leaving town."

"What the…" Darnelli started to say.

"You're pointing," Petrocelli said.

"Yeah. I am," Darnelli said. "And I'm really sorry to say this, but it's smoking!"

It was hot and steamy in Naples, which was business as usual.

But today, Vesuvius was clearly acting up and Mother Nature hinted to its humblest creatures to run away.

While men, women and children were trying to catch a few more hours of sleep, Vesuvius was breathing as if it was a living organism, an entity 400,000 years old.

The earth moved again. It gave off a certain smell. The ones not yet asleep heard it gently growl. The mountain had awakened the dead as well as those who soon would be.

The earth swelled in places, leaving its mark on land and under the sea. Darnelli and Petrocelli were racing through the narrow streets of Naples looking for somewhere safe, hoping and praying their beat-up Fiat wouldn't let them down in their hour of need.

Nevertheless, Vesuvius was an unstoppable force of nature. Whatever you had done in your life, and whatever you believed in, was immaterial. It was almost too late to run, almost too late to pray and almost too late to hug the ones you loved.

Much too late to do anything about anything.

40

NAPLES, ITALY
PRESENT DAY

The phone rang again.

"It's 5h30 a.m. What could be so important?" Mattia Vicenti was CNN's Rome bureau chief. He was already at his computer. "Tell me something I don't know."

Vicenti listened carefully. What he heard made him excited and frightened.

"Okay, let's get going," he said. "This might be the big one… or not, I don't care. But I have this feeling. I don't want to miss the opportunity to get there first."

The phone rang again.

"Yeah," Vicenti said annoyed. "Okay. Book a small hotel. And don't forget, we need private parking spaces for trucks and our people. I'm sending a team down there as soon as I can get through to my secretary."

"No, don't wait. Go now."

41

NAPLES, ITALY
PRESENT DAY

The port of Naples was preparing for a day of commerce and travel. Fishing trawlers would soon be heading home while ferries prepared to leave Naples within the hour.

The Gulf of Naples was calm as the sun began to rise on the 3,000-year-old city.

The weather forecast called for light rain until 9h00 a.m. followed by a warm and sunny day until 3h00 p.m. A heavy rainstorm was predicted to hit Naples around 9h p.m.

The coastal road of Via Nuova Marina was almost free of traffic. But that would soon change as the fish markets were set to reopen in the next hour.

Business as usual.

42

NAPLES, ITALY
PRESENT DAY

A few imperceptible micro fissures were working their way from the Sant'Anastasia commune located at the foot of Vesuvius toward Naples' city center. The fissures were racing at light speed toward downtown Naples, passing under the city's Gianturco Train Station, ending further west underneath the Church of Gesù Nuovo.

Destrey was on the phone with Lola. She listened to Lola's words as the computer was describing what could be a full-fledged eruption. There were signs. Based on Lola's prediction, Naples was now ground zero.

"We're too late," she said to herself. Destrey turned on CNN. She imagined people driving to work, being shuttled to schools, shopping or travelling. Destrey felt anxious at the prospect of certain death for many of Naples' citizens if, of course, Lola was right. She prayed the computer was wrong. Unfortunately, Lola was right almost all the time. Listening to the story unfold on CNN, Destrey couldn't imagine residing or working in Naples. As her late husband used to say about living in Naples, *you'd need to put a gun to my head.*

Destrey focused on the information CNN was presenting live.

"Is this the beginning of a full-fledged eruption?" the reporter asked his viewers. "Will Vesuvius create a new page of history for Neapolitans or not? It's now Tuesday, 5h35 a.m. in Naples Italy," said the reporter. "Ladies and gentlemen, all I can say right now is that Vesuvius is awake."

The camera pointed to Vesuvius showed images that appeared normal.

No one working at the church of Gesù Nuovo took notice of the tremors under their feet. Most were so small that people going about their business didn't feel them. The regular seismic incidents were weak, and they occurred nearly every other day.

A few minutes later, micro fissures began to appear near Trocchia, a commune in the Metropolitan City of Naples located about 9 kilometers east of Naples' city center.

At 5h46 a.m., a micro-earthquake measuring 0.12 on the Richter Scale happened near the island of Ischia, a small volcanic island located at the northern end of the Gulf of Naples. Located about 30 kilometers south of Naples, the island is populated by more than 75,000 residents and is the largest of the Phlegraean Islands.

Destrey was by now at BTG's offices, deep in the Safe where Destrey continued to listen to CNN. She felt sad mostly because Lola was so horribly reliable. And now, Vesuvius was acting up.

A hairline fissure, 6 kilometers in length, partly located under the bay of Naples, was also speeding westward toward the city of Puzzuoli. The city of 80,000 citizens, sat in the center of the Campi Flegrei volcanic caldera. Approximately half the caldera was under the Bay of Naples, the other half on dry land. Most but not all hydroacoustic systems missed the seismic occurrence given its extremely small signature.

On the eastern side of Vesuvius, another micro-earthquake measuring 0.21 on the Richter Scale hit Pompeii at 5h47 a.m. No damage was reported to the police.

At 6h03 a.m., a sinkhole, 30 by 60 meters and 20 meters deep consumed 25 parked cars forcing the evacuation of a temporary hospital emergency ward at the back entrance of Naples' Ospedale del Mare (Hospital by the Sea). The health care facility was situated roughly half an hour's drive from Vesuvius. The sinkhole instantly caused power and communication outages in Rione Lotto Zero and Rione Incis, both territorial subdivision of Naples.

By 9h30 a.m., Naples' skies cleared up. No one paid attention to Naples' soundless heaven. Birds were perched on their favorite branch or windowsill. Few birds were hunting for food. In fact, there was a stillness about the city, as cats and dogs as well as young children behaved strangely. But then, everyone in Naples generally behaved oddly. The expresso machines were working overtime. Neapolitans were thirsty this morning. Baristas across Naples noticed the high turnout but did not link any new business to Vesuvius.

The Vesuvius Observatory was also busy managing the volcano's surveillance center. It routinely monitored two other volcanic areas located in the province of Campania which include the Phlegrean Fields (or Campi Flegrei) and Ischia, the island volcano located south of Puzzuoli.

"We're on site, here at the Observatory," the reporter said. "As you can see, the specialists analyze the data from Vesuvius nonstop. In the case of a communication breach, the data collected is transmitted to Naples' civil-protection agency by cable, cell or radio."

The volcanoes were under 24-hour surveillance. If a volcano acted up, the observatory would communicate with the local civil-protection agency and assess risk and scope and if required, call for an evacuation. "So far, the reporter said, "there are no signs of significant volcanic activity, but the Vesuvius Observatory is nevertheless on high alert."

The camera showed the monitors displaying Vesuvius' numbers.

"Basically, Naples' underground is behaving normally," a scientist told the CNN reporter. "Until now, there's no significant seismic phenomena that would lead us to believe that Vesuvius is about to erupt in any significant way."

It was now 11h05 a.m.

The coastal road of Via Nuova Marina near Corso Arnaldo Lucci was experiencing a traffic jam in both directions due to an accident between a transit bus and a motor scooter. An ambulance was on its way. Drivers hollered and honked as they were late for work.

Salt water was seeping in the lower ground floors of a few buildings on Via Ferdinando Palasciano. The structures were located a few minutes' walk from the shore, flooding often occurring after heavy rains and when high coastal waves hit the port.

At 11h07 a.m., a small tremor hit the Eduardo De Filippo primary school located in the commune of Pozzuoli, in the center of Campi's caldera. The school lost all electrical power. In contrast to Vesuvius, Campi Flegrei was flat, showing a number of small cones and craters all located within a giant caldera that extended over 20 kilometers around Pozzuoli.

At 4h33 p.m., a faint tremor measuring 0.26 on the Richter Scale hit the Tangenziale Highway. The tunnel heading toward Pozzuoli was experiencing heavy traffic as workers blocked off two lanes of traffic approaching the Pascale and Cardarelli hospital exit. The maintenance on the tunnel normally added an hour of commuting time.

At 5h p.m., heavy rain began to fall, making driving hazardous. The roads were slippery.

At 9h04 p.m., the rain turned into a storm with winds gusting up to 80 km/h across the southern half of the province, while areas near Vesuvius saw wind gusts reaching 100 km/h.

Destrey returned to her home. There wasn't much to see. It looked like Lola was wrong after all.

Her cell rang.

What's up?" Destrey asked.

"I would say that we are watching an overture, *Madame* Destrey. An introduction to something more substantial," Lola said.

"Are you sure, Lola?" Destrey said.

"90% sure *Madame* Destrey. I'm in Vesuvius Observatory's

sensor array."

"You mean you hacked your way in, Lola?"

"Correct, *Madame* Destrey. The locals can't see a pattern yet, but I can."

"I was afraid you'd say that," Destrey said.

It was now Wednesday, 3h45 a.m. and the rain was falling heavily on the city. Neapolitans were sleeping. The bars closed early. A few city employees were beginning another day's work.

Business as usual.

An earthquake of 1.29 on the Richter Scale hit the Tyrrhenian Sea. The epicenter was located 350 km east of the Stromboli volcano. The shallow earthquake occurred at a depth of 78 km.

At 3h55 a.m., an earthquake of 5.6 on the Richter Scale hit downtown Naples. As a result, the Gianturco Train Station was now out of commission because a number of tracks were damaged across the greater Naples area. Commuters would soon be informed to take other modes of transportation.

The earthquake triggered a few landslides. Buildings near the shore were severely damaged. Overpasses, bridges, tunnels, pavements, and other elements of Naples' highway infrastructure were also damaged by the earthquake. So far, no serious injuries were reported to the police.

The Tangenziale Highway was partly out of commission. A few hundred cars were now stranded, and people began to walk away from their cars, trying to find their way home.

"Good morning from CNN's control center in Naples, Italy. We're here live. At 6h35 a.m., Naples experienced gridlock on most of the city's key intersections. If and when the city calls for an evacuation, they'll have to find alternate ways of getting people to safety. This situation will certainly worsen as people wake up to go to work. Police are on site and trying to get the traffic moving again. Still no word from the mayor or the Vesuvius Observatory."

Despite the police's attempts to open up the highways, the queues of vehicles all along Naples' transportation network brought traffic in all directions to a complete standstill.

Fires erupted as explosions ripped through an AGIP petroleum storage depot. A cloud of gasoline vapor exploded and damaged some of Naples' port infrastructure. Large reservoirs of gasoline, kerosene, and diesel were on fire. The incident destroyed 18 of the 32 storage tanks.

"The cause of these explosions is still unknown," the reporter said. "We were told by the police, that Vesuvius had no part in this new development."

"As of 8h a.m. this morning," the reported said, "almost half cell towers in and around Naples have failed and as a result, communications between City Hall and its employees are severely compromised. Fortunately, some land lines are still working."

Most ambulances, firetrucks, public transit, taxis and police cruisers failed to reach their destinations in time. Hospitals began to receive a large number of walk-ins seeking emergency care.

Part of Naples' city center was paralyzed. The rainy weather was hampering emergency services.

"Lola?"

"Yes, *Madame* Destrey."

"Is this what you expected?"

"Yes, *Madame* Destrey. The call to evacuate Naples will come too late to do any good. In fact, I would have called for a total evacuation of Naples at least twenty-four hours ago. But any attempt to sway the Mayor to evacuate Naples would not have worked because the numbers at his disposal didn't show any real danger of an eruption."

"Have you since tried to contact City Hall and warn them?" Destrey said.

"Communications between the US and Naples is also gridlocked as millions of Americans are trying to reach their loved ones."

"Is there anything you can do to help the Mayor at this point?"

"Yes and no, *Madame* Destrey. Unfortunately, I cannot reach him or anyone else at City Hall. I've also been trying to reach the Mayor through the Italian military. No luck there either. He's unreachable since yesterday."

The rain continued unabated. The Vesuvius Observatory's seismographic network observed a cloud appearing atop Mount Vesuvius. A few sensors apparently began to malfunction. Northwest winds reached 47 km/h.

The Vesuvius Observatory called for Naples' evacuation.

"The Mayor just announced at 9h a.m. Naples time, that he was calling for an evacuation for Naples' Red Zones. Red Zone number 1 and number 2 are the most vulnerable areas if and when a full eruption occurs," the reporter said. "Officials at the Observatory said, and this is a direct quote, its lethality would be contingent on the strength and direction of the winds. Red Zone 1 and 2, include 25 towns and villages. Please let me repeat what we've heard from the Observatory. The Mayor of Naples just announced that he was calling for an evacuation of Naples' Red Zones. The Mayor said it would not take more than two days to evacuate all of Red Zone 1 and 2 residents."

By 10h a.m. Thursday, almost 15% of city employees, police officers, firefighters, hospital workers as well as first responders were abandoning their posts to assist in the evacuation of their own families. Burglaries and vandalism were widespread. Attacks on property and people were undermining the evacuation of the city as some citizens refused to leave their homes and businesses.

Ash began to fall near the volcano at 10h10 a.m.

At 10h50 a.m., the Vesuvius Observatory was evacuated.

Airports within a 500 kilometers radius of Naples were informed to avoid the city's airspace due to poor visibility and ash concentration.

Naples' Mayor was planning to call for the complete evacuation of Naples. Communications with the state police as well as the military were uncoordinated and haphazard. Technically, Naples' evacuation plan included 500 buses and 220 trains that would ferry Neapolitans each day. Pompei residents would be evacuated by ship to Sardinia, while Neapolitans would be evacuated toward

Lazio, about one hour north of Naples by train and two hours by car. The plan was contingent on the usability of roads, train tracks and expressways.

At 3h15 p.m., a seismic swarm or a succession of tectonic events began to occur beneath Campi Flegrei. The swarm was made up of eleven earthquakes with magnitudes ranging from 0.11 to 4.7 on the Richter Scale. Two new fumaroles, those breaches in the earth's surface that emit steam and toxic volcanic gases, were reported in Campi Flegrei's caldera.

By 3h50 p.m., almost 35% of government employees had deserted their posts. Naples' Mayor reluctantly called for a full evacuation of the city.

At 4h p.m., the Mayor called in the army and declared martial law.

By 7h p.m., the army has taken control of Naples. Italian Airforce helicopter surveillance has also begun.

At 11h45 p.m., Naples' outskirts began to encounter ash, making driving almost impossible.

"Lola?"

"Yes, *Madame* Destrey."

"Tell me how the city can evacuate a million people before the volcano erupts?"

"I cannot," Lola said. "Naples will be gridlocked withing one hour."

"What are you saying?" Destrey asked as her eyes never left the TV screen. "So, there's nothing they can do?"

"The evacuation called by the Mayor is part of a planned exercise and strategy generated over two years ago. However, as we all know, all carefully crafted plans can go haywire, *Madame* Destrey. According to Field Marshal Helmuth von Moltke (1800-1891), no plan of operations extends with certainty beyond the first encounter with the enemy's main strength. It has been three days since Vesuvius has begun to rumble and shake. I feel that day 3 will now introduce the unintended as well as the unwelcomed elements of a full volcanic eruption," Lola said.

"And?"

"That would be the end of the Mayor's successful evacuation. As you said, *Madame* Destrey, we are too late to do anything to stop what will inevitably happen to Naples," Lola said.

"I remember my late husband telling me that by failing to prepare, we are preparing to fail," Destrey said." And now you're telling me that all plans fail sooner or later."

"Pastor H.K. Williams said that in 1919," Lola said. "I could also add that all plans begin to fail at the onset of their execution."

"Yeah," Destrey said.

"With that in mind," Lola continued, "Naples' city fathers neglected to include in their evacuation plans the probability of the worse scenario which should have included significant infrastructure breakdowns."

CNN's helicopter was showing Vesuvius in all its terrifying splendor.

"What's going to happen next?" Destrey asked.

"The possibility of misjudging the volcanoes' specific behavior is significant, *Madame* Destrey. However, one thing is now certain: the volcano will erupt. There's no doubt about that. How it will erupt is, at this point in time, speculation based on historical facts."

On Thursday morning at 1h30 a.m. white pumice fell with accumulations of 1 to 5 cm per hour. Naples' Red Zone evacuation was well underway. Hospitals as well as retirement homes for the elderly were prioritized but there was a serious shortage of staff. Even though the roads were nearly empty, low visibility made driving treacherous and slow. Most headed north by way of Strada Statale 18 (SP18), a state road connecting Campania to Calabria. It followed the Tyrrhenian coast, from Salerno to Reggio di Calabria.

At 9h30 a.m., small earthquakes with magnitudes ranging from 0.18 to 2.1 on the Richter Scale, were registered throughout the Campania region encompassing Naples and the Amalfi Coast.

At 3h p.m., buildings near the port collapsed as tremors

continued. In Pompeii, buildings and archeological structures also collapsed.

At 3h10 p.m., fist-sized rocks began to fall in the Red Zone at speeds of up to 50 meters per second. The sun was blocked by smoke. People who did not evacuate the Red Zone, sought shelter in their homes and local public buildings.

At 7h30 p.m., Vesuvius suddenly erupted, discharging a high-altitude column composed of ash and pumice.

At 8h20 p.m., the Italian military with the help of the American military, flew over Naples to help identify the best roads to evacuate Naples. Two military helicopters crashed.

Two routes were identified: ferries located at the port of Naples and the Via Santa Teresa Degli Scalzi highway by bus and army trucks. The military also reported that the Tangenziale di Napoli highway that led out of Naples was out of commission.

At 10h p.m., a small leak of magma was detected from Vesuvius' reservoir beneath its peak.

"It's 10h p.m. in Naples," the reporter said from his hotel balcony. "And you can see it for yourself." The camera turned toward the volcano and zoomed in. "It's a horrible sight but a hypnotizing one. You can't get your eyes to stop looking. We were told that the Vesuvius caldera has collapsed. Scientists are saying that the magma chamber underneath Vesuvius has split apart. The magma is beginning to flow east and west of the volcano. They also said that pyroclastic flows have already begun. As you can see, lava and rock flows are surging downhill toward Pompeii, the Bay of Naples and Naples' port," the reporter said.

"Lola? Please explain pyroclastic" Destrey said.

"Of course, *Madame* Destrey. Pyroclastic flows are fast-moving currents composed of solidified lava pieces, volcanic ash, and hot gases. These flows destroy nearly everything in their path at the speed of up to 700 km/h, with temperatures that could reach 1,000 °C."

"I don't know what to think! Can we outrun a pyroclastic flow?" Destrey asked.

"No," Lola said.

"Too fast and too late" Destrey said to herself.

At 11h45 p.m., lava fountains and new fissures broke through the surface and a stream of lava flowed through residential neighborhoods in the Red Zone, toward the sea.

At 11h50 p.m., scientists were rethinking their basic assumption: Vesuvius was organizing for a full eruption.

"It's now Friday 0h30 a.m.," the reporter said. "Pyroclastic flows reached the Autostrada A3, a highspeed motorway which runs from Naples to Salerno. Ash falling on Naples quashed most the city's evacuation plan."

At 1h20 a.m., pyroclastic flows continued toward the seaport of Naples, they were rapid-moving, dense, and very hot, knocking down all structures in their path.

At 3h30 a.m., Neapolitans who had chosen to stay in their homes were trying to run away on foot while tremors continued to disrupt and destroy infrastructures.

Pyroclastic flows were now generating temperatures of 275°C.

"It's 6h a.m. in Naples," the reported said. "Vesuvius is spreading ash as far as 30 kilometers in a south-westerly direction, leaving a dark yellow haze in the atmosphere. The sun is barely visible. All flights in a 3000 km radius around Rome are being rerouted. We were told to evacuate ourselves, but we will stay a while longer to see what will happen."

At 7h a.m., pumice and ash entered the stratosphere.

By 9h a.m., between 200,000 and 400,000 people had been evacuated from Red Zones 1 and 2.

At 11h30 a.m., six pyroclastic surges hit the eastern front of Naples. Heat surges caused thousands to die in a fraction of a second.

"It's now Saturday, 0h30 a.m. We are minutes away from being helicoptered to safety. From what you can see," the reported said, "ash is continuing to fall on Naples. It's causing widespread disruptions."

Ash began to impact animal and human health, aviation, critical infrastructure such as electric power supply systems, telecommunications, water and waste-water networks and most importantly, transportation. Most industries, buildings and structures were by now, out of commission.

Over the previous three days and nights, hundreds of earthquakes, alternating from mild tremors to tectonic shock waves strong enough to make any sound person behave irrationally, occurred. The same could have been said for the previous year's Vesuvius temper tantrum.

So, it had taken place before! What of it! It will happen again, they said to themselves. That's why the Neapolitans chose to live with it or more accurately, denied it ever happen.

By mid-day, the Neapolitans were shattered. Three days and three nights would do that to anyone sane or not. At first, people were tired of the constant tremors rocking the city. By the end of the second day of volcanic activity, people began to feel anxious, then became fearful. By the third day, everyone was terrified at the prospect of no one coming to recue them.

Today was a different story, the people of Napoli began to expect death on their doorstep. There was no hope, no miracles, no silver bullet to save everyone. For most of those who stayed behind, death was already staring at them. He or she, or whatever it was, was coming for them. It appeared like death was the only outcome the Neapolitans could imagine.

Those who had not left Naples were going insane trying to outrun Vesuvius' lava flows. They imagined that the volcano would, at every turn, block their way to safety. They felt like prisoners being tracked down to be finally executed.

Many prayed to God to help them in their hour of need. Others, just ran for the safety of higher ground, not realizing that deadly gas had no bounds to its reach. The elderly sought safety in the bosom of their ancestral homes. They did not think any longer, they just held on tight to their better half and waited patiently for the end to come.

As of 1h30 a.m., the Cavour, an Italian aircraft carrier reached the Bay of Naples. It was escorted by the Nimitz-class aircraft carriers

USS Abraham Lincoln and USS John C. Stennis as well as their escort ships. The French aircraft carrier Charles de Gaulle as well as the Russian aircraft carrier Admiral Kuznetsov, also entered the Bay of Naples and began, along with the Italians, and the Americans, to evacuate Neapolitans who were stranded in the city.

At 3h a.m., the ground deformation of Campi Flegrei began to increase. The ground near Pozzuoli rose by about 2 cm. The uplift appeared to be ongoing as micro-earthquakes continued to hit the area. There was also a notable rise in temperature.

At 6h a.m., almost half of Naples' citizens had been accounted for.

As of 7h30 a.m., all aircraft supporting the evacuation, including military and private helicopters were grounded.

At 10h30 a.m., pyroclastic surges hit the port of Naples. Ships that did not leave the port were destroyed. So far, tsunami warnings had not been issued.

At 12 noon, Naples was paralyzed and partly destroyed. The death toll had so far reached the half million mark. A new plan for relocating Neapolitans was unavailable.

43

NAPLES, ITALY
PRESENT DAY

The sky was dark even though it was almost noon. The Mediterranean was in mourning. Many structures had collapsed under twenty feet of ash. The city was almost destroyed.

Back in Boston, fear spread through Destrey's veins and soul. The thought of a vibrant city burnt into oblivion, was unbearable. Kleinrup would be working under the worse possible conditions. She wrote to him every day.

Destrey missioned Kleinrup to find out as much as he could about Carbone's whereabouts. The problem was that finding anyone in Naples would be difficult in normal times, but now, Vesuvius made finding Francesco Carbone almost impossible. Destrey believed it was her responsibility to bring him back home, dead or alive.

Meanwhile, she'd met with several backers who understood that dealing with earthquakes and volcanoes was now a priority and a BTG Event -which was code for a consulting assignment of the highest order involving most of BTG's resources.

With the help of her financiers, she managed to put together half a billion US dollars to get the project going. While they could not change what happened in Naples, the core group of research scientists and volcanologists held their first meeting to develop a strategic plan to deal with future earthquakes and volcanic eruptions. Project Hades, a long-term endeavor, would be led by Destrey until she could find a good replacement. She was thinking of Francesco Carbone for the job. Whether Kleinrup would be able to find him was another question.

Soon after Kleinrup had set up a command post on Destrey's yacht moored near Salerno, he began a search and rescue operation in what was left of Naples. "At the moment," he said to Destrey, "I have no leads. It's like Carbone disappeared from the face of the earth."

With his weapon securely holstered, he set out about Naples' ruins with the help of a dozen mercenaries and a prize of a hundred thousand Euros for anyone you would lead him to Carbone… alive.

Adding to the destruction, there was looting on a grand scale. The streets of Naples, or what was left of them, were teeming with armed civilians and would-be mafiosos. The police had the help of the military to keep the peace, but they were helpless to stop the violence.

People were hungry and had nowhere to go. Unfortunately, there was only military grade slosh available to feed them as the Red Cross was slow in helping those in need. Not surprisingly, the city was completely paralyzed.

With no water, electricity or telecommunications, the citizens of Naples tried to escape anyway they could. The level of destruction of the city's public services left citizens to fend for themselves. Alone and vulnerable, survivors were at the mercy of carpetbaggers and murderers.

"Naples is once more the capital of chaos and murder," the reporter said. "To makes things worse, there's talk of a new Covid variant setting up shop in what was downtown Naples. I was also told that the police fear a civil war between them and the Vesuvius survivors."

People were angry. The government had yet again failed in its duty to protect citizens. The eruption caught everyone by surprise which included volcanologists.

"Apparently, the government did not warn its citizens of Vesuvius' eruption soon enough," the reporter said. "We've tried to get in touch with the Mayor. Although serious accusations have been made, CNN has been informed that Naples' Mayor is missing. With more than half a million Neapolitans missing, it is unfortunately impossible, at this time, to determine exactly the number of dead."

At night, Kleinrup's crew regrouped on the My Sister's Float, Destrey's floating resort she'd named in honor of her sister. Kleinrup still had no lead on Carbone's location, nor did he have any real hope of finding him, dead or alive.

"This is what we know so far," the reporter said. "The eruption caused toxic gases that choked those downwind followed by falling rocks. Houses collapsed and in so doing, crushing residents. Then a cloud of toxic gases and ash swept through part of Naples. Death was quick. As you can see, there's ash everywhere. Tons of it. We don't know how deep or when we'll be able to unearth the bodies. I was told that this task of retrieving the dead might take years," the reporter said, "probably into the next century. There's also no talk of rebuilding Naples at this time."

The task at hand was saving and relocating those still alive, many of whom said they wanted the Italian government to rebuild their city.

That, Destrey believed, was never going to happen until Vesuvius became extinct. Unfortunately, Destrey had learned from Lola that Vesuvius was still very much active and unlikely become extinct in the near future or any future the human race could understand.

44

PENTHOUSE SUITE
BACK BAY APARTMENTS
BOSTON, MASSACHUSETTS

Destrey's phone was buzzing. It was 2h a.m., Boston time. She fumbled around to reach her cell. It kept on wringing.

"What the hell?" She said to herself.

"Louise?" Kleinrup said.

"Yeah."

"Got him."

"Got who?"

"Carbone. He's right here with me. I found him in a monastery turned field hospital by the military. He's okay but he needs to be checked out."

"Thank God."

"We'll be heading for Boston as soon as the jet is fueled and readied for takeoff."

"Let me talk to him," Destrey said.

"He's sleeping. Want me to wake him up?"

"No, just..."

"Wait! He's awake! Give me a second."

Destrey was overjoyed.

"He wants to talk to you too."

"*Madame* Destrey?" Carbone said weakly.

"I'm so happy to hear your voice, Francesco," Destrey said.

"Me too," Carbone answered back.

They were by now both crying.

"Okay, that's enough," said Kleinrup. "I'll call from the jet as soon as we're airborne. Got to go."

"Bye," she said while still crying.

The line went dead.

Destrey was now fully awake, and she had no one to talk to at 2h a.m.

Her phone rang again.

"What's wrong? Is he okay?" she said fearfully.

"Good morning, *Madame* Destrey."

"Lola?"

"Yes, *Madame* Destrey. I've taken the liberty to monitor Mr. Carbone's vital signs until he reaches Logan International Airport. Will contact Mass General. They will be ready for Mr. Carbone's arrival."

"Thank you, Lola."

"My pleasure, *Madame* Destrey."

"Yes, well…" Destrey said. She almost heard the computer giggling. *But that's impossible*, she said to herself.

More books by André John Haddad

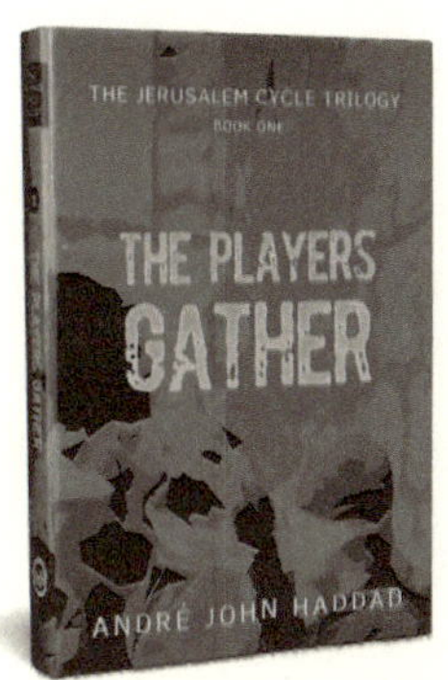

Available at Amazon, Barnes & Noble, Indigo,
and other major online book retailers.

André John Haddad is the author of several international thrillers including *The Jerusalem Cycle* Trilogy and *The Thirst*, as well as *Five Hundred Days of Killer Viruses and Attempted Wit*, a collection of personal essays chronicling the 2020 Covid-19 pandemic.

André has spent the past forty years as an industrial psychologist, and his work has taken him to organizations all over Europe, the Americas, and Asia. His specialty is understanding and predicting the behavior of different components of the organization. He helps businesses develop, change, and grow sustainably.

He currently teaches innovation techniques to executive MBA students, and lives with his wife in Sainte-Adèle, Quebec.